Acclaim for Melissa Ferguson

Meet Me in the Margins

"*Meet Me in the Margins* is a delightfully charming jewel of a book that fans of romantic comedy won't be able to put down—and will want to share with all their friends. Readers will lose themselves in Melissa Ferguson's witty, warm tale of Savannah Cade and the perfectly drawn cast of characters that inhabits her world. This literary treat full of missed opportunities, second chances, and maybe even true love, should be at the top of your reading list!"

—Kristy Woodson Harvey, *New York Times* bestselling author of *Under the Southern Sky*

"Ferguson has penned a lively romance for every bookworm who once longed to step through the wardrobe or sleep under the stairs. *Meet Me in the Margins* brims with crisp prose and crinkling pages as Savannah Cade, lowly editor at a highbrow publisher, secretly reworks her commercial fiction manuscript with the help of a mystery reader—and revises her entire life. You'll want to find your own hideaway to get lost in this delightful, whip-smart love story."

—Asher Fogle Paul, author of *Without a Hitch*

The Cul-de-Sac War

"Melissa delivered a book that is filled with both humor and heart!"

—Debbie Macomber, #1 *New York Times* bestselling author

"Melissa Ferguson delights with a grand sense of humor and a captivating story to boot! With vivid detail that brings the story roaring to life, *The Cul-de-Sac War* brings us closer to the truth of love, family, and home. Bree's and Chip's pranks and adventures turn into something they never expected, as Melissa Ferguson delivers another heartwarming, hilarious, and deeply felt story."

—Patti Callahan, *New York Times* bestselling
author of *Becoming Mrs. Lewis*

"Melissa Ferguson's *The Cul-de-Sac War* is sweet, zany, and surprisingly tender. Bree and Chip will have you laughing and rooting for them until the very end."

—Denise Hunter, bestselling author of *Carolina Breeze*

"With her sophomore novel, Melissa Ferguson delivers hilarity and heart in equal measure. *The Cul-de-Sac War*'s Bree Leake and Chip McBride prove that sometimes it isn't the first impression you have to worry about—it's the second one that gets you. What follows is a delightful deluge of pranks, sabotage, and witty repartee tied together by heartstrings that connect to turn a house into a home worth fighting for. I was thoroughly charmed from beginning to end."

—Bethany Turner, award-winning author of
The Secret Life of Sarah Hollenbeck

"Witty, wise, and with just the right amount of wacky, Melissa's second novel is as charming as her debut. Competition and chemistry battle to win the day in this hilarious rom-com about two people who can't stand to be near each other—or too far apart."

—Betsy St. Amant, author of *The Key to Love*

The Dating Charade

"Ferguson's delightful debut follows a first date that turns quickly into a childcare quagmire . . . Ferguson's humorous and chaotic tale will please rom-com fans."

—*Publishers Weekly*

"*The Dating Charade* will keep you smiling the entire read. Ferguson not only delights us with new love, with all its attendant mishaps and misunderstandings, but she takes us deeper in the hearts and minds of vulnerable children as Cassie and Jett work out their families—then their dating lives. An absolute treat!"

—Katherine Reay, bestselling author of
The Printed Letter Bookshop

"*The Dating Charade* is hilarious and heartwarming with characters you truly care about, super fun plot twists and turns, snappy prose, and a sweet romance you're rooting for. Anyone who has children in their lives will particularly relate to Ferguson's laugh-out-loud take on the wild ride that is parenting. I thoroughly enjoyed this story!"

—Rachel Linden, bestselling author of
The Enlightenment of Bees

"A heartwarming charmer."

—Sheila Roberts, *USA TODAY* bestselling
author of the Moonlight Harbor series

"Melissa Ferguson is a sparkling new voice in contemporary rom-com. Though her novel tackles meaningful struggles—social work, child abandonment, adoption—it's also fresh, flirty, and laugh-out-loud funny. Ferguson is going to win fans with this one!"

—Lauren Denton, bestselling author of
The Hideaway and Glory Road

"A jolt of energy featuring one of the most unique romantic hooks I have ever read. Personality and zest shine through Ferguson's evident enjoyment at crafting high jinks and misadventures as two people slowly make way for love in the midst of major life upheaval. A marvelous treatise on unexpected grace and its life-changing chaos, Cassie and Jett find beautiful vulnerability in redefining what it means to live happily ever after."

—Rachel McMillan, author of *The London Restoration*

"Ferguson delivers a stellar debut. *The Dating Charade* is a fun, romantic albeit challenging look at just what it takes to fall in love and be a family. You'll think of these characters long after the final page."

—Rachel Hauck, *New York Times* bestselling
author of *The Wedding Dress*

Meet Me
in the
Margins

Also by Melissa Ferguson

NOVELS
The Cul-de-Sac War
The Dating Charade

STORIES
Pining for You included in *This Time Around*

Meet Me in the Margins

A Novel

MELISSA FERGUSON

THOMAS NELSON
Since 1798

Published in Nashville, Tennessee, by Thomas Nelson. Thomas Nelson is a registered trademark of HarperCollins Christian Publishing, Inc.

Published in association with Hartline Literary Agency, Pittsburgh, PA 15235.

Thomas Nelson titles may be purchased in bulk for educational, business, fundraising, or sales promotional use. For information, please email SpecialMarkets@ThomasNelson.com.

ISBN 978-0-7852-3107-3 (trade paper)
ISBN 978-0-7852-3108-0 (e-book)
ISBN 978-0-7852-3109-7 (downloadable audio)

Library of Congress Cataloging-in-Publication Data
CIP data is available upon request.

Printed in the United States of America
22 23 24 25 26 LSC 10 9 8 7 6 5 4 3 2 1

*To all the wonderful people at my own publishing house,
with a special tip of the hat to Kim Carlton and Mike
Bzozowski for living out their own inspiring love story.*

Prologue

From: Claire Donovan
Received: 9:17 AM
To: Savannah Cade
Subject: Manuscript?

Savannah,

Have you made any more progress on that book idea you brought up to me at conference last year? I was just sitting in an editorial meeting, and your story came to mind. Would love to take a look.

Best wishes,
Claire Donovan
Chief Editor, Romance
Baird Books Publishing

....

Draft
From: Savannah Cade
Saved: 9:21 AM
To: Claire Donovan
Subject: Re: Manuscript?

| Dear Mrs. Donovan

....

Draft
From: Savannah Cade
Saved: 9:22 AM
To: Claire Donovan
Subject: Re: Manuscript?

| Dear Claire Donovan

....

Draft
From: Savannah Cade
Saved: 9:24 AM
To: Claire Donovan
Subject: Re: Manuscript?

| Dear Claire,
|
| Thank you so much for your email! I'm so, so sorry I didn't
| get to it right after conference as I said. I promise I'm not

one of those aspiring writers who unloads a thousand details of the story in their heads on every stranger they land upon at conferences but then can't follow through when an editor actually requests to see the manuscript. Truly.

It was just that I realized after talking with you that the final scene was missing the big bang at the end, and Cecilia's character really wasn't all that likable after all, and then when I finally managed to amend those issues my manuscript was twelve thousand words over. So then I spent the next month agonizing over where to cut (you know, King's whole "kill your darlings" thing is really true from the writer's side—here I'd been casually telling my own authors to slash their manuscripts for two years and never really understood how truly GUT WRENCHING it is. I killed off a whole character and am still weepy for him).

But I am in edits now and just need to go over it a couple more times. So sorry again to have had you waiting on it. I'll be sure to have it to you in ~~two weeks~~ ~~three weeks~~ one month, tops

Delivered
From: Savannah Cade
Sent: 9:26 AM
To: Claire Donovan
Subject: Re: Manuscript?

Dear Claire,

How thoughtful of you to reach out. I plan to have the manuscript to you by the end of the day.

Warmest regards,
Savannah Cade
Assistant Acquisitions Editor, Pennington Pen

Chapter 1

*P*acing the back corner of the packed meeting room in *outstandingly* uncomfortable heels, I move as silently as possible along the three feet of available aisle space between my begrudgingly accommodating coworker, Clyve, and the horde of beady-eyed osprey staring down at me from the vintage wallpaper. I frown at the eerily stenciled birds, like I always do whenever I'm called to the Magnolia Room. There is a pause between Ms. Pennington's words, and I sense the need to nod with the others as I check my watch. Only 3600 steps for the day, and it's already nearing noon.

I pivot dangerously on one thin heel and take a smaller, quicker step on the thick red carpet, all while slashing three words at the end of a paragraph. This is one of the benefits of being an assistant acquisitions editor at a publishing company more vintage than the eighties-styled jumpsuits circling back into fashion among teens. Editors here are constantly lugging around thick stacks of paper with pens behind their ears, jotting last-minute notes on authors' manuscripts, looking harried.

In fact, at Pennington Publishing, you'd look noticeably off if you *weren't* dragging around at least one manuscript to one of the half dozen meetings making up your day. Hence why none of the eyes in the rows ahead or around me so much as flicker as I flip from one page to another during this meeting.

Plus there's the fact that I'm not an inch over five feet tall. And one of the benefits of not being an inch over five feet tall in a publishing house whose "conference room" is a converted living room of an old Victorian mansion is that half the staff has to stand, and I can multitask my heart out behind them without being seen.

And I do try to multitask. At least on good days when I feel one of those rare bursts of genuine motivation—or at least when my sister prods me until I give in. Because I am a Cade. Specifically, Savannah Cade. And the Cades are a pure breed distinguished by indefatigable energy, marked enthusiasm, and a dash of insanity. Seamlessly exceeding expectations is what we do.

It's just . . . a little more challenging for me.

"Pennington Publishing has been a cornerstone of the nonfiction and literary fiction markets for over fifty years," Ms. Pennington, CEO of Pennington Publishing, says, gripping the podium. Her eyes glint like the six candle-like lights on the antique brass chandelier hanging in the center of the room. "Why? Because Pennington doesn't bow down to pressure. Because Pennington won't conform by throwing away our high-standing principles for a mere dollar in our pockets. Here at Pennington, we actually believe in the *content* we produce as a means of evolving and fine-tuning the minds of our readers and the culture at large. Unlike other houses lining the grocery-store shelves with"—her nose wrinkles, as though she can barely handle spitting out the words—"*commercial fiction* as quickly as they can, Pennington works tirelessly to produce only the most curated, thoroughly vetted manuscripts worth printing on the page. Only the most curated, vetted manuscripts we believe the world *needs* to read."

I raise a brow as I slash another word.

It's a nice sentiment, but I don't know if the *whole* world needed to have in their possession my latest edit: *The Incredible World of Words: An Epistemophiliac's Guide.*

"And that's why, despite the onslaught of crises thrown our way last year, Pennington Publishing will continue to be *the* foundational place readers and booksellers look to for the coming year. And it's for that reason I want you all to give a warm welcome to the newest employee of our team."

My pen slips on the underlining of a word. I lift my head. A new employee?

Through the sliver of space between two elbows I see Ms. Pennington holding on to the podium with two strong hands as she looks down at her employees, her sharp blue eyes narrowed as if reading all our minds: *Someone speak up. I dare you.*

Slowly, a round of applause picks up around the room.

The thing is, the past few years have been hard on Pennington Publishing. Not just us, really. It's been this way for most smaller publishers not yet swallowed up by one of the Big Five. Despite Pennington's years of glory (of which Ms. Pennington is only too quick to remind everyone at every turn), it hasn't been able to keep up with the solid chugging of the bigger, well-oiled machines. Pennington is a sailboat. A beautiful Pen Duick regatta cutter whose owner slides his hand over the rosewood, mahogany, teak, and other exotic tropical woods of the hull with pride while watching the vast white sail overhead billow in the sea-salt breeze. Intricately detailed. Unlike any other.

But still just a bobbing speck compared to the ocean liner charging through.

Which is why everyone inside these popsicle-green, osprey-ridden walls claps now like obedient penguins on cue at a waterpark show. It is why Terry in Accounts smooths down his Moby Dick *Thar She Blows!* whale-spotting necktie every five seconds whenever Ms. Pennington is in the room. It is why Lyla chucks her AirPods beneath her desk whenever we hear Ms. Pennington's nails tap impatiently on the casing of a neighboring office door during one of her spontaneous "visits." It is why I have to keep Band-Aids in my purse these days to handle the torment caused by these diabolical, aka "professional," heels.

Because we are the ones left. The survivors of the great Pennington bloodshed.

"I'm aware that we have lost quite a few dedicated employees in the past calendar year. The 29 percent reduction in staff has been . . ." Ms. Pennington's long, slim nostrils flare slightly as she breaks down the word into each clear syllable. ". . . chall-en-ging. Each one of us has been required to take on additional tasks."

Her pitch heightens as she lifts a finger in the air. "*But* that is precisely why we will rise again beneath Mr. Pennington's expertise."

Wait.

Mr. Pennington? As in . . .

"A man whose experience of ten years in one of the most successful publishing houses in the world," she continues, "will provide fresh insight and new angles." Her eyes grow steely.

"Helping us to *prune* when and where necessary in order to *blossom* for years to come. Mr. Pennington, we are thrilled to have you join us as VP and publisher of our most revered line, Pennington Pen."

For a second, there is nothing but stunned silence as those seated in the front turn their heads and those sardined in the back crane their necks to see the man, melted into the audience just a moment prior, stand. My pen, forgotten in my hand, slides across the page, leaving a long streak of black.

"Sssssssuper."

Lyla, sitting casually on the deep windowsill of the expansive window in front of me, rolls her eyes, revealing the glimmer of last night's metallic eyeshadow.

Lyla is one of the many in Nashville whose long blond hair accounts for half of her body weight, whose circle of friends who know her real name grows smaller by the year, and who, like the Nutcracker, only really comes to life when the clock ticks some insanely late hour. Only instead of waking up to battle rats and tour children around some bizarre dreamland, she can typically be found down at the strip, perched on a beer-stained barstool, singing her heart out. Lyla is to Nashville what skinny waitresses in their twenties are to New York City. A dime a dozen, starry eyed to the bitter end, and positively certain their current day job to fund things like food and clothing is only a momentary pit stop on the road to freedom. And while you can see Ms. Pennington's eyes twitching with desire to chuck Lyla and her laptop on the street just about every meeting, her cover designs and digital marketing are second to none. And I mean that. Second to *none*. She has literally rolled two full-time jobs into one.

"Well, at least someone can go tell Harry it wasn't about

his little run-in with Ms. Pennington over those galleys," Lyla mutters—loud enough that several in the row beside her turn their heads. "Just some good old-fashioned nepotism."

"*Shh*," Jeanna Banks (Pennington Trophy division, six years) hisses before turning back around.

Harry—dear old Harry, who brought the same egg-salad sandwich to work every day for the past twenty-two years—got The Email four weeks prior. Nobody wants to get The Email. The last thing any employee of Pennington Publishing wants to receive is the email addressed to them with the subject line: MEETING REQUESTED.

I turn from the wall and pace back, and Lyla, with her apathetic, I-hate-these-meetings gaze, sweeps her eyes over my manuscript. As she does so, her face clears. She raises one perfectly arched brow. "Is that . . . ?"

"I promised I'd turn it in today," I reply.

"Yeah, but . . . *here?*"

So this is what it feels like, being the one on the receiving end of a raised eyebrow.

All our lives it has been the other way around. Me, the rule keeper, the one staying tightly within the lines. Lyla, the free spirit. Smuggling in her diary—vibrantly pink and covered in hearts on the outside, secrets within—into middle school in seventh grade and holding it brazenly open during lunch period while I silently have a panic attack on her behalf. Lyla, gaily pitching in with the other seniors to fill up Principal Peterson's office with orange cones during spirit week, all while I stand guard, listening to my knees quake.

"I have to send it in today," I repeat swiftly. "I just need a few minutes to squeeze a last edit in."

Out of the corner of my eye, a man steps up to the podium beside Ms. Pennington, and she shakes his hand.

Like they've never met before.

Like this isn't the only human being standing before her with half her chromosomes.

I stifle a grin and keep on.

The thing is, everyone knows Ms. Pennington's son got sacked from Sterling House three months ago. Everyone was on high alert the day we got the mass *Pub News* email. It informed not only the employees at Pennington but every reputable publisher, literary agent, film agent, and everyone else related to the industry down to the aspiring author tapping away in some basement that Sterling House's newest editorial director was Jim Arrowood. Ms. Pennington's beloved son had not simply been on furlough during the pandemic of 2020. He had been *replaced*.

The son of the Queen of Hearts had been tossed out of New York City and landed here, back in Nashville.

And now Ms. Pennington is patching up her son's situation.

"Thank you for the introduction." William Pennington clasps both sides of the podium, just as his mother did. His posture is as perfect as his mother's, as though they both have rods attached to their spine. They look like a couple of penguins standing side by side in impeccable gray suits—the kind that are sleek and mind-numbingly dull and that few in this room could afford. His striking icicle-blue eyes—also the same as his mother's—pierce the room. And like her, he frowns.

Gazes at us as if we're juvenile delinquents trying to break out of the bus.

"I'm William Pennington. Some of you may remember me as a child."

"Little Willy!" In the front, old Bernie Peterson (Pennington Trophy, thirty-four years) waves, and William, without smiling, nods curtly.

"I won't keep you unnecessarily. Authors are now making their way to us for the conference, and we all know how imperative it is to prepare as much as possible. From what I've gathered, nobody wants a repeat of two years ago."

I halt.

Great. Just grrrreeeat.

My stomach lurches, just as it always does at the mention of my first Librarians of America Conference and Exhibition—or, for short, LOA. I raise my manuscript higher to avoid anyone's eyes.

So, I had done this tiny, innocuous thing of losing four hundred books and the entire set of promotional materials for my author, who had flown across the country for his signing. He'd ended up signing bits of scrap paper and bookmarks that were actually promotions for other authors and—in one incredibly uncomfortable moment—one man's bulging bicep.

There's a *lot* to remember for these big events. Not easy when you've only worked for the company a total of two weeks, okay?

4200 steps.

Maybe Ms. Pennington hadn't specifically said who'd done it, I tell myself, moving my eyes from my watch and flipping a page. Maybe William had just been told the story in an off-handed way, like, "Yes, one of our employees—who turned out be quite bright, really, an invaluable employee during these harsh and trying times—had the unfortunate experience of being undertrained as a new hire, and, poor thing, she ended up having to . . ."

I half listen as I march on, my eyes scanning for any misspellings or glaring errors. There aren't many, only one or two notes every dozen pages, which only fuels the inner fire hungry to run up to my office and email the manuscript right now.

Ms. Pennington wouldn't fire me for a bathroom break, would she? I mean, yes, technically Donna got The Email two days after dashing to the bathroom with the stomach bug. But that was coincidental. Right? That had to have been coincidental.

And how many times have I edited this manuscript at this point? Two dozen times? Fifty times? A *hundred*? Whatever it is, it certainly feels like a thousand.

And that feeling, as I've told my own authors so many times, means it's done. It's finally ready. That's the telling moment.

Or when the deadline hits. Whichever comes first.

"So let's stay sharp, people," William Pennington says as I pivot on my heel. Less than twenty minutes on the job and he's already the perfect replica of his mother, droning on about razor-thin budgets and how he won't hesitate to "prune us back" at the slightest error.

I lick the tip of my index finger and flick the current page over my paper clip. It's not just any paper clip, mind you. Fourteen karats of antique rose gold intricately twisted into the shape of a sparrow, this oversize clip is the one Mom gave me on my first day in a "real job." It's the clip she herself used for over twenty years on her most promising papers and projects as chair of her department at Belmont University. One passed down from her own mother, who used it to keep her papers in place while fighting against health inequities among the poverty stricken as the first female surgeon in her state. And *her* mother who—I'm still a bit hazy on the details—apparently more or less ended the war.

You know, typical Cade-level stuff.

While I may not be shattering glass ceilings left and right like my ancestors, I have reserved the paper clip for only the most promising of stories out of respect for its heritage.

And now, with its golden wings clinging tightly to the papers, it is reserved for the story that is my own.

"Tonight is a big night," Pennington continues.

I flip another page. I'm so close to the end my heart starts racing in step with my pace.

"The eight authors attending this weekend's conference represent 46 percent of our sales. To lose their trust in us through our own performance is to potentially cost us one of our four imprints. We need them. But right now, Pennington authors are afraid. Most authors across the board, for that matter, are afraid. Tensions are high. The publishing world is more competitive than ever. People everywhere are wondering about the stability of their own jobs."

"That's hitting a bit too close to home for him, isn't it?" murmurs Lyla.

"People want to know they are standing on solid ground. So when they get here, they're going to be looking around for clues about the status of Pennington Publishing. And it's absolutely imperative we give them nothing to worry about." William Pennington levels his gaze. "*Imperative.* So, Marketing, get those displays looking perfect. Assistants, make sure they want for *nothing.* And editors, do whatever it takes this weekend to keep your authors happy. Whatever. It. Takes. If these authors want to spend two hundred dollars on dinner at Fleming's Steakhouse, whip out the company card like we're made of money. If they want to meet you at five in the morning this Saturday to spend the next twelve hours dissecting their next work-in-progress, you'd better be sitting in their hotel lobby at four thirty, perky and with a second cup of coffee in hand. I don't care what you do so long as at the end of the weekend they get on their planes remembering Pennington Publishing as the most dedicated, engaging, *stable* publishing company giving 110 percent to ensure their books outsell any others in the market. I want them to come away from this visit incapable of thinking anything other than one word: perfectio—"

I reach the wall and pivot but then, in a blink, hear a rather peculiar sound from below.

It sounds like cellophane paper crinkling.

But that can't be right, I find myself thinking as I turn my eyes toward the floor. After all, where would the cellophane paper be coming from? Who would bring cellophane paper into a meeting room? And why on earth would it be directly under my feet?

And then, in that nanosecond in which everything makes terrible sense, I feel it.

The lightning strike upon my ankle. My bones crackling as they grind against each other in ways the bones of no ankle anatomically should.

I look down and see my foot overturning, as if in slow motion, as the dagger of my thin black heel flips sideways on the plush red carpet. I throw my left foot forward, trying to stabilize myself, but in lunging only manage to land on Yossi's heel in front of me before that ankle gives as well.

With both ankles collapsed I fall forward, heads and suits rising on either side of my periphery, the carpet rushing toward me—one gigantic pool of red. I throw my hands out just before my body hits the floor in a tangled mess.

The carpet burns against the side of my face, my arms, my shins. Dimly, I hear the sound of my pen landing and clicking off on the carpet a couple of inches from my face. Feel, to my fresh horror, the breeze on my backside where my skirt has flipped up and is now revealing the poorly chosen underwear I put on this morning. Of *course* this moment couldn't have come during my cheeky bikini streak of 2019. Of *course* this had to happen when I'd pretty much given up the paranoia that this exact situation could one day possibly come to fruition. When I'd decided that nobody would ever need to cut through my clothes in a car crash. That there was never really going to be a moment in the dead of night when the fire alarm went off through the entire building and I was left stranded in the middle of the street in my granny panties making small talk with the neighbors.

And there was certainly no reason to fear I would trip on my own feet during an all-employee staff meeting and faceplant on the ground with my skirt flipped up.

Anyway, here I am.

Maybe the best thing to do now would be to play dead.

Yes, that seems like a good idea. After all, possums do it, and it seems to work for them. It's even a biological method of survival. It's *innate*. That really should count for something. Besides, nobody makes fun of people who pass out. It's like a "Get out of jail free" card. You can tease behind closed doors all you want when somebody falls flat on their faces, but try that when the situation seems remotely serious, and you are a horrible, insensitive person.

That's it, then. I'm going to have to play possum.

I'm just resolving to get comfortable on the carpet when a

different sound filters through my brain. A much, much more devastating sound. The sound of flapping, like a hundred doves overhead.

Oh no.

No, no, no, no, no.

My eyes flit open, and there they are. Each leaf of my 234-page manuscript soaring through the air, freed from the golden paperclip that had hitherto clipped their wings.

Any thought of previous embarrassment dissolves, and springing to my knees, I snatch at the sheets of paper wafting down around me. Vaguely, I hear William Pennington in the distance continuing his speech as I reach between one man's shoes for a few pages and clutch them tightly. Out of the corner of my eye I see Lyla making a grab for the ones scattered at her own feet.

Of all the moments . . .

My forehead starts to burn as I see staff around me leaning down, picking up sheets of paper at their feet.

"Thank you," I say, rising and seizing pages from each of their hands. "Perfect. Thanks. So sorry. Bless you, Marta. Thanks."

I'm a hoarding dragon, smuggling paper as fast as I can, grabbing pages in all directions and, whenever someone bends to pick one up, breaking stride to grab it from their hands.

I scan the perimeter.

Half the pages secure and protected.

Thirty seconds go by.

More than half.

Another twenty seconds.

Eighty percent.

At this point I volley every new sheet to Lyla, who crams

them into her giant leather tote. It kills me to see the pages wedged inside her bag, but I don't have time. It'll be a bear sorting them later, but I have to keep my priorities in line.

I spot five pages out in the wild and lunge for them.

The light at the end of the tunnel is starting to shine through. My rib cage is starting to loosen.

Three pages.

Two.

One.

I throw the last sheet at Lyla.

None. All of the manuscript safely crammed into Lyla's bag. Done.

I sit back on my heels at last, kneeling on the carpet, exhaling for the first time in what feels like years.

I did it. I came close—too close—to the biggest mistake of my professional career, but I escaped. There's a temptation to let out a hysterical giggle of relief.

Only . . .

Vaguely I note the silence around the room, like a little tap on the shoulder saying, "Hey, now that you've gotten that fixed up, you may want to have a look around."

So I do. I look up. And catch everyone's stares. Recall the little mishap over my skirt. Feel the general need to pretend the last sixty seconds didn't just happen.

"Thanks, everyone." I press both palms on the carpet, my fingers going deep into the plush, and start to push myself up.

Creepy Rem's (Pennington Scribe, four years) eyes are glued to my skirt, and I frown and tug it down another inch.

"Sav!" Lyla hisses.

She points over my shoulder. Her eyes are wide, blue, and

unnervingly crystalized on a single point in the distance. I jerk my head around and follow the direction of her finger.

Ten feet over, a single sheet of paper lies in the center of the aisle—and a dozen eyes rest on it like vultures about to dive.

I scramble to my feet.

"Excuse me," I say, touching shoulders as I rush past bodies. My legs feel like soft macaroni with each step. The row is packed. People are everywhere. People and laptop bags and purses and stray books and—

Finally, I hop over the last travel mug, untangle myself from a final computer bag trying to latch onto my heels, and emerge into the aisle.

At last, I'm free.

I stop.

Freeze.

Because *the* William Pennington is standing squarely in front of me.

He's even taller up close, his chin a solid foot, if not more, above me. I'd wager he has just a handful of years on me, given the single slight—though not, I have to admit, wholly unattractive—crease across his otherwise smooth forehead. A baby crease. The kind of crease that says, "I've reached a point in my life where I won't try to take you to Sonic for a first date, but not the point where I go to bed before ten." Mature in a way that, if he was placed side by side with some frat boy, he'd come out ahead, looking wholly more dependable but not so much older he was less attractive.

His eyes are even bluer this close, as shocking and pristine as blue ice on the frozen lakes of Michigan. Even his irises seem to be covered in crystals, as when snow descends on a glacier and air bubbles are squeezed out. (This, by the way, is what I get with my job: loads of random trivia stuck in my head to use on a whim.)

But at this precise moment, I have a hard time thinking about icebergs or the Jökulsárlón glacial lagoon in Iceland. Because right now, William Pennington is staring at the sheet in his hands. And right now, I have only the ability to focus on the overwhelming feeling reverberating up my spine: terror.

Hair-raising, mind-numbing terror.

I'm paralyzed.

I am going to get fired. This is it. I, Savannah Cade, am going to lose my job over a stupid, *stupid* piece of paper.

Why did I doubt myself at the last minute and smuggle my manuscript into work?

Why didn't I just press Send on that email this morning and let things lie?

But while I wait in agony, his arctic-blue eyes scan the page as though he has taken no notice of me or the fact that the whole room is silently watching. No emotion plays on his face. Nothing, except for the small frown nestled between his brows. His eyes dance from line to line, word to word.

With every muscle in me, I manage to put my hand out, my fingertips silently begging for its return.

He ignores me. Reads on.

The room is deathly quiet.

Everyone is looking at us—him and me.

Although, where else would they be? This is the moment of the beheading.

I'm going to be the next one axed.

Out of the corner of my eye I see Maggie (Pennington Arch,

eight years) looking at me with huge, doleful eyes that say, "I'll always remember you and that time we shared that yogurt in the kitchen."

It's too much to bear.

"What's going on?" Ms. Pennington's voice crackles from the front of the room.

Her voice seems to break the spell, and William Pennington blinks.

He looks up and for the first time takes me in properly. My face, like all good-southern-girl faces, doesn't seem to know how to respond to direct eye contact with anything besides a smile, and to my horror, I feel my lips begin to creep up on the sides.

Stop it, I tell my lips sternly, to which they sort of halt halfway and slowly, with incredible effort, tug back down.

Perfect. Throw *insane* into his growing impression.

He blinks again, his expression unchanged.

It's the pinnacle moment. The moment that, with no exaggeration, will decide my future at the company. Because Ms. Pennington doesn't just not like commercial fiction. She *loathes* it. And romance, according to her, is the lowest form. It is, according to Ms. Pennington herself, the stuff read aloud in Dante's lowest level of hell. On par with pink Moscato, girls in wraparound scarves holding pumpkin-spice lattes, and country music.

And yet here I stand, in possession of "literature's kudzu."

Standing before her own totalitarian son, a complete stranger brought in from the big city to swing the ax, and I'm wearing a weak, semi-unstable smile.

I may as well start thinking about how to pack up my office.

He holds out the sheet, still expressionless.

Dumbly, I take it. "Oh. Thank you."

For a moment there is silence.

"Nothing," he calls over his shoulder at last and turns on his heel. "Just some paper on the floor. Now," he says, raising his voice once again to executive status as he paces up the aisle, "as I was saying . . ."

I watch William Pennington stride back to the front of the room, his voice distant and commanding as he continues to forecast dire numbers and the tragedies that will ensue if we don't up our game. I creep back to my position beside Lyla and, after several seconds, glance down to the sheet he has read.

The second I see it, any lingering hope that he didn't recognize it for what it was bursts into flames.

My eyes graze along the header splashed across the top center of the page in neat Times Roman type: WORKING TITLE: PINING FOR YOU. The name in italics along the top right corner: *Holly Ray.*

My jaw tightens intuitively as I read the paragraph beneath it: "Time slowed as he slipped one hand to her shoulder, then cradled her neck as they stood there beneath the maple tree, the whisper of passing cars all around . . ."

There is no doubt about it.

William Pennington knows.

Chapter 2

"There's no way he knows."

For the first time in our lives I am outstriding Lyla as my heels make their wobbly way down the hall. Up another layer of stairs, and we enter the second floor with its own set of plush carpeting—royal blue this time—and wallpaper alternating between men in caps pushing ladies on swings and maidens dancing round and round to what must've been quite the lively jig.

I round the corner.

"It was just one page—"

"One page is enough," I interject.

"He barely looked at it. Not to mention we work in a *publishing* house, and every other sheet of paper in this building is a manuscript." Lyla levels her gaze. "C'mon, Sav. You don't even use your real name. You've just exercised the whole *point* of a pen name—"

"That's not the issue," I say without slowing. "The issue is he read enough to know it wasn't Pennington Publishing material.

He knows it's romance." I lower my voice to a meaningful hiss. "*Romance.*"

This must be what it feels like to be a criminal. I'm about as straitlaced as the Keds tucked inside my lower desk drawer waiting for the second the clock ticks to 5:00 p.m. Never skipped a class. Never cheated on a test. But now, harboring . . . fiction? And not just fiction, but *romance?* And not just romance, but *my* romance—*my* romance that I was not only reading, not only writing, but working on during *work* hours?

If Ms. Pennington had picked up that sheet, that would've been it.

I'd have been chased out the door, dodging copies of *Medieval Limericks for Lovers* and *The Practical Houseplant* chucked at my head.

I need to get this somewhere safe—now.

We pass doorframe after doorframe of entrances to various offices. There's a hum in the distance of people downstairs, the shuffling of bodies slowly moving outside, everyone with a job—picking authors up from airports and hotels, heading to the conference center to set up.

The hallway up here is unusually quiet.

I'm going about fifteen miles an hour, easily toe-to-toe with any Olympic walker, when Lyla grabs the tote strap across my shoulder and yanks. My heels tangle in the carpet.

I stop. Turn around, careful to keep a protective hand over the bag.

"Ooooookay, dearie," Lyla says. "I hear you. You don't want to lose your job to domineering overlords. I get it. But if you want to keep it, that means you actually need to follow directions. Which, at this moment, is going outside."

"I have to find a place to dump this," I say, hearing a creak and darting my eyes over her shoulder, then behind. "If I get rid of all the evidence and act nonchalant, maybe he'll forget what he saw. Or I can insist he didn't see what he saw."

Lyla raises a brow. "So . . . you want to . . . gaslight . . . your new boss. You do hear yourself?"

I can tell by her eyes. I know it. I know I look like I've lost it. But anyone would if they'd spent every spare minute of the past three years talking to imaginary characters in their heads, dreaming about the story they'd created, staying up late on more nights than they could count putting that story onto paper.

Being an editor at Pennington Pub is my job. And being a writer is my dream—my very personal dream.

And I can't risk both by letting my manuscript fall back into his hands.

Lyla blinks, charcoal-black eyelashes drifting down and then back up to meet her eyebrows. It looks like it's taking absolutely everything in her to avoid rolling her eyes. "Fine. Just stash the goods in your desk and let's go. Okay?"

She waves an arm down the hallway like Vanna White showing off a yacht behind a shimmering curtain. "Before we really *do* get fired. You heard the new boss. Head to the lobby so we can stand around like sorority girls welcoming the newest pledges on the lawn."

"Right. But . . ." I pull away from her arm, backtracking out of her reach. "I . . . I forgot a book Oswald has been asking about. He wanted to see if he could get an advance copy of Jenny's February release—"

"*Thriving in Premenopause?*" Lyla asks. "Why would old Ossie want a copy of *Thriving in Premenopause?*"

But before she can say anything more, I turn and book it down the rest of the hall.

"Are you at least going to bring back my bag?" she calls out.

"Three minutes!" I repeat over my shoulder and turn the corner.

As my footsteps widen the space between Lyla and me, I feel as if I've entered the last moments of the *Titanic* before it completely submerged. In a world typically humming with conversations and people passing to and fro, all the hallways are dead. The wallpaper—probably dating back to *Titanic* days itself—doesn't help the mood. Everything around me screams the same vibe I would've felt had I been a passenger back then, recklessly running back, deep into the lower levels of the ship, to grab one last priceless thing.

I wind around the corner and take my first step onto the small spiral staircase in front of me. The tiny, ornate steps barely contain the balls of my feet. Halfway up and my breath comes in short spurts as I grip and regrip the curving railing. Had this not been my home, my refuge, had I not ventured up this very staircase so many of the last 687 days, I would've without question lost my footing.

A stretch of faded yellow wallpaper greets me at the top of the stairs. There is no carpeting on this floor, only creaky hardwood screeching like an off-key violin with every step. I can only assume the unusual lack of maintenance on this floor is because nobody ventures up to the attic level. Who cares about improving a floor nobody except the rare visiting author treads on?

I move to the door at the end of the hall and check my watch.

Two minutes and twenty seconds. Perfect. If anyone asks, I just had to step away for a twenty-second bathroom break.

The door is closed. There is a simple black plaque beside it, just as all the rooms at Pennington Publishing are marked. In small gold script it reads *Storage*. It's not what we actually call it—we all call it the ARC room—but at any rate, that's its given name.

Nothing wild. Nothing out of the ordinary from any publishing house. Just . . . an ARC room.

But even as I grab hold of the old glass knob, I feel a tingle.

Magic.

The door creaks in a kind of screeching harmony with the floorboards as I push it open. Inside, the ceiling slants precariously low this way and that, matching the exterior of the old Victorian house and its multigabled roof. The room is dark in the windowless space, but without hesitating I take three steps forward, two right, sidestep a cardboard box, and reach blindly up for the chain. The lightbulb flares to life, illuminating everything in a vintage yellow hue.

Books.

Rows and rows of books.

Aisles of books. Shelf after shelf, crate after crate of books as far as the eye can see.

I inhale the smell of old pine, baked insulation, and freshly printed paper and move to the next aisle, where I pull on another string. The light roars to life, then another. Floorboards creak as I pass aisle after aisle, trying my best to ignore the glinting hardcovers and sheening paperbacks of new releases.

I can't help it. There's something about being in a room filled with *free* books that always makes me feel like a kid in a candy shop.

Every publishing house has an ARC room—a place dedicated for advance review copies of books about to be released.

Influencers and bookstagrammers need to see advance copies so they can polish and post their reviews on time. Authors need ARCs for endorsement blurbs. Magazines and publications need a lengthy lead time in order to get their articles lined up for release. And yes, on the rare occasions Pennington authors visit the office, their book-loving souls always spring to life at the mention of a trip to the ARC room. In fact, on more than one occasion I've had to drag an author out of the room when he or she took my words "Take whatever you want" to heart.

(And no, as I've had to explain multiple times, taking six copies of the same book for "Christmas presents" isn't what we have in mind when we offer.)

But I can never be too hard on them. I understand them.

Free books.

Free prerelease books.

Only a true reader would understand. Saying the music-to-ears words, "Browse around. Anything in this room is yours"? Well, the cobwebs bordering the bookshelves and hovering around corner crevices always start to glint like gold. The room suddenly smells like a field of tulips. Every creak in the floorboard is a choir singing, "Hallelujah."

Even if books were all the room contained, it'd be magical enough.

But . . . it's not just books.

It's more.

I stop before three identical filing cabinets against the slanting wall of the farthest corner. The cabinets themselves look as old as the house. The metal is cracked and rusted on every corner. Cobwebs cling to each handle. The whole thing looks like nobody has touched it in a hundred years. Just how

I like it. Just how, I know instinctively, the one before me liked it as well.

With one swift glance behind me and the same growing anticipation I always have, I grab the center handle and give it a tug. Feel the drawer give.

I still remember the shock the first time I opened this drawer. I was just a little fledgling at Pennington at the time, and it had been a particularly hard day. Ms. Pennington had just given me a public tongue-lashing over my "overuse of useless and distracting flower pictures" on a PowerPoint during an editorial meeting. This had come right after my supervisor, Giselle, had thrown out some not-so-subtle clues that I'd taken a major misstep in going on a date with her ex-boyfriend the week prior. When someone asked if we could get rid of a leftover box of books from the previous meeting, I jumped at the opportunity to be alone.

I remember how I crept into the room, barely making a sound, feeling that with one small creak something sinister would surely jump out from behind the shadowy bookcases. I remember seeing the metal cabinets in the corner and how I thought it looked like a good spot for storage. How I tentatively gave that little handle a tug. And how, instead of what I'd prepared for—the single drawer scratchily sliding out, revealing a bunch of forgotten files—the *entire* face of the file cabinet swung open. It took everything within me not to cry out as I stumbled back, tripping on a box of old books in the opposite corner along the way. My head had grazed a massive cobweb on the wall, and I'd spent the rest of the day breaking out into fits imagining spiders crawling through my hair.

But the discovery I made in that moment was well worth it.

Pulling Lyla's tote close, I hunch to half my height and carefully step through the open door.

One push against the back of the metal cabinet, and it swings open as well.

My personal wardrobe to another world.

And suddenly I'm here.

The room is dark, illuminated only by the window and its streaming light just below the cone-top roof. I glance at the stained-glass sparrow, the purple of its wings shading the beanbag in the center of the small turret in violet hues, as my fingers find the chain and tug. The lightbulb swings as it comes on, revealing the beaten, wine-red Persian rug in the center of the floor and the curved bookcases rimming the shoebox-size room.

Books. Dozens of them, brought here—like the rug, like the beanbag—not by me but by someone before.

Covers of books framed in cheap wood hanging along the wall, all signed by their authors. Stacks of books forming a sort of side table on either side of the beanbag. One half-read overturned book with cracking spine waiting impatiently on top of a book stack for me to return and finish.

Slowly, over the past two years, I've been adding to the books, inserting my own favorites into the treasures harbored here. Ones I love. Ones that mean something to me as well.

I've always felt it was our little secret—mine and the mysterious person who made this their secret refuge before me.

Our little sparrow room.

Our little hideaway.

I check my watch. Three minutes and twenty seconds. (And 4678 steps! I may just hit 5K by lunch!) Not even time to organize the mess. Only time to drop and go.

I feel exposed flipping the tote over and spilling the crumpled, beaten sheets all over the rug. I've never left my manuscript here before. For that matter, I've never brought it to work at all, until today.

And yet, where better to hide your secrets than in your secret hideaway?

With one more long look at the papers at my feet and with the silent promise of return as soon as possible in my heart, I pull on the string to turn off the light and leave it all behind.

Chapter 3

I t's the Griswold Family Christmas reunion.

Boisterous greetings echo around the vast foyer of the old mansion, bouncing from the polished marble floors to the frames of bestselling Pennington releases lining the walls. Several silhouettes are in view through the windows, framing a crowd chatting on the creaking planks of the wide, wraparound porch outside. Old brass sconces, faithfully keeping their posts, glimmer softly. The chandelier, with its 352 crystals, high above quivers with a booming laugh.

Arms are thrust out and hugs in dripping overcoats passed around as Pennington's authors escape the freezing rain and step inside. Conversations like "How was your trip?" and "I saw your post about your missed flight, poor thing" and even "I'm sorry, Tabby, but I really don't think trying to conceive is a permissible excuse for missing your deadline" float all around me. Cheeks are flushed, partly from the excitement, partly because the foyer is so hot and crowded.

And me?

I'm just about quivering with excitement. Or at least my stomach is.

Because today is a *free* day. And not just any old free day, but a free day with a company card. A free day where I literally get paid to take authors out under the illusion of company grandeur to eat at that new restaurant I've been eyeing for months and can't afford. A free day to prance around the city with whichever author I'm hosting—making sure they have a good time, sure, chatting over their newest ideas, yes, but also *eating*. And sightseeing, sure. But then *eating* some more.

I can almost feel the silver company card in the large pocket of my pea coat throbbing like a heartbeat. Ready for action. Chanting, *Free. Free. Free.*

I haven't eaten all day in anticipation.

I feel like a kid at Christmas.

"Delilah! Over here!" One shrill voice overshadows the others, and I feel an elbow jutting into my side. I stumble forward as Giselle, completely ignoring me, wiggles her outstretched fingers toward Delilah Ray until she's hugging her like a beloved sailor returned after a decade.

It's been two days.

Delilah Ray, posh Instagram influencer with about a million followers watching her every move (and, in turn, buying her book describing her every move), lives in Nashville.

Giselle is my boss. Actually, one of my many, many bosses, but specifically the one directly above me. She is five ten. Her hair is a sheet of platinum blond. And after one semester abroad a decade ago, she still likes to tell everyone to be quiet when she's on her "mobile" and how "knackered" she is after a night on the town. Oh. And she loathes me.

But honestly, how was I supposed to know, my first week in, that Sam in Contracts was in an on-again, off-again relationship with Giselle when he asked me—also reeling from my own on-again, off-again relationship—out? To borrow Giselle's words, it bloody well wasn't a picnic for me either. Nobody likes to be used as bait to lure in a jealous ex-girlfriend who just so happens to be your new and extraordinarily spiteful boss. Anyway, two years later, despite the fact that we are all adults, she still hasn't forgiven me.

Giselle and Delilah Ray are locked in one of those exhausting, ignore-everyone-else-in-the-place-while-talking-at-top-volume sort of greetings, taking up so much space that it's hard to see the new figure who has just stepped inside behind them. I perk up, however, at the hint of a red knitted sweater in the distance and step on tiptoe for visual confirmation.

Sure enough, Oswald pops out from behind them, looking around in bewilderment. In fact . . . he looks a bit like a flight risk. Oh dear.

At once, I hurry over to greet him.

"Oswald, so glad you could come," I say, closing the gap between us. I grab his hand and give it a hearty shake, partly in greeting, partly to keep him from retreat. "And look at you." I take in the thick red turtleneck curling around his neck. "Is that a new sweater from the missus?"

His huge eyes blink behind his round glasses as he struggles to focus on me. Poor Oswald. Brilliant with words. Incredibly knowledgeable of his craft. Terrific in sales. Terrible with people.

"My turtleneck?" he says at last, looking dubiously down at his sweater. "Well . . . yes."

I smile patiently. "And did you get all settled in at the hotel?"

Another lengthy pause. At last, a nod.

"Wonderful." I smile wider. "Wonderful." The next twenty-four hours are going to be a breeze, *clearly*. I strike for another topic. "I'm sorry your wife wasn't able to make the trip. What's she going to be up to this weekend? Something fun, I hope?"

The pause is excruciating, nearly as long as his page-long descriptions of deciduous trees. "Reading."

"And?" I nod encouragingly, waiting for more.

Oswald blinks, and I realize that's the end of his story.

Well, enough chitchat. It's time to get down to the fun part anyway.

And besides, there's a real plus here, I remind myself. The bright side of having an Oswald—and not, say, a Delilah Ray—is that Oswald is, above all things, compliant. Passive to the point of me begging for his opinions on marketing strategy and cover designs. I've always had to be careful when editing his latest books (covering topics like "Is the variegated liriope really the best way to color the border of your woodland garden?") because he, master of horticulture, with a surprisingly large social media following that tracks his every garden-loving move, would take even the slightest question in my edit to heart and completely flip his world upside down to agree with me (who, for the record, can't keep a succulent alive).

Being an editor is a dangerous position of power, really. One snap of my fingers and he'd be making "Concrete gardens: the way of the future" the subject of his next release.

But today?

Today I'm going to use my power to its full advantage.

"Now, for our afternoon," I say, scrabbling in my bag for my keys, "I found this lovely little bistro downtown and took the liberty of snagging us some reservations. I thought we could start things off with a nice cup of coffee and brunch and go from there. Are you a fan of fish? I hear the flounder with shrimp stuffing is something else—"

"I'm allergic," puts in Oswald, and he looks so startled at his own interruption that his mouth claps shut.

"Allergic," I say, fumbling momentarily, then see he's starting to turn red. Not to worry. I pivot with ease. "That's fine. *Completely* fine. There are plenty of other specialties there as well. I'm sure—"

"I can't eat there," interrupts Oswald again, and just as before he pops his mouth shut.

"Oh." Given the man is so passive he once tried to tell me "not to worry about that next book advance" (to which his agent swiftly stepped in, negating everything Oswald said on his behalf), I have to admit his response is a bit surprising. I once saw Oswald interviewed on a morning coffee show where the host mistakenly picked up the script meant for the following week and, for thirty minutes straight, asked him about some book called *The Murderer's Dilemma*. Did Oswald correct him? No. He just sat there, ears flaming red, answering to the name Skippy G and giving mumbled responses about what he was going to do now that he was released from prison after thirty years behind bars.

Oh, for goodness' sake. Sweat's starting to bead up on Oswald's receding hairline.

"This is not a problem, Oswald," I say as soothingly as I can manage while putting a hand on his shoulder. "We can go absolutely anywhere you like. Anywhere at all. The day is yours."

My stomach rumbles.

Anyplace, Ossie. Before my stomach growls so loud it makes a scene.

But amazingly enough, he shakes his head.

"C'mon, now." I nod encouragingly. "You just name the place. We'll go anywhere."

At last, he speaks. Granted, it's so quiet that I have to lean in, but he speaks. I frown as I hear a few unclear words.

"What was that?"

With my ear practically pressed to his mouth, and his hot breath tickling my ear, he whispers, "I'm fasting."

I step back and look him in the eye. "You're on a . . . fast. Well . . ." My thoughts begin to churn madly. "That's okay. In fact, that's *great*, Oswald. Really *great*. Good for you." And I'm about to say something like, "We can just pop in and you can talk about your new release over a glass of water (while I try out the champagne, chicken gumbo, mahi, and tiramisu)," when I feel a presence over my shoulder.

I turn my head.

William Pennington is standing behind me, his hands stiffly at his sides, clearly waiting to step into the conversation. I don't know how long he's been standing there, but in the moment's pause, he steps forward and stretches out his hand.

"Mr. Makers. Such a pleasure to meet you. I'm William Pennington, the new VP and publisher of our Pennington Pen division."

Oswald blinks up at the tall man and hesitatingly reaches out his hand. "What . . . what happened to Harry?" he asks.

"Are you getting your plans all sorted out for the day?" William says, pressing on as though he hadn't heard him at all.

Oswald blinks. Looks at me.

"We are," I jump in enthusiastically. "We're just planning to . . . to . . ." But all that's coming to mind is biscotti. And manicotti. And lattes with swirly foam art in the shape of a leaf. In restaurants where the tab is a week's worth of pay. All *free*.

I can see William looking at me expectantly. *C'mon, Sav. You did plan this out. You had a whole list of things to do outside of food. Think. What was on your list?* Brunch at Butcher & Bee. Drop in to scout around Parnassus and the Bookshop (because . . . books). Lunch at Margot. A quick drink at Attaboy before returning to hear Trace Green for LOA commencement.

Now *that* is one thing I am particularly excited about. I mean, Trace *Green*. I've loved him since college. He was actually what started me on writing in the first place.

I was in the middle of yet another breakup with Ferris when I read one of his books. And became hooked. *Hooked*. Flew through all twenty-four of his novels in the span of two months and spent the next three wandering around morosely, craving more. Everybody thought my slump was because I missed Ferris. But no, it wasn't. Not that time. I mean, of course, the breakup was *hard*, but it wasn't nearly as heart-wrenching as the fact that there were no more Green books to read. The reality that I was going to have to wait a whole nine months before another of his releases was almost too much to bear.

I mean, what, after all, *happened* to Clara in *The Woman on the Train*?

Would she *ever* get out of that manhole?

The whole experience of stumbling into his books made such an impression on my life that I went down to the registrar's office, set one of his books on the counter between me and the registrar's assistant, and declared I wanted to change majors. No more nursing for me. My life was going to revolve around *words*.

A total stranger had given me solace through the power of words, helped me escape the troubles of my world if just for enough time to get a much-needed breath, and even—through several quietly uplifting messages threaded throughout his fast-paced novels—showed me what it was like to pursue my dreams. Try new adventures. Dare.

The written word became my passion. And from that moment on all I knew was what an incredible honor it would be to bring that adventure, that life, that joy, that hope, that *world* to somebody else.

To pen novels—to play any role in bringing fiction to life, for that matter—is to wield a superpower.

"Le Écureuil Volant!" squeals Giselle from across the room, her bony fingers jubilantly clasping Delilah's. I haven't seen her this happy since Trina from Accounts got fired and freed up that parking spot. "And after we go *there*, Parnassus wants to talk about your Sunday signing. Then, if you're game, I booked a *fantastic* package at the Paintbox for a mani-pedi."

"Mr. Makers." My attention is drawn back to William, and although he's smiling at Oswald, I can see a steely flash in his eyes as they dart momentarily my way. "You flew in from Nevada, is that right?"

Oswald gazes up at him like this is a trick question. "Yes," he says uncertainly.

"And you plan to leave tomorrow?"

Oswald's slight double chin wobbles while his eyes dart from William to me, hesitating as though trying to make out where the trap lies.

At last he gives the slightest of nods.

"Well, we at Pennington would love to make the most of your efforts in traveling here," William continues. "So please tell us, what is it that *you* would like to do before tonight's welcoming banquet?"

The previous long pause seems like a snap in comparison to the one that follows, and for what feels like an eternity we stand there, watching the man think. As his teary blue eyes swivel round the room as if this is the deepest question he's been asked all day, I feel an odd sense of trepidation rising. What will he say? With anyone else, I could predict an answer. But with Oswald? The man's a shot in the dark. You never know where he's going to land.

But . . . this is okay. There is *still* a win here. The point is I have the company card. I have the day off from my desk to tour Oswald around. And I do look pretty sharp in my outfit, if I say so myself: a deep maroon cardigan, white blouse, black tights, and trendy gray skirt with just enough twirl to show I can be fun while professional. My celebratory outfit for the eventual victory in sending in my manuscript tonight and, on top of that, snagging the free day. It took quite a while to squeeze myself into this thing, but even Olivia had to compliment me on it this morning—and that's really saying something.

"I . . . I believe you have one of those swimming tanks around here."

My thoughts halt. I see out of the corner of my eye one of the dark locks I painstakingly curled this morning start to fall. What did he say?

William's brows are pinched. "I'm sorry, I'm not sure I know what you mean. You'll have to clarify. You want to go swimming?"

"The Float Spot?" Oswald says at last. He blinks at me.

I stare for a moment, letting the words sink in. The Float Spot. Of all the thousands of wonderful things to do today, he wants to go to *the. Float. Spot.*

The newest sensory-deprivation saltwater tank in town, where you strip down to nothing, squeeze yourself into a tiny capsule, and, worst of all, shut the door. To *nothing.* Lyla introduced this bizarre hobby to me a few months ago on a holiday. She asked me if I wanted to go with her, and I went along, thinking the whole time we were going to a spa full of ordinary things like, oh, I don't know, relaxing music and pink nail polish and foot massages. Instead, where did I find myself? Sitting in an itchy robe in a cold room, waiting for my turn in the alien birthing pod. I distinctly remember this terrifying sign on the opposite wall in bold red letters:

EXTENDED SENSORY DEPRIVATION CAN RESULT IN EXTREME ANXIETY, HALLUCINATIONS, BIZARRE THOUGHTS, TEMPORARY SENSELESSNESS, AND DEPRESSION.

For the record, they forgot to add *NAUSEA* to the list.

I cannot possibly think of a worse idea.

"What a terrific idea." I snap my head to see William Pennington smiling brightly. "I can imagine few things more relaxing after a long flight. I'm sure Ms. Cade would love to join you. Wouldn't you, Savannah?"

He's looking at me expectantly. He's waiting for me to reply. He's waiting for me to say, "Oh, what a dream!" while Giselle is off in the corner with Delilah Ray somehow justifying the need to purchase matching Tory Burch bags to hold all their bookmarks.

Well, I'm just not going to. That's all there is to it. I'll drive Oswald to the crazy station if he wants, and then I'll sit in the lobby with a gas-station hot dog for three hours while he enjoys his silence. Oh! I *could* possibly even sneak back into the office, grab the manuscript, and work on it while I'm waiting. With any luck I could have it sent off to Claire Donovan even before the welcoming banquet tonight.

But as William's cold blue eyes peer into mine, I hear my plans sputter until they die out. I feel exposed, as though every thought is streaming across my eyes for him to read. Somehow, he knows what I'm thinking. From the frown tilted ever so slightly upon his lips to the crease between his brow, he *knows*, and he, the boss, *cares*. I can hear the words replaying in my own head: *"And editors, do whatever it takes this weekend to keep your authors happy. Whatever. It. Takes."*

A cold feeling comes over me, the air dropping fifteen degrees within a dark, ominous shadow.

I'm not going to get food.

I'm not going to get biscotti at 8th & Roast.

I'm not even going to get to listen to Trace Green.

No, what I'm going to do is get in that stupid tank.

My voice strangles as I turn to Oswald. "That's a brilliant idea, Oswald. I can't wait."

"Trace Green?" I hear Giselle's voice ring out, her Botoxed forehead struggling in vain to crease. "Yes, we can hear him, I suppose. But it might cut into our pedi time . . . Is he the one who wrote *Amber Waters*?"

"*Tides*," I mumble bitterly. "*Amber Tides*."

Well. It's settled, then. While my supervisor is off getting her perfectly manicured nails repolished and half listening to one of my favorite authors share powerful, never-heard-before tales while she is also scrolling through the J.Crew website, I'll be starving. In a lukewarm tank. In the dark. Hallucinating.

I look up and realize William Pennington is gazing at me. This time, however, it's in a way that isn't altogether . . . well, terrifying. "So. You are a fan of Green?" he says.

I stiffen. Green isn't exactly . . . literary. More like read-him-if-you-want-to-go-on-a-stay-up-till-dawn-ignore-all-family-and-friends-call-in-sick-for-two-days-fictional-adventure-of-your-life. That type of fiction.

"Oh," I say, shrugging. "I may have read him at some point years ago. I'm more of a . . . a Chaucer fan myself nowadays."

There's a long pause.

"Chaucer," he repeats.

His lips twitch. Is he trying not to smile?

"Yes," I say, lifting my chin a millimeter. "I adore Chaucer. Chaucer's . . ." I scour the crevices of my brain for that new Word of the Day I learned recently for just such an occasion. ". . . phantasmagorical." I wave my hand around. "I can read Chaucer's tales for hours."

And believe it or not, there it is again. The lip twitch.

"Really. And which tale is your favorite?"

Shoot, Savannah, now you've done it. But I know this. I read Chaucer in English Lit my freshman year. Or part of it. Or at least what I could understand through all the "ful ofte tyme he hadde" and "gentil knights." Now, which tales . . . which tales . . .

At last, like a blessed dove from above, a tale comes to mind, and I snatch for it. "Well, if pressed, I'd have to say 'The Miller's Tale.' Excellent message."

His work frown has apparently lost the battle against amusement entirely now, because the twitch gives up and finally concedes to a grin. "The drunken miller's fabliau about a carpenter and the two men who want to sleep with the wife. That message?"

For a moment, our eyes are locked. He's daring me to answer.

"Yes," I say, trying hard not to grind my teeth. "Yes, that's the one. Positively riveting stuff. And, of course, there are my other passions as well, like those books on"—my eyes dart to Oswald—"landscaping."

"Well, of course." William's eyes turn to Oswald as he puts out a hand. "Landscaping. So. Chaucer and . . . landscaping. You must have a sizable yard, then. For all that gardening."

"Not at the moment," I hedge. "But I do have a window box that's very inviting."

For the birds, who have built a nest on last year's dead pansies.

"Oh, right. Yes. I have seen some rather elaborate ones. There's really an art there." But for all his polite words, William's temples are crinkling, his eyes looking dangerously close to being outright mirthful. "I commend you for your efforts to educate yourself. Pity, though. I'm a bit of a Green fan myself. Would've been nice to meet another."

I can see the challenge in his gaze. He's waiting for me. Waiting for me to crack.

Now it's my turn to pull an Oswald and be wary of the conversational traps.

"What's the name of the one he put out last year?" He frowns as though talking to himself, trying to remember. "*Treacherous Games*?"

Lies. The book is *Treacherous Lies*, and he knows it.

I narrow my eyes.

For all I know, this is a test, and William Pennington is even more insane about the evils of commercial fiction than his mother is. After all, he was brought in to be the hangman. He is here to save Pennington and make the hard choices. I'm one of the newest employees to the company after all the others have been cut. First he sees me smuggling in romance on the job. Now, perhaps, he's gathering final evidence before the kill. Playing a little good cop before slamming the cell door.

"Anyway," I say loudly, "we've got a big day ahead of us, Oswald. We'd better be off."

For a moment William surveys me, looking as though he's working out whether he wants to pursue the conversation some more or let it go. But then he blinks, and with it, his expression vanishes. He turns his attention to Oswald.

"I look forward to hearing about it tonight," William says and gives Mr. Makers one final shake of the hand.

Oswald and I have just taken our first steps toward the door when William adds, "And Savannah?"

I pause and turn my head.

"I am particularly intrigued to hear how your experience goes in the pod today. Please be sure to update me. Perhaps it'll be something for the company to consider adding as a benefit in our health plan."

And there it is again. The merest twinkle in his corporate eyes. If I didn't know better, I'd even call it a dare.

I plaster my smile firmly in place, partly because I refuse to admit a dare from my boss and the CEO's son could even exist, partly because the mere thought of adding float tanks to the corporate health plan is so revolting it threatens to make me nauseous. "Of course. I'll be looking forward to it."

Eight long hours later, my hair *still* clings wet and tangled in a tight bun on the top of my head. Not the cute kind of bun. Not the oh-look-at-me-in-my-slouchy-sweater-and-ballet-flats-while-carrying-a-coffee kind of bun. The other kind. The I-was-locked-into-a-small-wet-hole-and-stared-into-the-abyss-for-an-eternity kind. And for the record, the answer is no. No, I never actually relaxed. Not for one millisecond.

I spent the bulk of the time thinking about my manuscript. And the more I thought about the manuscript, the more I itched to retrieve it. And the more I itched to retrieve it, the more anxious I felt about turning it in.

What if the banquet this evening takes so long it goes past midnight? What if everyone gets really excitable and talks on for ages, and I'm expected to just sit there, playing the good host? What if after the banquet Oswald says he wants to go over some concerns about his newest work-in-progress, and I come to find out I'm trapped with a regular Vladimir Nabokov insomniac, brainstorming with him in his hotel room while he taps feverishly on his computer keys until dawn? And most important of all, *What if I never get out of this tank?!*

I did get out of the tank.

I did make it back to the banquet with Oswald (where a meal has never tasted so good in my *life*).

I did drop him off at his hotel and manage some parting

encouragement about tomorrow's signing to a man who looked like he needed another hit in the sensory-deprivation tank just thinking about the chaos of the day to come.

And I have managed to sneak back in before the doors are locked up at Pennington for the night.

China clatters downstairs as I wind around the last of the staircase and stride down the hall. There's no need for pretense this time. The only people in the building are the caterers packing up what's left of the welcome banquet hours prior and Robby, Pennington's long-serving janitor, vacuuming somewhere on the second floor. I take solace in the humming below and push open the door to the ARC room, my steps determined. It's darker than usual as I pull on each lightbulb chain, blazing the path with light until I reach the metal filing cabinet on the other side. Once I've ducked inside, I push the door open.

A crescent moon shines through the stained-glass window, the sparrow looking as though it's balancing the moon on its pointed yellow beak. I smile to myself and feel myself exhale, as if for the first time that day. My stomach is pleasantly stuffed. Oswald is safely tucked into his hotel room. And here, at 10:30 p.m., I still have a full hour and a half to turn my manuscript in. I'm exhausted but finally ready to release it.

My fingers tighten around the string connecting to the lightbulb as I droopily look down at the floor.

I pause.

Squint.

And just as my heart starts to punch at my rib cage, I pull the cord.

Light floods the small room, and with it confirmation.

Because there, in the middle of the old Persian rug, is my manuscript, the papers no longer scattered and disarrayed, the corners of each page no longer folded in wonky discordancy.

No.

My manuscript. Sitting in a crisp, neat pile. A rubber band snapped around the middle. And worst of all—in bold black ink—are words. Dozens of fresh handwritten words, scribbled down the margins.

Words that are not mine.

Chapter 4

By the time I reach the pristine welcome mat of my apartment door (did Olivia really just clean it *again*?), I'm exhausted. Head-to-the-squashed-toes-I-limped-home-on exhausted. The wicked heels I spent the day in poke out from the thin leather of my laptop bag where I thrust them the second I managed to snatch my tennis shoes from my lower desk drawer on my way out of Pennington.

Eleven p.m.

With the busyness of toting Oswald around all day and the whole issue of stashing, then retrieving, my manuscript, I'm left with only one measly hour to look over my final edits and send it in. And then, of course, there is the whole issue of what to do about the scribbling all along my beloved manuscript's margins.

Despite how much my heart is racing me forward, I pause. Press my ear close to the door. Listen.

There is the whizzing of one Peloton bike inside. Just one. Not two. I exhale.

But then I check my step tracker and see the number there: 6670. I feel my rib cage compressing again.

Perfect.

I can only hope she's so engrossed she doesn't notice me.

My key slides into the lock, and as quietly as possible, I inch the door open. Directly across the room Olivia cycles on her bike beside the second, currently unoccupied one, sweat beading on her model-high cheekbones, a book propped on the handlebars that looks thick enough to hold open a bank vault. She's so deep into it she doesn't look up. Good.

I haven't always lived with my sister. No, for over six years Lyla and I shared a tiny garage apartment. We'd scored it from my mother's Belmont colleague, who was on the hunt for a pair of bright young students who prized the peaceful solitude of historic little homes over, say, belching contests in the hallways. And we did love it. Loved it with every fiber of our being. Until they sold the house. And with it, our garage-apartment bungalow. Which for Lyla worked out seamlessly, as she married her college sweetheart just three months after we got the boot. But as for me, it left me dangling.

And looking at house ads after splitting $550-a-month all-inclusive rent for six years was, let me say, the worst reality check.

So, after being told by several prospective landlords to "Just ignore the smell, we're bombing for roaches again" and "Now, just know the biohazard cleanup specialists will be coming in on the fifteenth to clean up that blood left over from the . . . [clears throat] previous owner," I resorted to calling my mom—who within twenty-four hours had Olivia calling me, offering up her spare room. Now, mind you, Olivia's lips were pressed together pretty tightly when she said, "No, no, I don't really need a room dedicated to a home gym," when I questioned her. But, given it was move in with her or back with my parents, I didn't press that much.

See? You do for family.

The Cade way.

I tiptoe toward my room and am just reaching the wall-to-wall bookcase, the only space in the apartment that is allowed to exist in disarray—with cookbooks and classics, books on French and dictionaries in Spanish, thick volumes on law and ancient hardcovers on the principles of economics, and even a few glossy ones on fitness poking out from the lowest corner, all stuffed in a puzzle-like manner both horizontally and vertically—when Olivia calls my name. "Oh, Savvy!"

I squeeze my eyes shut. Turn and see her pulling out an AirPod from one ear.

I loathe being called Savvy.

"You get your steps in today?" she says through pants, her forearms slick with sweat as she sits upright and presses both hands to her hips. Her legs are so skinny in her black leggings they look like a granddaddy longlegs racing on a hamster wheel.

I hesitate. "Nearly," I lie.

Olivia lifts an eyebrow. Her spindly legs slow. She checks her watch. "You've got an hour left."

"I know."

"Will you be able to meet your quota for the day? Exactly how far off are you?"

"Not too far," I say.

Olivia sighs. "I can make up for the shortage if you need me to, Savvy. I mean, as long as it's not *too* far off—"

"I'll handle it," I say firmly, but even as I'm saying so I feel a faint pulsing heartbeat in my ears, like a ticking bomb. My hands move instinctively to my laptop bag and the manuscript inside.

"Yes, but . . . you've said that before," Olivia says dubiously.

This is what you get when you live in an apartment with your hyperactive, perfectionist sister. Olivia is three years younger than me, graduated summa cum laude from Vanderbilt at twenty, and has been working on dual PhDs in law and economics since August. Because why get one doctorate when you can get two?

And this whole tracking-steps thing is Olivia's baby. The Steps-4-Life Step-a-thon runs each February. One month of tracking and logging steps every day in order to reach a monthly goal. What's even better? You can't fib. It syncs from your watch to your app, and then you're stuck. Being honest. With an obsessive-compulsive micromanager for team leader. Who lives with you. And monitors quite literally, your every move.

It started three years ago after Olivia got the flu for a week and was in bed for five days. So what did she do? Sit in bed for five days watching *Frasier* reruns? Make horrible online purchases at 1:00 a.m. only to wake up to Amazon boxes on her doorstep she couldn't recall ordering? Sleep?

No. What Olivia did was use the time stuck in bed as a springboard to brainstorm, figure out the logistics, secure the money, build the app, and ultimately put the stamp on Steps-4-Life, her own nonprofit organization dedicated to conquering seasonal depression by encouraging togetherness, healthy weight loss, and self-esteem. To Olivia, every problem can be cured with exercise. And as people weren't exactly stampeding with enthusiasm over her first idea, Ultra-Marathons-4-Life, she eventually whittled down her expectations to "meet the lower people [aka normal humans] where they are" and settled on walking.

In three years Steps-4-Life has raised over three million dollars and has become a yearly tradition in over thirty-six states across America.

I, too, had the flu that week three years ago. I ended up with a humidifier in the shape of an elephant, three shirts from Aerie, and a crate of dark chocolate from a fair-trade organization in Ghana.

"I don't want to pester you about this, Savvy," Olivia continues. "It's just that, you know . . ." She swings her arm in a hearty way like she does whenever she gives her slogan. "We're all in this together. And you did say you'd get twelve thousand steps each day. You did"—her voice lowers solemnly—"make the pledge."

Oh, geez. Now she's looking down on me as if I've enlisted for war, arrived at the front lines, and am considering hightailing it for the woods.

I don't have time for this.

I'm just about to open my mouth to tell her I'm *sorry* that I was stuck in a sensory float pod with an author, trying not to hyperventilate, and I'm *sorry* about the banquet afterward—all the while knowing she still won't be able to fathom why I didn't just run in place at dinner while chewing my asparagus—when a voice speaks up from behind.

"Leave her alone, Olivia. The Cade ranking isn't going anywhere tonight."

I stiffen as I feel his breath so close it lifts the hairs on my neck. He must've come from the hall bathroom, but to me, who didn't hear him over the whizzing of the Peloton bike, he might as well have emerged from thin air. My reaction would've been the same either way.

"'Xcuse me, Savvy."

I feel the lightest touch of his fingers on my hip, and it takes everything in me not to jump a foot. *Do* not *move*, I tell myself firmly. *Do* not *react*.

But despite myself, my heart thuds against my chest as he begins to move past me in the slim hallway.

As if in slow motion, Ferris turns his head and looks down at me. His long, careless brown locks drift into his equally brown eyes. His lips turn up slightly. "And by the way, hi."

"Hi." My voice is more breathless than I intend.

No.

I ball my hands into fists at my sides and try again. I'd take one giant step back, but my back is against the wall, and he seems in no hurry. "I didn't know you were here, Ferris."

"Yeah. Just getting some work done. Big deposition Monday." He moves another step forward, and I take the opportunity to slide out of the way.

"Sure. Sure," I repeat and move swiftly for my door. Before Olivia can call out to me again and make more guilt-inducing remarks, I slip inside my room.

Bringing people together, yeah, right. If I didn't know the creator of Steps-4-Life myself, I'd say it was designed by desperate family therapists and divorce lawyers needing to drum up business.

"You don't want to stick around for a movie?" I hear Ferris call from the hall. "C'mon, Sav, it's Friday night. Don't go to bed yet."

"No, thanks," I call back through the door.

I take a breath and exhale and, after a second's hesitation, turn the lock.

Ferris is my ex-boyfriend.

Ferris is Olivia's fiancé.

I try very, *very* hard to be an adult about it.

And while I would typically spend the next two hours on the couch downing extra-buttered popcorn while the whizzing of Pelotons goes on behind me and calories sweat off the two of them like raindrops, proving I really am *com-plete-ly* fine in the company of the man who has consumed all my firsts—first date, first kiss, first love—I have more pressing issues to attend to.

Like this.

Gingerly I take the manuscript out of my messenger bag.

Set it on the bed.

Press my finger to my lips.

Stare.

Well, as I see it, I have three options.

One. I can take in the full fact that someone (a) was in my little sparrow room today, and (b) read my manuscript. But that would lead to a nervous breakdown, and I'm too pinched for time for that.

Two. I can table the issue that my beloved room is now compromised for a later date (say, 3:00 a.m., when I'm staring at the ceiling) and instead look at this from the angle that is most natural to me. This is just someone's edit. Someone's typical edit for a manuscript I'm looking at. I'm an editor. I do this for a living. This is not a big deal. All I need to do is read through as many comments along the margins as I can in the short span of time I have, find what comments I align with, and edit the manuscript accordingly.

Three. Ignore the crazy bat who dared touch my manuscript and send it on to Claire.

I inch toward the manuscript and play with the rubber band.

The handwriting looks pretty pretentious, doesn't it? Cursive and short in width yet still making a show of all the *t*'s and *d*'s and *b*'s. All in a bold black ink. The dot of each *i* is missing, as if the writer was too busy and important to worry about such insignificant details. Pretty annoying, actually. I have a sudden itch to dot each one.

My eyes, having squinted to avoid reading any of the actual words, widen slowly, taking the sentence in.

Start is weak.

I stare. *Start. Is. Weak.*

What does that mean, the start is weak?

This is the first page, practically the first paragraph! The mystery editor hasn't even gotten to the good part where they meet.

My eyes drop to the bottom of the next page, and I read the note there: Unoriginal meet.

Unoriginal? The pair of them getting their drinks mixed up at a coffee shop is *wildly* original. And what makes it particularly cute is that they order the *same* drink. Not some "Oh, dear me. Here's your black coffee. I don't know how I mistook it for my venti Frappuccino with extra whip" nonsense you see in some romances. What's so cute and, most important, realistic is that they both mistook the barista calling out their double Americano with pumpkin spice as their own! It was a natural mistake, given the order was identical. And only when they see the other person's name on the cups they're holding do they make this really *adorable* remark to each other.

I was actually so proud when I thought of it—

Nauseating and directly plagiarized from every Hallmark movie in the last ten years.

Okay, that's it.

I flip through the pages, cheeks growing hotter as I read each word along the margins.

Slow beginning. Get to the meat. Give readers a reason to stay. If you bore them, you lose them.

Awkward word choice?

Drop this paragraph.

We don't need this character.

Rabbit trail, stick to the point.

Change of POV.

Have you considered shifting the manuscript to present tense?

Alright. That's *enough*.

I slam down the pages I hold, my whole body flaming. Only as I see myself in the mirror opposite do I realize I'm panting as if I've sprinted a mile. But, honestly, who is this person?

Deluded, that's what they are. Deluded and haughty and a hater of all things happy. And most significant of all, dead wrong. *Dead wrong.* The person probably doesn't even *like* romance. They're probably like every other editor at Pennington, poring over books about existentialism and the history of dog shows like it's the most riveting stuff in the world.

On impulse, I pull open my closet door. The metal rail

screeches as I push the overstuffed mass of sweaters, shirts, and dresses to the right, revealing a large cardboard box on the floor. With one hand pressed to my clothes, holding them back, I open the crisscrossed top of the box and throw the manuscript inside.

There. Discarded like all the other pieces of junk in my life.

In one seamless move, I slide the closet door shut and slip into my desk chair. Click on the mouse as the desktop screen comes to life. Tap swiftly on the keyboard to draft an email.

Realistically, there's no way I can get to all the little markups I made today anyway. Most of what I noted was just second-guessing actions and word choices. Phrasing. It's better to just follow my gut and send it. Better not to make any hasty moves. Better to trust the writer I was when I was working slowly and clearheadedly without a deadline instead of the one now exhausted and confused and feeling pressured to change it all in the last second of the game. And really, this is exactly how my authors say they feel before they turn in their manuscripts to me. I should pat myself on the back. I'm doubting myself, ergo I must be a real writer after all.

Clinging to that short and momentary encouragement, I press Send and hear the email zoom off toward its final destination before I can backpedal.

For a long moment, I stare at the computer, hardly able to believe what has just happened.

Such a small act, just one little button pressed, and yet . . .

Done.

No turning back now. No regrets whatsoever. What-so-ever.

It's an unsteadying feeling. A feeling I wasn't expecting.

I stand up from my chair, and as I do so, my eyes are drawn

toward the closet door. The bitterness is starting to settle in. Whoever took my manuscript not only read it without permission but stole my moment too. I'm *supposed* to feel elated right now. I'm *supposed* to feel like a load has finally been lifted off my shoulders. I've been dreaming of this particular moment for months now. No, *years.* But now? Now all I feel is a growing sense of panic.

So much for my celebratory day.

I hear a light knock on the door. "Sav?" Ferris's voice is gentle on the other side. "Sav, you sure you don't want to come watch the movie? I'm about to start some popcorn. If you come, I promise I'll keep her from making you do steps."

I take a breath. Turn my eyes from the closet door and rise up from my bed, hauling along all the emotions of the day as I drag my feet toward the door.

"I'm coming," I call through the door.

I've done it.

I've sent my manuscript, and that's the thought I'm going to choose to hang on to, no matter what.

Celebration.

Chapter 5

I wake up just like I do every morning of my life, to the *stomp-stomp-stomping* of Olivia's 5:30 a.m. sprint on the treadmill in her bedroom. You'd think I'd be used to the noise a year after moving in. Or better yet, you'd think I'd have had a clue as to what I was in for when I watched Olivia tear the wrapping paper off the treadmill last Christmas morning.

Anyway, here we are, a year later, and the first thought bubble still to form in my mind is, *Why the* heck *couldn't Ferris have bought her the quiet one?* Followed shortly by another mental favorite: *And it's Saturday, Olivia. Can't you sleep in, just once, on a Saturday?*

But today new thoughts greet me, and with a jolt I sit upright, the memories and actions of the previous twenty-four hours lined up for me to reconsider one by one. It's not a typical Saturday, and I have so many things to prepare for today. So many things to do.

The LOA conference.

Oswald's signing.

The ARC room.

The *manuscript*.

Finding out who exactly tampered with my manuscript.

Last night I stayed up watching the movie with Olivia and Ferris. And even while I shed tears into my popcorn (unlike Olivia, who takes a firm stance against crying), my thoughts were also far away. *Was it creepy Rem? He does lurk a lot around the building. But doesn't he have that thing about heights? Wasn't that why Pam championed moving his office to the first floor? Because he kept looking out the window and passing out?*

What about Lyla? No, no, of course not. She'd never write those things. I don't think she even knows how to spell the word sesquipedalianism.

Which, for the record, my mystery editor declared in one of their handy margin comments is something I do. And which, for the record, I most certainly do *not*. The insinuation that I would scour dictionaries to find obscure, five-syllable words to throw into my manuscript just to puff myself up is so laughable it's insane. It's farcical. It makes me repine for the days readers were erudite and could appreciate a well-chosen word . . .

Okay, it's a tiny bit true. But nevertheless, it's a good true, not a bad true. After all, there's nothing *wrong* with fine-tuning a paragraph, and frankly, I work in a building full of people who are smarter than me. I need the big words. People prize the people who pull out the big words.

Could it be Giselle? Ha. Who am I kidding? I wouldn't be surprised if she's outsourcing her own editing to some unpaid college intern in the back booths of some salty saloon, let alone voluntarily reading someone else's manuscript.

And the more I thought about it, all the while munching on my popcorn, the more furious I became. What right did this mystery editor have to read my manuscript? *Munch.* What sort of crazy person would walk into someone else's room (okay, even I know that's stretching a bit), plonk down on the rug, and proceed to tear someone else's manuscript apart? *Munch.* It's narcissistic. *Munch.* Sadistic. *Munch.* They probably loved seeing my manuscript in disarray, sheets out of order and piled on the floor. *Munch.*

I mean, it's not like what I do for a living. I get paid to edit. I get asked to edit. My authors *want* me to edit. And most important, I'm *kind.*

These are the thoughts that transfix me two hours later as I sit on a barstool in the kitchen, manuscript in front of me, frowning at a sentence in Oswald's latest. A bit aggressively I underline a paragraph, then scribble the words in the margins in my untidy handwriting: *I'm not understanding the point of this paragraph here. Clarify.*

I bring the coffee mug to my lips, then set it down.

Please, I add.

See? I'm kind.

"Still in your jammies?" Olivia hustles to the fridge and opens it up. There's a stack of twenty meals neatly lining the left-hand side of the refrigerator. She pulls one out. "I thought you had to go to work today."

"I do. But I don't have to be there until nine. And . . . seeing as I couldn't sleep"—I lift my eyes from the manuscript to give an accusing look to the back of her head—"I'm getting some work done before I go."

"Oh?" Olivia's damp ponytail swings as she turns her head.

She looks at me with fresh eyes, as though there's hope for me after all. "What a good use of time. Where's the conference?"

"Music City Center." I feel a rush of anxiety as I say it.

Claire Donovan will be there. For the first time in a year, we'll be in the same building. She'll be busy at her own Baird Books tent, I'm sure, but we could run into each other. Probably will run into each other. I could probably even "happenchance" bump into her. But then what will I say?

Oh, hey, Claire. Have you read my manuscript in the last twelve hours?

I can't be *that* author. I can't.

It takes me typically a full twelve weeks to get to any new manuscripts that aren't from my authors. And we're a small house. It's ridiculous to think it'd take her a mere twelve weeks, positively ludicrous to think it could be done in twelve hours. Between midnight and noon. The evening before conference.

Olivia checks her watch. "You know, if you decide to walk, you could not only get ahead of work but reach your daily step goal too." Her eyes positively sparkle. "Talk about a win-win before noon, am I right?"

My own expression tightens. Leave it to her to always think I should be doing one more thing. "Gee, Olivia. What a wonderful idea."

Olivia gives a modest shrug. "You can never be sure how the day will go, so . . ." She snaps opens the container, revealing two perfectly portioned squares of dried fruit and Greek yogurt. "Best to get those steps in early. And then, not only will you have the satisfaction of knowing you are successfully working toward a healthier body, but you'll find it easier to retrain your mind to—

"Climb the other mountains in your life," I finish in unison with her and take another sip of coffee.

I am the recipient of one of Olivia's Steps-4-Life speeches once a week.

"Well?" Olivia says, scowling. "It *is* scientifically proven. Honestly, Savvy, if you just tried it for a solid month . . ."

But as apathetic as I act, I can't help watching her figure as she turns toward the silverware drawer. Olivia, in her maroon running tights, calves perfectly sculpted. Her back muscles, exposed by her crisscross tank top, rippling delicately beneath flawless skin as she reaches down for a spoon. Her neck, long and lean.

She hasn't always been this way. Back in our school days she used to be the shy one. The one with a little bit on her hips. The one with the mouth full of braces for an inordinately long period of time. Following me—with the brighter smile, better grades, smaller pant size—through school. But then I left for college, and at some point in that gap of time, things shifted. Slowly she started taking on extracurriculars. Learning to play new instruments every few months. Taking on internships. Then after-school jobs. Thinning as she took up track. Then cross country.

By the time she graduated from university, top of her class, I hardly recognized her.

While somewhere in there I settled into mediocrity, she burst forth as the next shining Cade star.

Olivia pulls a box of oatmeal squares from the overstuffed cabinet as she turns to me. "Really? Another box? Don't you have another twelve of these shoved in the pantry?"

"It's healthy," I protest and then rub my nose as she makes a face. "Comparatively, anyway. And I like them."

"We don't have room for them," Olivia retorts. "For goodness' sake. Do you ever *look* in the pantry anymore? If you just checked the kitchen while you make your grocery list at least every *once* in a while—"

"It's just a box of cereal, Olivia," I reply, bristling. "Just a couple boxes of cereal. I think the pantry can manage."

"Yes, well, I could line up all your 'couple boxes of cereal' and play dominoes across the apartment." Olivia waves an arm at the living room.

"And what about your precious container meals?" I say, standing with my mug. "You stuff the entire fridge with them and leave me enough space to squeeze in a block of cheese—"

"It's *my* fridge," Olivia replies, her voice louder now. "I think I've been pretty generous with *my* fridge—and my whole apartment, for that matter—these past twelve months."

My face grows hot. Is she really going to prick at my insecurity like that, here, before I've even finished my cup of coffee? Does she really want to try to play this game? Before second-guessing, I blast back with my own trump card—the card I never wanted, the card she, by her own actions with Ferris, handed me. "Oh yes, Olivia. I'm well aware of just how *great* you are at sharing *everything*—"

"Ladies!" a voice booms from behind us, and we simultaneously turn to see Ferris stepping into the living room from the front door, a coffee tray carrying three sage-green cups in his hand. His cheeks—ruddy from the wind outside—are nearly as red as the maroon sweater he's wearing. He smiles broadly, as though he hasn't heard my subtle remark aimed at him. "Who'd like some coffee?"

While Ferris hands out the usuals—a small nonfat latte with

one tablespoon of honey for Olivia, a medium white-chocolate mocha for me—I notice mine is larger than usual. Ferris catches my eye and gives a lopsided smile. "I know we kept you up too late last night," he says quietly. "Figured you'd appreciate a size up for your big day."

As tight as my chest is from dealing with Olivia (a condition I experience at least once a week), my lips can't help curling upward as I set down my mug and accept what he's brought me from the Raven. Already, I feel my insides defrosting as I hold the toasty cup in my hands.

For all our patchy times, I couldn't ever deny that Ferris, when he's wanted to, has always been the one who could walk into a room and calm me down. Whether with a timely proffer of a caffeinated beverage or a willingness to sit down for hours and hash out a whole situation, he has always been there for me. A listening ear. An active participant. And this is exactly why I love him.

Loved him.

And now appropriately appreciate him as much as any mature woman would appreciate her ex-boyfriend-now-sister's-fiancé.

Was it hard to lose Ferris to my sister after the long history we had together? Sure. Was I full of throw-your-computer-out-the-window blind fury at the discovery that, after he civilly broke it off with me one evening in my bedroom, he declared his undying affection for my sister twenty-four hours later in hers?

Ab-so-*flippin'*-lutely.

But it's not quite that easy to block a person like Ferris out of your life, as it turns out. Not when he has been a part of the family on and off the last ten years. Not when he asks your sister to marry him three months after they get together. And not, principally, when you are a Cade.

Because we Cades live by three life words: *Generosity. Persistence. Family.* You live each day looking for an opportunity to serve another. You persist in achieving the best for your life come drought or high water. And you stick to family. Always and forever, you stick to family. We're like the mafia. Only . . . nicer.

And while, yes, my sister initially played the black sheep by breaking the Cade code and allowing the man who had broken my heart to capture hers, the moment he dropped down on one knee, the situation changed.

In fact, the situation required an intervention. Precisely twelve hours after the engagement announcement, my parents "dropped" by the apartment. Sat me down (on Olivia's couch). Insisted they hear out the whole story. My feelings. My claims. My hurts. Then, with half a box of tissues used up, Mom patted me on the hand, gave me the biggest sympathetic eyes she could, and said, "Darling, we've got a wedding in four months. We're going to have to speed things up."

This was followed with a lengthy, statistics-laden explanation that they had passively watched as bystanders, wanting to give me room to move through the five stages of grief, from the first denial phase (aka a full month of bubbly overenthusiasm and overbright statements to anyone within earshot that we were just "on a break") all the way toward acceptance. Only apparently, according to my parents, I was stuck on stage two—the anger stage. You know, where you are discovered sitting cross-legged in your closet, cutting old letters to shreds by the light of the old photos of the both of you at prom now in flames on a dinner plate. That stage.

Which was all fine and well, except now he was going to be

a Cade, and by golly, Mother had a dress fitting at Harold's on Monday. They were going to have to help me along.

And so, after many such lengthy discussions, I eventually did come to terms with things.

Even, bizarrely enough, started to see everyone else's point of view.

After all, for everybody except me it did make sense. It was quite romantic, even.

The boy who had dated the older sister all through high school and never noticed the one three years younger with braces, watching them through the stair rails while they went off to their proms and parties. The younger sister who eventually grew up and went to her own university, gained her independence, blossomed into her own strengths, and then, nearly a decade later, ran into the boy-now-man she'd (apparently, as I was to discover in the glowing how-we-met stories they like to share at parties) had such a crush on before. How, when I moved into Olivia's apartment last year after my financial crisis, their eyes locked that first evening. And while I—sweat soaked and panting in stained T-shirts—hauled boxes up to my room, they apparently had "hilariously" stumbled into one another in the hallway, where she had "the cutest lock of hair that had fallen out of place" and he had "fallen in love with her at first sight."

He was, as he says, "captivated against his will. Love had chosen him. Cupid had shot his arrow."

And there was nothing he, nor I, could do about it.

Like I say, it's romantic. For everybody but the girl who gets dumped and replaced by her successful, beautiful, younger sister.

But I will say that for his part, Ferris does feel terrible about what it did to me. Even now, he always tries to make up for how things happened. Always tries to include me. Make sure I feel important. Make sure I know I'm loved and not alone. I honestly think that's why they've pushed the wedding out twice now. For me.

I look at the clock. Ferris sees my fingers fidgeting on the counter.

"You're going to do great, Sav," he says, giving me a little smile. "You've mastered the ropes. Could probably run the whole conference by now."

I give him a smile back. He's assuming I'm nervous about the LOA wreck from my first year. The assumption is off base—I've double-, triple-, and quadruple-checked that all the books, bookmarks, and bookplates will be safely secured beneath the booth table by the time we get there. Still, it's thoughtful.

He's trying.

He just wants us all to get along.

"You know what? I may just walk down there after all," I say, scraping together as much kindness toward my sister as I can muster. It only, all collected, comes to a pinch worth, but it's enough. "May help with the jitters."

Ferris's smile widens as Olivia turns from the fridge where she's holding a glass under cold running water while jogging in place. "Yeah?" Her eyes flicker from the clock above the sink to me, then brighten. "Yeah, that's a great idea. And . . . good luck today."

I manage a tiny smile. "Thanks."

There, I think, my grin broadening as I look to Ferris. *Olive branch given. Olive branch received.*

The Cade name preserved another day.

But the noble gesture looks awfully pale by the time I stride, freezing fingers wrapped tightly around the waist of my coat, through the twentieth stoplight and up the steps of the Music City Center. And thanks to an unforeseen 5K, with the street taped off and a mass of runners sprinting by with country music blaring, I was forced to detour an extra dozen blocks I hadn't accounted for.

I'm painfully late. I can feel it. I know it so deep in my soul I'm afraid to check my watch.

As I reach the doors, I clench my jaw and dare a glance.

Nine-oh-three a.m.

Shoot.

As I follow the signs, Music City Center is buzzing with activity that, after only two years, still makes me feel a bit like a kid in a candy shop.

Oh! Look at that banner! I didn't know Sophie Kinsella had a new one coming out.

Oh! That person has an entire suitcase of books! What did they find . . .

Oh! Is that the Fonz?! Here?! SIGNING BOOKS?!

And just as I'm about to veer off to follow the old *Happy Days* icon into the bathroom for an autograph, I'm funneled into an even smaller hallway and pop out at the top of an expansive exhibit room. Banners cover booths as far as the eye can see. Books spill from every inch of available space. Stacks lie on tables. Beside tables. Beneath tables. It's only 9:00 a.m., and already the crowds swarm.

Everything as far as the eye can see is the librarian's dream.

The booklover's dream.

The dream.

And sure enough, I can see hundreds of librarians racing

around like ants from my perch at the top of the stairs over-looking it all. It's that old TV show *Super Toy Run*, where one lucky kid races through a toy store in five minutes, throwing anything he can into a shopping cart. Everything free. Except instead of toys, it's something much, much better.

Books.

Hundreds and hundreds of crisp advance copies of books, free for the taking.

Beside a large HarperCollins banner I spot a smaller one, the sparrow logo next to the neat words *PENNINGTON PUBLISHING*. Lyla is bouncing from one end of the booth to the other in a pink pantsuit and three-inch heels, trying to stop the woman in the corner who's currently trying to sneak all the copies of one book title into her bag. Giselle is sitting off to one side, sipping coffee as she scrolls her phone. And William Pennington has his hands on his hips while he stands beside Oswald, look-ing around impatiently.

Shoot.

Shoot. Shoot. Shoot.

I dart down three steps, one hand holding on to the railing. A woman in a T-shirt that says *WILL BRAKE FOR BOOKS* takes up the stairway with a rolling suitcase by her side.

"Excuse me," I say, trying to squeeze by. "I've just got to—"

"We're all here for the same thing," the woman says gruffly, pushing out her rolling suitcase and blocking me from the poten-tial foot of space between her and the man on the other side.

"No, you don't understand," I begin but then spot, over the woman's shoulder, the booklet detailing the schedule of events. Hour-by-hour events are noted over the course of the next three days on the left-hand side, but it's the headline covering the right-hand side that grabs my attention. "Green? Green's got a new one coming out?"

"Only two hundred copies too!" the man beside her says, to which she eyes him, then me, suspiciously. She folds the booklet up.

Two hundred copies? I can't help thinking. *Are they signed?* But no. I mentally shake myself. I need to stay focused. I need to remember why I'm here.

I glance toward my tent again and instantly regret it. Oswald's hands are now gripping the back of the table, and he's inching his way toward the exit. As for my new supervisor? Well, maybe that face is always the face he makes when he's doing business. Maybe that murderous-looking frown as his eyes dart around, one hand gripped on Oswald, is just business as usual.

Maybe.

I check my watch. Nine eleven.

I want to wail, *Move it, people!* but then spot the situation: an elderly woman getting settled into a wheelchair at the bottom of the stairs. Knowing this place, she probably took one look around, spotted from a distance that sporting young man in the neon staff T-shirt now helping her into the wheelchair, and realized he could whip her around three times faster than the competition.

I force a calm breath.

Isn't that nice that all those people are helping her into her chair? I force myself to think. *Isn't that just so nice that we are all here . . . at this event . . . all together . . . right before I get fired! Get out of the way, everyone, or I'm going to scream!*

I grab my phone from my bag and whip out a text to Lyla: **Stuck at stairs in a pileup. Can you tell the boss?**

Most people wouldn't hear their phones in the chaos of the room. Most staff, for that matter, wouldn't even have their phones on their person while they danced around during such an event. But not Lyla. She could hear the single *ding* of a text across a stadium during the Superbowl.

I watch as she pulls the phone from her pocket, reads the text, and hustles over to William. Good ol' Lyla.

A moment later he turns his head toward the stairs, and after several moments of scanning, his eyes land on me.

No.

I've made it worse.

I shrink under his volcanic glare, wishing in that moment for an escape. *Any. Escape.* Backward. Forward. I don't even have to go to this event. After all, I don't really need this job, do I? Really? I could just squat in my sister's spare bedroom forever, wallowing in self-loathing while Mom and Dad tell Olivia, "Your sister just can't cut it in the real world like you, honey. But remember, you do for family."

The elderly woman in the wheelchair points ahead at last. "Start at the Berkley tent!" she declares, and moments later the staff member in neon races her into the crowd, prodded on as the woman pushes people out of the way with her cane.

Now, where were we? Oh, yes, trying to face Ms. Pennington's son.

By the time I reach the tent, Lyla has given up on the librarian in the corner and appears to have cornered Oswald, talking avidly while his bifocaled eyes dart around for a means of escape.

I face William.

"That was a madhouse—" I begin to say, but he cuts me off.

"Do you think this is unimportant, Ms. Cade?"

His voice is eerily calm. I don't think I expected it to sound like that, I realize. I think I was suspecting it to sound more like his mother's—loud and quasi-hysterical and attention-grabbing. But calm? Somehow, it feels worse.

"Do you think we are in some sort of shopping mall, where you can just float in when you please?" he continues.

I open my mouth, but he lifts a finger.

"Was I not *absolutely* clear yesterday when I stated just how significant this event was today, and how imperative it would be to go above and beyond?" My eyes dart to Giselle, who has now taken out a file from her purse and is frowning at a nail. "If this was my staff at Sterling, if I gave them a time to be somewhere—"

"Will! There you are!"

William's eyes dart up, followed by mine, as two men approach. As they saunter toward him, with enough lackadaisical confidence in each step that others slide out of the way, I feel the tension in my chest releasing. I'm saved. Momentarily, at least, I've been spared.

Unlike those surrounding the pair of them in colorful cardigans and clever bookish shirts and pins saying things like *Never Judge a Book by Its Movie* and *Abibliophobia: noun. The fear of running out of books*, the two men wear gray. Suits that are utterly free of any sort of emotion. As if the very idea of accidentally causing a smile is repugnant.

I'm just trying to inch my way backward and out of the scene when the tallest man claps William on the back, his smile revealing the whitest, straightest teeth I've ever seen. "We've been all over this place looking for you. I kept saying, 'Pennington Publishing. I know it's small, but it has to be *somewhere*. Surely it isn't such a small pub they don't actually get'"—he laughs as he says the word—"'invited.'"

His companion chimes in with a soft chuckle.

"Anyway," the man continues, his hand turning from a clap to a grip and shoulder shake, "with a little squinting we found you."

"Jim. How good of you to come over." If I'd thought William was intimidating before with his eerily calm behavior, I now see he's only been using quarter strength. His eyes have all but crystalized into two sharp, piercing icicles—but not the nice kind, no. Not the kind where you touch their dribbly tips as they dangle off tree branches while saying, "Aw, look! Icicles." No, the kind that are so big and sharp people snap them off and use them as weapons. That kind.

And his back, for that matter, is starting to look like an upright cutting board. His body is so rigid I feel like if this guy shook him hard enough, he wouldn't bend, he'd tip over.

There's a painfully silent pause, wherein Jim overtly begins looking at me, no doubt awaiting introduction. Stiffly, William puts out a hand toward me. "Savannah, this is Jim Arrowood and Jenson Forbes, former coworkers at Sterling." His chin barely moves an inch their way. "This is Savannah Cade. Acquisitions editor for our Pen division."

I almost put in, "Actually, it's assistant acquisitions editor," but hold my tongue. Now's probably not the time to correct the new boss.

The tall one, Jim, puts out a hand. His smile has grown to full-on used-car-salesman status, and for a blink of an eye, I wonder what exactly would happen if I refuse to shake it. Reluctantly, I give in.

"Nice to meet you, Savannah," he says, giving my hand a hearty squeeze and shake the moment it grips mine. The next second he's whipping his other hand into his chest pocket and pulling out a business card. "Editorial director at Sterling House. We're always on the lookout for the next generation of great editors."

I look down at the card in my hands. Read his name and title below the classic outline of the dignified old mansion that is Sterling House's logo.

Unbelievable.

Not only is the man using me to loudly remind my new boss that he took his job, he's openly discussing poaching me in front of my employer. As though my place of employment is of such little regard it couldn't possibly be considered offensive.

My lips tighten.

I don't know this man, and I certainly don't know William Pennington, but I do know Pennington Publishing. I do know Patricia Pennington, terrifying as she may be, and the long-standing grit, determination, and integrity she has poured into her company. And I do have some self-respect.

Etiquette can take the back seat on this one.

The Cades do for family, and for me, even if it be in a smaller way, Pennington Publishing is family.

Even as my cheeks pink, my grip on the business card tightens. Before I know it I'm holding it out to him, a polite smile on my face. "I'm happy where I am."

There's an enormous pause as all three men look down at me, fresh shock in varying degrees on their faces.

I sense the pressure to add to my words, to backpedal quickly in both professional and good southern fashion, but I stand firm, smile stamped in place. In my periphery I see a flicker in William's eyes.

He doesn't look like he's about to brim over with happiness or anything, but there is a spark.

Good, I think. *Remember this moment, William, instead of the ire of the last five minutes.*

Slowly, Jim reaches out and takes the card.

"So," he says, stuffing the card quickly back into his chest pocket and shuffling his gaze to the tent behind us, "how have you been these past months? When I heard you left the City . . ." He shakes his head. "I couldn't imagine. I would kill myself."

William's smile tightens. "Yes. Well. It's not for everyone."

Jim gives a bark of laughter and tries to give William a loosening-up shake. It doesn't work. "Oh, come now. Let's not be like that. Who do you have lined up for the day?"

Jim looks at the foam board in the center of the tent, where a large headshot of Oswald's face is plastered beside his newest book. Jim's brows furrow. *"The Complete Guide to Pruning Technique,"* he murmurs. "That's quite the change from Green, isn't it, Will?" he says, his eyes mirthful.

Green.

. . . Greeeeen.

Trace . . . Green?

My eyes swivel back to William.

William Pennington was the editor for *the* Trace Green? The one I adore wholeheartedly and yet so forcefully refused to admit knowledge of yesterday? And William was demoted to *this*?

Even I can't help feeling a little disgusted at our booth as Jim's eyes slowly rove around it, clearly neither familiar with nor impressed with any title. Then they stop, and a flicker of amusement ignites in his eyes.

"Uh, Will," he says, pointing toward Oswald. "You might want to do something about that."

Both William and I turn at the same time and see Oswald, who, with eyes wide and unblinking, is pressing himself against a wall of books. He's staring at Lyla, transfixed, as though caught in her web.

William starts to turn toward me, but I head him off. "I'm on it. Good morning, Oswald!" my voice rings out as I spring into action.

And for the next ten minutes I stand beside Oswald, alternating between peeling him off the wall of books and jumping in front of any passing librarians who slow their canter to gaze at his poster, shielding him from those who might recognize him and unintentionally cause him to throw himself under the table the rest of the morning. It's consuming work, but I still catch the conversation going between the three men.

All their words are barbed, each carrying their own insinuation.

Frankly, it's fascinating.

It's like they're playing two games of tennis at once, a racket in each hand. One conversation volleying back and forth across the net is the surface discussion about business and home and New York life, while the other is a stab. And while William does make his fair share of jabs, it's the ones from the tall guy, Jim, that I feel in my gut.

Jabs that William is not missed.

Jabs that he, William's replacement, is far superior in every way.

Jabs that, with William gone, headliners are flocking to Sterling in droves.

By the time the announcement goes over the room about Green's signing at Booth #207 and the two men set out with self-importance toward their "abandoned" (and yet, as stated three times, apparently run by an onslaught of lower staff tripping on themselves to fulfill their every wish) booth, even I have forgotten all about William's piercing words about me being late.

As the two men fall into the crowd, William turns, and for a moment his expression has fallen. He looks ragged. He looks abused. And even I, in that moment, can't help feeling for him.

But just then he catches my eye, and I turn and dive headlong into my duties.

Now there are four things I'm going to hope he henceforth forgets about and never brings up: the manuscript page he read yesterday, my response to meeting his former coworker (even if he was ghastly), my tardiness, and the way the entire conversation played out about Green.

I don't know why I'd just assumed he had headed up some upscale fiction branch back in New York.

I take that back. Of course I know why I assumed: because he is Ms. Pennington's son. Only son. And for her, taking on commercial fiction would be like being a Montague and jumping the fence to hang out with the Capulets. And look how well that turned out for Romeo.

Truly, I'd be afraid to sit in on the Penningtons' Thanksgiving dinners.

Oswald's signing comes up shortly afterward, and with it a lot of heavy lifting on my part—serving both as the bodyguard ensuring people keep a solid two feet from the anthropophobic man and as a sort of translator between his readers with their fandom-speak and Oswald with his mumbling. The intensity of the next two hours saves me from any more conversation with my boss, and by the time I am giving well wishes to the last stragglers in line, William is nowhere to be seen.

"Nice job," Lyla says, patting down my hair. "You'd think five hundred copies would be enough for this lot."

"Then you've underestimated the power of properly treated hydrangeas," I reply. I turn my face toward the podium. "Isn't that right, Oswald?" I frown. "Oswald?"

Oswald is staring bleakly out at the crowd, as if he's resigned to his life sentence in the chair. "Okey dokey. C'mon." I move away from Lyla and take him by the hand. I give it a soothing pat and then reach my arm out behind me. "You did so well today. Didn't he, Lyla?"

Lyla gives a generous nod and promptly slides my purse up my arm.

"Let's get you to the hotel."

And with one arm holding lightly to the elbow of his sleeve, I wind through the crowd, guiding Oswald toward the double doors. Once we're back into the convention hallway with its expansive ceiling, I let go. There are only a few people shuffling about now, most having gone down to the exhibit hall or to the conference rooms to listen to the speakers. Oswald, for his part, is perking up like a water-deprived flower. He's doing so well, in fact, that I'm about to ask him if he'd like to sit down for one last cup of coffee at the onsite coffee shop when a familiar patch of brown hair with several strands of glinting gray catches my attention. The same small, petite frame. The same short, blocky blue heels.

In that moment, time freezes.

I can't decide whether I want to grab Oswald by the arm and drag him into the coffee shop or leave him then and there and make a mad dash for her. Or run away myself, for that matter. Maybe I don't want to face her at all.

But before I can thoroughly think it through, I realize my body has made the decision for me, because it's taken up Oswald's elbow once again and is now all but rushing for the door. Claire Donovan has her back to us. She is the last in a small line waiting to place an order. If I hurry, my body—and my mind, as it's slowly realizing—knows I just might make it to her before she slips away.

"Off we go," I trill, speeding us up even more as we hurry down the stairs for the double doors. "As I was saying, Oswald, it was so good to see you. You were fabulous today." I push open the doors, and a gust of wind bites at our eyes. "Please thank your wife for letting us steal you away."

"My coat," Oswald says, struggling to take it off his arm to put it on.

"What's the use when you're about to get inside this cozy taxi?" I say, already raising my arm and waving at a slowing cab coming toward the curb. As it halts, I pull open the door, then stretch my arms out wide with a large smile. "It was so *good* to see you."

Dumbly, he receives my hug. "But we were going to talk over the sales channel report . . ."

"That? Let's not worry about that today. Not on the heels of such a triumphant signing. I'll be sure to email you all about it Monday."

His puzzled expression is somewhat adorable, like a puppy

staring at his own tail, dumbfounded as to why it keeps following him around. But as I pat the top of the open door invitingly, he blinks and follows my orders.

"Have a good flight!" I call as I shut the door. I force myself to stay planted and wave while the taxi rumbles off, counting to five with a smile pasted on my face, then turn and race back up the stairs.

My heels clap loudly on the marble floors of the empty hall. I'm a terrible host. I gave a terribly rushed parting. But if there was anyone I could shove off like that who'd respond with a five-star review, it's him.

And this? This matters.

When I'm close enough, I scan the line at the register. The line has moved on to new faces, and for one dark moment I think Claire has gone.

Then, over by the sugar station, I spot her.

She's opening a packet of honey and pouring it into her cup, a slight frown on her face as she takes a wooden stick and begins to stir.

My pace slows. Why is she frowning?

This must be a bad time.

This *is* a bad time. She's no doubt on her way to some grand and serious lecture, somewhere only fitting for the literary elites of the biggest houses. Like a VIP room. Yes, a VIP room that nobody else knows about, where only the biggest professionals in the business gather under soft lighting and discuss the future of the industry. A circle of plush red couches. Sconces glowing. Waiters serving them food on silver trays because they are too busy determining the future of culture and literature everywhere to deal with the hassle of deciding where to dine—

And then, as if she feels eyes upon her, Claire turns and looks me directly in the eye.

She blinks, and then her eyes crinkle in recognition. Her frown dissolves as she tents up a smile and starts walking toward me.

This is it. I'm bound now.

I follow suit and move toward her.

"Savannah," she says, her voice warm. "I was actually just thinking about you." She waves at a nearby table. "Have a minute?"

I hesitate.

And by this I mean I force myself to hesitate.

My immediate, natural reaction is to hop the railing and sprint toward her until I'm hugging her knees. But instead I give a slight nod, hoping I'm communicating something halfway between *Oh, what does it matter?* and *Oh my gosh, yes! Yes! YES!*

"Sure, I'll just . . . get a cup of coffee and join you," I say in my poshest, most casual demeanor, like we're old friends who do this all the time. Like I always have coffee with the chief editor of Baird Books. Like we email Pinterest recipes to each other late at night with messages like, "This'll be perfect for our brunch next week."

No. Big. Deal.

I've only dreamed about this moment every single day since last January.

I get my coffee and slide into the chair across from Claire just as she finishes taking a sip of her tea. As she sets it down, I see the same down-to-earth warmth in her eyes I found last year as we stood in that long line, chatting for the hour we waited for a moment with Margaret Atwood. We were such kindred spirits then, just two editors enthusiastic about the same literature and dogs and movies. When she said she acquired romance authors, I told her about my manuscript. At first I didn't claim the story, leaving it open as just a manuscript I was looking over. But eventually she probed. And eventually I told her the truth. That it was my own. That I'd been working on it since college. That my dream was to see it out in the world one day, just like I cheered on my authors as their books went out in the world. She liked the hook enough that we exchanged business cards, her telling me to send it over when it was ready. It was only when I looked down at her card that I realized exactly with whom I had been speaking. Not just a nice editor at a nice house. The chief editor at *the* house. *The* Baird Books. The house to beat all houses. Even Sterling Publishing walks in Baird's shadow as far as romance is concerned.

And those same warm eyes are looking into mine now, easing all my fears. *What have I been so worried about?* I think, taking my first sip of coffee. *Why have I built this whole thing up in my head?* This isn't scary. This isn't intimidating. She simply called out to me.

Asked me to sit for coffee.

She's smiling.

It's alllll going to work out—

"I got your email last night."

My attention snaps at her words. "Oh?"

This is it. The moment of truth. The moment all my dreams come true. Or don't.

And then, with those warm, down-to-earth eyes, Claire Donovan blinks, and in that moment the corners of her eyes dip ever so slightly down. As though she knows what she's about to say.

Knows it. And hates it.

But of course she does.

Because we are kindred spirits.

And I, too, hate with every empathetic fiber of my being this part of the job.

Delivering . . . rejection.

"We need to talk."

Chapter 6

I force myself to stay glued to my chair, hands clasped neatly on my lap, ankles crossed politely beneath my chair. Even though every part of me wants to run.

The volume in the world around us has turned down, lowering to a quiet hum. Time slows. My palms feel warm and sticky as they clasp one another, like two hot pancakes stacked together. I'm suddenly kicking myself for putting on that expensive, made-from-organic-tree-bark-while-saving-Liberian-puppies deodorant Olivia prodded me into buying so I could "do my part to save the planet" while ensuring the aluminum in the regular stuff didn't seep through my pores and give me dementia. Right at this moment, I'd give anything for a good, cheap, all-body rubdown of aluminum.

"Sounds good," I say at last, forcing the conversation to come to its inevitable destination. My voice is almost normal, except for the raspy rise as I finish the word. What I'd intended as a carefree tone turns out be to an anxious, mousy squeak. I lower my voice an octave and press on. "I'm impressed you're even checking your email given everything going on this weekend."

She waves a hand with a companionable smile. "Oh, you know how it is for us workaholics. It's never that easy to leave the work behind." She gives a little self-deprecating laugh, and I chuckle along.

"Isn't that the truth," I say and try my hardest to muster up the biggest smile I can—which isn't saying much. I feel I can't keep up with this shabby attempt at lighthearted preamble. It's time to get on with it. Both thankfully and horrifically, she senses it too.

"Anyway," Claire says, her voice instantly more businesslike. "I opened your email last night for a reason. When you shared with me the hook of your story last year, I was intrigued. A recovering shopaholic and your personal finance radio personality fall for one another in a coffee shop, only to then have to settle out their differences? It was so charming. Truly. But the story you told me last year and the story I saw on the page last night are two very different things. What I wanted—" She pauses. "What I really hoped for was *that* story."

That story.

She wanted *that* story.

My stomach drops to somewhere around my feet. I'm not even sure what she's saying. My manuscript is not the same as my manuscript? Of course it's the same. Everything about it is the same. The only things that changed were a few revisions here and there because I was wise enough to know I was no expert in the romance-writing department and consequently took up as much reading on the subject as I could.

I'd read a new book on the craft of writing and realize a

ghastly amateur move, then shift the manuscript to parallel the winning wisdom within that book.

I'd read another book, realize another major flaw, and adjust my manuscript accordingly.

Yes, at times the books would contradict one another, and that was, I admit, confusing. But I worked through it. My manuscript worked through it.

And came out *stronger.*

I think.

"Oh," I say feebly, trying hard not to fidget with my hands. Trying just as hard to form cohesive, intelligent words while keeping my face and voice from giving away just exactly how I feel. Which is as though a lightning bolt has struck overhead and a telephone pole has bludgeoned me.

"Now, I didn't get through all of it last night, of course," she continues.

"Of course," I say, a bit of hope rising. Of course she didn't read the whole manuscript. *Of course.* "How far along did you get?"

She hesitates. "Enough."

Her word falls like a massive blow.

Enough.

She'd read . . . enough.

I feel sick to my stomach.

This author side of things is *awful.*

I've never been on the receiving end of manuscript rejection before. It's dreadful. Nobody should write.

"But there are pieces there. Potential. And"—she pauses thoughtfully—"under normal circumstances, I think I saw enough potential in your story that I would've welcomed the opportunity to continue working with you on it, getting it into tip-top shape."

I raise my eyes. Yes. Yes, that would be a good idea. I myself do that sometimes when I get particularly keen on a potential client. We'll just . . . exchange emails. We'll volley them back and forth until it's right. And then she'll take it to her team. And then it'll move on to pub board. And then I get a contract.

The sweet words echo in my ear. *And then I get a contract.*

"But," she continues, "the fact of the situation is that I'm not under normal circumstances at this point in time. Had I gotten this email last year—even six months ago—things could've been different."

Claire shifts in her chair, clearly trying to be as subtle as she can in the reminder that I should've sent her this manuscript sooner, like we discussed.

But I *tried* to send it sooner.

I really did. It just never was *quite* ready back then. Never quite perfect.

"I'm retiring at the end of March," she continues. "As such, I am in the midst of offloading my authors onto other editors, not taking on any new ones. And the reason I took a look at it last night was because I liked your hook. I like you. And were . . ." She hesitates, as if considering if I'm emotionally able to handle what she's about to say. "Were the manuscript in prime condition, I would've considered taking it on. Just"—she gives a wry smile—"get it through contracts and then hand it over to an editor on my team. But . . ."

She trails off, and while that little shrug she's giving may seem like a good enough finale for her, I feel my anxiety rising.

But . . . *what?*

What?

You can't just leave off our conversation with, "Well, I could've made all your dreams come true. But . . . ," and then shrug and ask me to pass the sugar.

You're the editor, for crying out loud! I want to wail. *You need to know how to end a scene!*

"I hate to have to throw myself out of the ring before the bidding gets started, though." She smiles at me as though she's the one to be pitied here, not me. Which . . . now that I think of it, I may be a tiny bit to blame for. I may have touted myself just a little after I got her business card last year, ballooning up the fact that one small press almost certainly working out of its garage had expressed interest into the illusion that dozens of New York houses were knocking on my door. Oops. "Anyway, you probably wouldn't have wanted to dissect all the pieces of your manuscript with me anyway. Especially when I'm only one opinion."

You're the only voice I want to hear! my brain wants desperately to blurt out, and I squeeze my hands together tightly to keep from doing so. *You're the only voice that matters!*

It's time for another tactic.

"What," I begin as lightly as I can, "sort of things did you notice?"

"Hmm." Her eyes dim slightly. She takes an extra-lengthy time to reply. "Well, for example, the meet." She puts up a hand. "Now, meeting in a coffee shop is a wonderful idea," she says encouragingly. She gives a gentle smile as she waves a hand around. "We're meeting in a coffee shop here, just like thousands of people use the coffee shop as an extension of their living room. There is always something lovely about the ambience. But," she says after a pause, "it's just . . . a bit overdone."

My mind flashes to the words my mystery editor inscribed on the manuscript: Wildly unoriginal.

"I just thought," I venture, "perhaps it was original considering the way the two characters mistakenly mixed up their cups when they picked them up, only to find out, you know . . ." I shrug with a smile. "They actually ordered the same drink . . ."

"Yes, and I believe Hallmark has enjoyed that opening as well. Time and time again."

Her smile is tender. I know she's trying to make light of it all, make it a joke for my sake. And for hers I smile back as the words on my manuscript's margin flash across my eyes: Nauseating and directly plagiarized from every Hallmark movie in the last ten years.

"Interesting," I say, nodding as though I'm casually digesting this information and it's not feeling in the slightest like glass shredding my insides as it goes down. "So the meetup needs some attention."

"And the characters," Claire adds, nodding back.

"The characters. Yes. Of course. The characters." I pause. "How exactly . . . with the characters?"

"Well, for example, Sloan."

"Sloooan," I repeat. "Yes. Sloan. Exactly what about Sloan?"

"Sloan has to go."

Claire delivers the fact of the matter just as easily as she would say, "You know, I think that table lamp has to go. It's throwing off the vibe in the living room."

Sloan. The quirky woman desperately in love with Renaldo. The one who inserts herself in every other scene in one bumbling way or another. The one threaded expertly into the story to highlight the movement and growth of the other characters. Sloan.

And precisely how, I want to yell, would I manage taking out a major character without the entire story collapsing?

The mystery editor's words—We don't need this character—are crackling through my brain, but I don't have time to dwell on it.

"And I did have one thought," Claire continues, her eyes brightening. "Have you ever considered shifting the manuscript to the present tense?"

Have I. Ever considered. Shifting to present tense.

Claire Donovan is replicating the words and thoughts of my mystery editor so well she practically *is* the editor. Who knows, maybe she actually *is* the editor. Maybe *she* is the one who stole into a foreign publishing house in order to sneak up into a secret room, scribble hateful comments on my manuscript, and steal away again. That seems like the only logical conclusion here.

That or, I feel with sickening dread, my mystery editor was right.

Everyone around me is right, and I'm the only one who can't see the flaws in my own work.

I've heard this from my authors before, at least a dozen times. How blinded they get to their own writing. How hard it is to see the story from the reader's perspective. In my mind, I *live* in the world of Harpwood, Indiana. I've worked so hard and for so long on this story, I know every intricate detail—both written and unwritten.

A sudden mood of despair hits me, and I can't help but feel my shoulders beginning to slump. All this time I thought I had something. An idea. A spark. All this time, I thought, *I may just be able to do this! I may just have a writer's soul after all!* But what am I, really?

Just a girl, sitting in a coffee shop, who's completely deluded herself.

"Well, I'd better be getting back," I say, shifting my knees out from underneath the bistro table to stand. I force a little laugh. "And I'm sure you have much more important things to attend to than talking with me all day." I smile as I speak, my cheeks plastered into formation, although I'm finding it hard to look her in the eye. "Thank you so much for everything, though, Mrs. Donovan. I know I am . . . very small . . . compared to you, and yet even I understand what it's like to have your in-box flooded with proposals and ideas. I'm truly honored you chose to consider mine."

I move to stand, all the while gazing fixedly at the floor.

"Savannah, wait just a moment."

I pause.

Force myself to meet her eye. When I do, her gaze is steady, open.

"Your story does have promise," she says slowly, as though hoping with each measured word I fully absorb and believe it. "It truly does. You just need to get that story, the one I heard last year, on paper. That's all."

For a long moment, I pause.

And there, looking into her warm eyes, all the while trying to absorb her words as she intended, I'm aware of a new thought forming. And for a moment, I push away the doubts flapping their large, thunderous wings.

This is not someone trying to butter me up when I'm feeling low. This is Claire Donovan.

The Claire Donovan.

And we may have had a jolly chat in line last year, yes, but the fact is this is her job. She gets hundreds of supremely vetted, hand-selected manuscripts to peruse each year from the hands of a few select literary agents. And while, yes, we did have one nice chat last year, the fact is she wouldn't have sat here, wasting twenty minutes of her precious time, if she didn't actually think my story had an inkling of potential. She wouldn't have wasted the time opening that email if she didn't really believe there was something there. She wouldn't have read at least a few pages by computer light near midnight if the hook hadn't grabbed her. And she certainly wouldn't have taken the time to pull me aside and talk today instead of shooting off a sympathetic email.

Contrary to the chant pulsing in my ears, I am not doomed.

I might not have a good enough manuscript here to get a deal on the spot, but I have a start. A good start.

And I need to make a decision. Right now. Because it really might be now or never.

The smile I had plastered on before falls, my expression replaced with a serious brow.

"So, you said that if my manuscript was up to the quality you had hoped, you would be willing to push it through pub board before retiring at the end of March."

She eyes me warily, clearly noticing the change in my own tone. "If. Yes. I would've. *If.*"

"So, *if* I can get this manuscript perfected by your next pub meeting, you'll consider it."

She hesitates. Takes a breath. "Well, Savannah, I—"

I raise my hands in the air. "I know you are talking about a major rewrite here. I am in no way misunderstanding the level of work you're asking for."

"It would take quite the upheaval," she says. "More than, I

fear, you may be able to do in such a short time. Our pub board meets the first Tuesday of the month."

"The first Tuesday of the month. I can *do* that," I say, nodding, more to myself than to her. "I *will* do it."

She peers dubiously at me for so long, I scramble and then throw out the words. "I even have an editor working with me now. Someone who agrees with all the pointers you've just given."

She pauses. "You have someone helping you?"

"Yes." Help. Criticize. Same thing.

I can see her expression slowly turning, my own eager expression and confidence causing her to budge. "I can't promise anything. You know that."

I nod fervently. "I do."

Several seconds of silence pass. The hubbub around us grows—classes out, halls filling up with people.

"Alright, Savannah. Get it to my in-box by March 1, in the best condition you possibly can, and I'll give it another look." And with those words our meeting is over. She's rising to her feet.

I shower her with a dozen "Thank yous" and "I wills." As we part, she doesn't smile quite as confidently and carefreely about our interaction as I would have hoped, but it doesn't matter. The point is I now have *time* to prove she's made the right decision in giving me another chance. I have *time*.

As we separate in the sea of people and I follow the stream back toward the exhibit hall, my head races as I process what just happened.

My dreams were dashed. Momentarily.

Then they came true. Sort of.

And now I have exactly—I check my watch—forty-four days

to completely rewrite a book that took me four years to write in the first place.

Forty-four days.

Forty . . . four . . . days.

Six Mondays.

Six Tuesdays.

Six Saturdays.

Just six.

I can't be sure—I only edited *Breathe Your Way Through Panic Attacks* last year—but if chapter 4 is any indicator, I believe I feel a panic attack coming on as the status of my situation starts to settle in.

I step into the aisle with booths on each side.

The Pennington booth is still packed, the crowd less angsty here in the afternoon (no doubt because everyone has already cruised by the booths at least once) than it was this morning. People now are actually perusing the stacks of books on the tables, making the atmosphere more like that of a bookshop and less of a hijacking. I squeeze between two women holding up a black-and-yellow-striped disk as they discuss Linden's new audio.

Out of the corner of my eye I spot Lyla, whose typically glossy curls now look like they've been beaten in a windstorm. Her smile looks like she's put Vaseline on her teeth (one of several odd cheerleading tricks she once used in high school to keep smiling for long periods of time). She holds a scanner out to a man's badge as she talks, but when our eyes meet, she breaks off her speech to give me a look that says, *Run, Sav! Run for your life!*

I halt immediately.

"Savannah!" Just as the librarians in front of me break apart, Giselle's figure comes into view. "Tom was just asking about you."

Tom.

I frown.

Who's Tom?

And then the bell clangs loudly in my head.

"Tom?" I say, suddenly on the receiving end of a hug. As his rather round, Santa-bowl belly bumps into me, I inhale the distinct smells of sour-cream-and-onion chips, cigarettes, and ancient recliners. I squeeze out words while he squeezes me: "*Tom*. I didn't realize you were going to be in town."

"I wasn't," he says, then lets go to step back with a huge grin. As though this was his little ruse. As though he's just given me the best surprise. "But then I thought to myself, what's six hours for a fine opportunity like this? You didn't get my email?"

"Uh . . . no," I hedge, taking another step backward for good measure. Tom is one of those authors who likes to send me thirty emails a week, mostly about cats. "I must've missed it."

"Ah, well, I thought that's what happened. Anyway, here I am!" he says and throws his arms out grandly, causing at least three people to duck.

Tom Haggerty was picked up by another editor, Siri, a handful of years ago. When Siri got the boot six months ago, Giselle divvied up his authors among the team. Which meant she gained Francine Thomas, a perennial bestseller who sends Giselle cupcakes on her birthday. And I got Tom, a perennial bestseller who prefers really tight, full-frontal hugs lasting thirty seconds too long.

"Don't mind me, though," Tom says, scratching the fabric on

his stomach. "I know you'll be all kinds of busy at these things. I won't get in the way."

"Nonsense," says Giselle, sidling up beside him and giving his shoulder a pat. "You're part of the Pennington family. I just *know* Savannah would love to tour you around."

Forty-four days.

"Actually," I begin, but then I see a familiar pair of oxfords stepping up beside me. My teeth are clenched so tightly I can barely force out my own Vaseline smile. "I can't think of a single thing I'd rather do."

I try to ignore the ache in my sternum.

Forty-four days. That's basically a chapter a day. A brand-new chapter every single day.

With a meet cute that needs a total transformation.

Characters that need slashing.

Dialogue that needs a total override.

And language that is, apparently, snobbish and utterly *dénué de sens.*

"Terrific." Tom has thrown out his hands again, this time toppling a whole stack of books onto my feet. I gather them up in my arms, and when I stand, I discover Tom has slid into the remaining inches between us. His eyes are a twinkling mossy green, matching both his moss-green collared shirt, of which he's ignored the top three buttons, and his rather gloomy, philosophical Camus-style books that discuss—far too often, in fact—moss. His voice is low. Sort of purring. "That's just terrrrific."

"I believe we haven't met."

And suddenly I see the sleeve of an arm being thrust between us and Tom taking a step back. He turns and, with a slight frown, surveys the man who has just intervened.

William—clean shaven, poised, and with an expression that conveys a thinly veiled *Who the heck are you, and why are you talking to my editor?*—stands eye to eye with Tom. The sameness of their height is, most refreshingly, where the commonality ends.

"William Pennington," William says, taking a slightly dazed Tom's hand. "New publisher of the Pennington Pen division." His eyes dart down to Tom's name badge. "And you must be Tom, one of our authors. What a surprise to see you."

And now it's my turn to feel a flash of delight sparking in my eyes.

"Yes, well," Tom says, his eyes brightening. He shakes William's hand heartily. "I had the weekend off, and I thought to myself, who's the only person in the world I want to see?" He turns his gaze on me. "And of course I knew the answer immediately."

I give a little smile in return. I seem to be one of Tom's favorite people.

My ankles throb at the reminder of that hideous evening just a few months ago. I look down at Tom's shoes and grimace. He's wearing them. The pointy red cowboy boots with at least a dozen rhinestones.

"Ah. Yes," William says, retracting his hand and putting it in his pants pocket. "So you have some work to go over together, I gather?"

That's funny. William didn't ask once about work with any of the other authors.

"Work. Of course. Yes. And then"—Tom gives a cheeky grin while he surreptitiously pulls up his jeans to highlight his boots—"I imagine we'll paint the town red again like last time. That was one-of-a-kind fun, wasn't it, Savannah?"

"One-of-a-kind, indeed." In reality, the idea of heading to

every karaoke bar and line-dancing saloon in Nashville is so unoriginal it's laughable.

I spot Lyla in some sort of altercation with an elderly woman, the librarian's beaded eyeglass chain swinging as she tries to yank back the massive foam board of Oswald's face from Lyla's hands.

"Excuse me, I'm going to have to . . ." I trail off as I move toward the couple, and both men's faces turn. William's expression, for his part, doesn't flicker. Clearly he's been to so many of these things he's come to expect the odd librarian-trying-to-make-off-with-our-cargo situation.

"I'll just wander around for a while, then!" Tom calls merrily, and stuffing both hands into his pockets, he drifts out of the booth. "See you soon, Savannah!"

I force the smallest smile that could still pass for professional interest and call back, "Okay, Tom."

Tom Haggerty. Line dancing.

And forty-four days.

Chapter 7

The music inside the Painted Pony Saloon crackles so loudly over the speakers I'm going to need aspirin for days. Between the noise, the swirling kaleidoscopic lights on the dance floor the past three hours, and the calluses currently forming on my inner thighs from their consistent rubbing beneath my jeans, I would gladly dive into one of those sensory deprivation tanks over this.

"Whooooeeeee!" Tom hollers. My ears quake with the thunder of his clap by my head as he follows the line dancer demonstrating onstage.

He grabs me by the hand and throws me into another twirl.

I could have taken an editor position at another publishing house two years ago. A nice, sane house, with sane bosses and sane editors and sane authors who, when they come to town, want to do things like eat asparagus wrapped in bacon while discussing possible endorsements.

But noooo.

Instead, I get Tom. And a publishing house that wants me to tour Tom around like I'm some kind of line-dancing hostess at—I check my watch—eleven o'clock on a Saturday night. When I'm already exhausted. And overwhelmed. And have to deal with a full day tomorrow as well.

The song ends and transitions into a new one, and as a single note slowly rakes across a violin, the man onstage holds the microphone to his lips and tips his cowboy hat down. His voice lowers as though he's got an intimate secret to share. "Ladies and gents, we're gonna take this one easy. So slow 'er down, hold your sweetheart close, and sway to an old country favorite, 'Just Another Woman in Love.'"

Tom spins on me, his thin lips lifting in a wiry smile as if to say, "Welp, I guess we have no choice but to do what we're ordered to," and I immediately put up two hands.

"Oh no, Tom. I think I'm going to sit this one out."

But even as I speak, I feel him tug on both of my elbows. "Aw, c'mon. Listen to this song." His eyes are brimming with elation as he tugs me an inch toward him. "This song is a *classic.*"

"Yes, it's very nice," I say, struggling to unwrap his fingers from my elbows. "All the same, it's getting late."

"*Late?*" His forehead wrinkles at such an insinuation, and I realize as the lights fall upon his glassy eyes that he may have snuck yet another pint of beer down somewhere in the last half hour. "No such thing as late when you're accompanied by such fine music and fine women."

"No, really—" I begin but, despite my protest, feel his hands grab onto my wrists and pull them firmly toward him.

As he does so my face grows hot—as hot as it can be on this packed dance floor surrounded by beer and cheap leather.

I feel myself finally losing my last, shaky grip on the self-control I've been warring to keep hold of all evening, and all thoughts of Tom's *New York Times* bestseller rankings and Pennington's profits and the world's tough economic times fly from my mind. I'm like a two-liter of soda that's been shaken one too many times, and cap or no cap, I'm going to explode.

I'm just about to make my stand, no matter *what* he might say to Giselle (who'd slay me) or William or even Ms. Pennington herself tomorrow, when I feel somebody step in and grab Tom by the arm.

"I think that's *enough*," William says, and my mouth practically falls open as I see him.

He's still clad in his blue suit and tan oxfords from earlier in the day. But he looks different now, less polished than the poised professional I saw this morning. His tie is crooked, the perfect creases in his perfect blue trousers gone. There's even what appears to be a bit of gum and torn-off paper stuck to the bottom side of one shoe. By clothing alone, he looks weary. But in his frank blue eyes there is an icy steeliness that says he can go all night.

Tom takes a step back, clearly seeing the same thing I'm seeing. "We were just having a bit of fun," he says, then adds an overripe laugh. He turns his head toward me. "Weren't we, Savannah? Just some good fun."

My eyes widen as I turn from Tom to William, unsure of how to respond. I'm about to open my mouth to give the best noncommittal yet professional reply I can come up with when I find I don't need to.

William takes a step in and faces him, completely blocking

me out. And then I'm standing there, staring into a sea of blue on the back of my boss's suit as colorful lights from above pan slowly by.

"Even so, there's an Uber waiting outside for you," I hear William say coolly. "It will take you wherever you need to go."

"But . . . Savannah was going to drive me back to the hotel. And we had some things to talk about for my next book."

"Good news, Tom. You will be pleased to know you have been promoted. I am now personally taking responsibility for you as editor, and unfortunately, I don't have time to dance with you. Good night."

For several seconds I stand there, hidden behind William's stoic hold on the dance floor, barely able to breathe from what I just heard. Did he just say that? Did he just *do* that? On my account?

When William does turn around at last, there is no sign of Tom anywhere.

I look around, but all I can see around us is a sea of slow-dancing couples.

Couples and slow-moving strobe lights and, most important, no more Tom.

I look up into William's face and for the first time all night feel my shoulders begin to droop. My pent-up breath exhales. When I do, a bubble of laughter wells up inside me. A bubbling of anxiety, of release from anxiety, of disbelief at what just happened. Just remembering the shocked look on Tom's face is almost too much.

William's face, for his part, is still steely as he keeps his eyes on the doors. Drawn. And frankly, exhausted.

I can't help it. My shoulders shake a little as I let out a quiet chuckle.

He turns as if noticing me for the first time. His expression shifts.

The single line on his forehead creases deeper.

Gone is his concern at watching the uncivilized, handsy man exit. Here is the concern at watching his petite, bizarre employee in the center of the dance floor, laughing.

"I can't believe you did that," I say, fighting a new round of laughter building up in the pit of my stomach. Boss or no boss, I can't help myself.

For a moment he just looks at me, frowning slightly, as if he's come across some small, odd creature and he's trying to figure it out. "I can't believe you danced with him at all."

The threat of laughter stops.

Surely he's not going to put any of the blame for tonight on *me*. "You said to entertain our authors," I reply. "You said it was vital to let them know how important they are."

"Yes, but not *that* vital," he says, raking a hand through his brown hair as he darts his eyes toward the doors. He throws an arm out. "For heaven's sake, Savannah. Surely you know it's never, ever *that* vital."

For a moment I'm stunned by the realization that he's criticizing me, as though I should've known it was *obvious* not to subject myself to Tom for the sake of performing well in my job. As if he's frustrated by the reality that he is clearly going to have to babysit the new editors under his wing, unlike the big, brassy, self-sufficient ones at the elaborate publishing house in New York City.

And I would be offended, except for the new question that suddenly crowds my thoughts. "How did you find us, anyway?"

"I did what every other bachelorette party in town does," he says. "I followed the strip."

A rush of emotion surges through me, and for a moment I forget his previous criticism and find myself surveying this man who moves his gaze back toward the doors. I'm finding it hard to believe the situation before me. So this guy, my new boss, battled his way through the crowded streets of Nashville, overflowing with drunk tourists moving from one noisy honky-tonk to another, to find me.

To . . . what exactly?

To make sure I was okay?

"Mind if we take this conversation . . . ," he says, nodding to the area off the dance floor.

"Oh. Yes." I all too readily start toward the bar. My feet ache in my boots, not worn so much for the sake of looking the part tonight but to protect my toes, given how much Tom stepped on them last time. "Please."

I try to hobble as little as possible as we weave our way around couples and find two barstools. Both of us exhale as we sit on the cracked red leather. A bartender comes over, and I glance at the rows of bottles on the shelves behind him. My brain, however, is too amped up to delegate time to the task of making a choice, so I throw out the name of the first drink that comes to mind.

"Gin and tonic for me," I say to the man on the other side, brandishing the ID out of my back pocket.

William seems to feel the same way, because without hesitation he adds, "Make that two."

And for a long moment after the bartender leaves we sit in silence. Both trying to find peace and our bearings, it seems, in the current environment.

"Why didn't you just call me?" I say with a sudden thought. I can't help feeling a bit rueful about everything as I glance over to the man who looks like he's just run a marathon. "Surely you have access to my number."

"I did," William responds. "Several times."

I reach instinctively for my phone in my other pocket and blanch when I see the missed calls from the unknown number line up on my screen. "Sorry," I say at last. "I didn't realize it was on silent."

He waves a hand as if done with the conversation. "It's fine. I just need to make a memo for the next company pep talk: *Do Everything within One's Power to Please Authors, Except Line Dancing with Scurrilous Men.*"

"'Scurrilous.'" I grin as my hand itches to type that one into my phone's notes app. "That's a good word. People should use it more often."

He pauses, and I see him smile lightly. "Or not." I raise my brows, a question forming, and he continues as he pulls his drink toward him. "Not when 'complete idiot' will do."

I smile, pulling my own glass toward me. "If you were so opposed, why didn't you just say something this afternoon? Save yourself all this trouble."

"Because I wasn't so opposed this afternoon," he says mildly. "Until I saw the way he looked at you as he followed you out the door."

I'm just starting to feel a little creeped out imagining what he witnessed from his point of view when William takes a thoughtful sip, then smiles a little darkly. "I am going to thoroughly enjoy being his editor."

The previous picture in my head slips away as I give an all-out laugh. "You do realize you sound terrifying."

"As an editor, I can be terrifying," he replies, and he says it so automatically and with such authority, I believe it.

Well.

If he wants to enjoy giving Tom a hard time via email in the coming months, by all means. And I have a feeling that those thirty emails Tom sends a week of cat memes and selfies will unexpectedly have a hard time finding the Pennington in-box.

"Well, for what it's worth, thank you. I was about to hold my own—"

"I saw the flash in your eyes. I don't doubt it."

"But I'm glad I didn't have to," I finish. I pause, then raise my glass. "To good bosses. Thank you, William Pennington. You're doing pretty good for your second day."

For a moment he almost looks like he won't play, but at last he clinks glasses with me. I can't be sure as we both face the wall of bottles and take our sips, but out of the corner of my eye I think I see a small smile on his lips just before he tips his glass. Good. He should feel good for what he did. Not many bosses would go to such lengths. Unless . . .

I feel the silent question rising with the beat of the next song, and with it a little flurry of activity in my stomach.

But no.

Surely he's not. Surely he wouldn't be . . . *interested* . . .

"Call me Will. And a good publishing house doesn't just take care of their authors," he says. "They take care of their employees too. I hope you know that."

I feel a momentary rise of disappointment but just as quickly whisk it away. Of course. Of course this was all about work. Or liability, even. Maybe he just wanted to make sure he wasn't going to step Pennington into a lawsuit. Enabling harassment. All of that. Of course.

As we drink in silence, I feel the need to turn the conversation. To say anything. Anything at all.

"So, I'm sure it was a big move coming all the way from the City," I venture. "Do you miss it?"

The second I ask the question I regret it. The man was fired from his bigger, better job in New York City. The only reason he has returned, most likely, is a lack of other opportunities. *Great, Sav. Just throw salt on his wounds.*

He raises his hand for the bill, the expression in his eyes unreadable. "Sometimes."

"I've been there a few times," I say, trying to keep the tone upbeat. "Once when my father ended up on the *TODAY* show to make some baklava and talk about his new cookbook, and once when my sister was marching in the Macy's Day Parade."

"Your father is a chef?"

"No. Dentist," I say, then catch myself. "A dentist with a penchant for pastries and a thriving YouTube cooking account with a Saturday baking class for underprivileged youths downtown."

"A dentist with a sweet tooth," Will muses, smiling slightly. "How ironic."

"Good job security," I say, grinning back.

"And your sister?" he asks. "What instrument did she play?"

"All of them."

He smiles politely as though waiting for my real answer.

"No, really, all of them. I mean, in the parade itself she

only juggled between flute solo and trumpet. But yes, all of them."

His brows raise, and I see the same look I see in everyone's eyes when I talk about my family. "A real go-getter family you got there."

"You have no idea."

"Well, I can see why Pennington Publishing must be glad to have you, then."

"Oh no." I almost choke on my gin. "No. I'm nothing like the rest of them."

Will's eyes widen, and a smirk slowly rises on one side of his face. "Ah. So you aren't a high achiever. Too bad."

"Wait, no," I amend quickly, setting my glass down to focus on correcting myself. "I don't underwork. I do just . . . enough."

"A very satisfactory level, you might say."

I see it now, in his eyes. They're mirthful. He's teasing me. My lips start to curl. "Pleasantly sufficient."

"Perfectly adequate," he says, his eyes crinkling too. "You could highlight that on your CV."

"How do you think I got this job?"

Our eyes hold, and for a long moment we just smile. A warmth spreads through me. I can't define it exactly, but if it were a scent, it'd be eggnog sprinkled with nutmeg. If a sound, it'd be the footsteps of a dear friend on your front porch.

"Or at least," he continues, "you can throw it in your CV when you email Sterling."

For a moment I'm so thrown by this comment in the midst of our banter I fumble for a response. He seizes the moment in stride. His expression shifts. "For the record, thank you also for what you did today. There aren't many people who would hand a business card back to Jim Arrowood. For what it's worth, I appreciated it."

He appreciated it.

Not Pennington. Not him on behalf of Pennington.

He.

Will.

"Well, your former colleagues are real scurrilous," I say, inwardly tucking away the compliment while, on the outside, brushing it off. "And besides, you now are subjected to being Tom's editor. I'd say tonight, your sacrifice was far greater."

"Ah, yes. Tom. Well, we'll just see how long Tom lasts with Pennington in the end. I have a feeling he'll be moving on soon, so I wouldn't worry too much about me."

He grins while I raise a brow. "You do know he's surprisingly successful, don't you? He sold a hundred thousand copies of his book last year, nearly out of the gate."

And there he goes again. The smile he's hanging on to drifting down like an autumn leaf off his face. "Yes, well, for the record, it was an editorial and publishing misstep to allow him to all but plagiarize Camus as his own. He walked a razor-thin line throughout the novel, particularly—"

"—with the quote, I know!" I interrupt. "He all but claimed, 'To be happy, it is essential not to be too concerned with others.' That's what I told everyone!"

Will pauses. Adjusts in his chair and looks at me, really looks at me.

"You told everyone what, exactly?"

His voice is so probing, I feel almost certain now I've made a mistake. My voice treads lightly as I respond. "Just that . . . it seemed dangerously close to a copyright issue for him to follow the same storyline and themes, and even title, as those in *The Fall*. Regardless of what Tom claimed, to even have the appearance of lifting Camus's quotes by replacing words with a few well-chosen synonyms was—"

"—absolutely reckless to allow," he interjects. "It was. And nobody agreed with you?"

I shrug. It doesn't seem wise to give the specific details of how Giselle had all but told me I was like a child in meetings: there to be seen, not heard. "I'm just an assistant acquisitions editor."

The crease in Will's forehead deepens. He doesn't respond right away, but when he does, it sounds as though he's made up his mind. "I see. Well, where I come from, everyone has a voice. Evidently, those in Pennington may need that reminder."

We let the silence linger.

What is there to say?

And after several moments pass of twisting my glass on the countertop, thinking of what topic to approach next while watching the condensation bubble up on the heavily polyure-thaned wood, I give in. Change the subject to the first reasonable thing that comes to mind. "At any rate, I hope you enjoy the shift from New York. I'm sure there's a lot to be missed, but hopefully you'll like the change."

"Thank you and yes." He pauses, and I can see thought clouds starting to form in his eyes. "Much to be missed, but at the same time, I hope, much to be gained."

What does that mean? Is this about more than his job? Does he have some long-lost girlfriend up there, perhaps? Someone he yearns to get back to?

But of course he left his life up there. He probably had a slew of close friends and, even though I don't find myself liking to admit it, a number of stunning girlfriends over the years. It's New York. They breed pretty people there.

Besides, it's none of my business. And more important, he's my boss. And classy. And sophisticated. And truly a *man*. Settled into a mature life, no doubt uninterested in someone who can't even pull together her life enough to move out of her sister's apartment.

But most pertinent here is the reminder that it doesn't matter, and I don't care.

At last the bartender comes over, and Will points at both our glasses. "I'll get these."

"Oh no, please," I say immediately and begin scrabbling in my back pocket. "I couldn't let you."

"On the company," he says, pulling out a flashy silver card. "Our apologies for one heck of a night."

For a moment I wonder if he's serious, if he's really trying to represent Pennington Publishing and make amends for the disastrous author in our house with a twelve-dollar cocktail. But then I see his name on the personal debit card and catch the light in his arctic eyes.

"You're all forgiven," I say, grinning as I slide off my seat to stand. "Consider the slate wiped clean."

A new topic looms over my head, and before I can wimp out, I snatch at the opportune moment. This is the time to find out what he knows. If I say it just right, I can ask without giving anything away. "And . . . about that manuscript I dropped at the meeting." My finger taps on the counter. "I'm sorry about that and—"

He stops me. "Don't worry about it, Savannah. It's an easy

thing to happen when working with all that paper. But you might want to consider using the binding machine next time. Or better yet . . . keep it out of sight altogether."

His smile grows. "After all, not everyone at Pennington shares the same appreciation of the more . . . adventurous fiction as you and me."

I slide my key into the lock thirty minutes later and find myself still a little amazed by how everything went down. Replaying the look on Tom's face as Will tore his hands off me and stepped in. Hearing Will's authoritative voice declaring he was taking Tom from now on. Hearing him exonerate me for my manuscript slip without any questions raised.

It was priceless.

All of it.

Priceless.

But as I play it all back in my mind, questions jump in here and there. Like what were all those thoughts so clearly occupying him half the time? And who exactly is up in New York that he misses?

But then, as I open the door, comes that other, higher-priority thought that I won't be rid of for a month. *Forty-four days.* It's nearly midnight now, yet again, but I can't be deterred.

I take a step into the living room and am greeted by the whirring of the Peloton. Olivia, in the middle of flicking a page of her book, pauses as she sees me come in.

"How many are you at?" Olivia says.

No hello.

I drop my laptop bag off my aching shoulder and wearily check my watch. "Nineteen thousand. And hello."

"*Nineteen,*" Olivia breathes, looking so proud she might cry. "Excellent work today, Savvy. What did you do today? Whatever it is, just repeat it every day for the month, and you're gold."

Right, I think, moving away from her beaming gaze and taking my poor, aching body toward my bedroom, along with the laptop bag I drag across the floor. *All I need to do is repeat the chaos of today and—*

I stop at the sight of the small bouquet of flowers on the table by my bedside. As I move toward them, for one insane moment I think with a stutter, *Did Will Pennington send these to me?*

But no, I realize, seeing the scribbled handwriting on the small card sticking out of the bundle. I take the note, flick it open, and read the inscription:

Hope you hit it out of the park today.

Leave it to Ferris to drop by some flowers on behalf of the two of them, just to make sure I cheered up from this morning. They aren't from Olivia, I know. But they are a team now, just like how Mom always adds Dad's name to the Christmas cards without his awareness. I'll have to thank them tomorrow.

I take a couple of moments to stop and smell them, inhaling the scent of the petite yellow roses. Read the card again. *Hope you hit it out of the park today.* Well, in a way, I did hit it out of the park, didn't I? I had a brave conversation with Claire; I asserted myself when I could have cowered, and now I have a *tremendous* opportunity before me. Not to mention I no longer have to deal with Tom. *Ever again.* It really was a home-run kind of day if you think about it.

Propelled by my momentary burst of self-congratulatory encouragement, I turn toward my closet and, after much yanking and digging, find the tattered manuscript.

As I settle down on my bed, computer beside me, stack of papers in hand, I feel instantly better. I have a plan. It may be hectic. It may be incredibly busy over the course of the next month. I may have to hunker down and set all the other priorities in my life aside for a while, but I have a plan. I will get through this. Just so long as I have the direction found in these—

I halt.

All this time I've been flipping pages, reading through to see all the notes my mystery editor left for me, how much work I'll have to do, how many words fill up the margins. But then suddenly, on page 16, it all stops.

Nothing.

I flip to the next page.

Nothing.

I flip three more and see nothing but the clear, clean white margin.

Nothing.

I flip through the rest of the manuscript, and all the while my heart sinks lower and lower. Why was I so stupid as to think whoever did this had actually read through the whole manuscript? Why would I be so ridiculous as to think they would choose to spend their afternoon jotting a thousand ugly notes in the margins?

I close my eyes. Take a deep breath. Assess the new situation.

So, my mystery editor only went through the first chapter.

Well, then, I have two options. Strike out on my own, trusting my—clearly blind—intuition to guide me. Or—

I gulp, already knowing what I have to do.

Ask for help.

And *hope* I get an answer back.

Chapter 8

Dear Mystery Editor and Intruder into
My-Most-Secret-Precious-Oasis-of-a-Room,
If you are reading this . . .
Help.

It's been three days. Or, as my mind prefers to think of it, 4,320 minutes. Four thousand three hundred twenty excruciatingly long minutes since I left the Post-It note on the manuscript in my hidden little sparrow room and waited for an answer. I live this way now. In minutes.

Lyla is convinced I have a urinary tract infection. I "visit the ladies' room" about fifty times a day, and then, when I escape our shared office and smile and give a little stroll-by wave to the others whose doors are propped open down the hall, I turn the corner and all but sprint up the tiny, twisting stairs for the attic. I've done it so much these days I've met my daily step goal each day and lost three pounds.

(But seriously. Three pounds. Olivia is thrilled.)

And now, this Wednesday, I sit in my office chair by the window, chewing my nails to the nubs (a disgusting habit, I know), while I do what I do every Wednesday morning for our editorial meeting. I click on Merriam-Webster's Word of the Day and try my best to focus on the task at hand and not the looming deadline and the desperation in my heart. I read the large, bold word: *bailiwick*.

Hmmm.

1. Bailiwick: law enforcement: the office or jurisdiction of a bailiff.

That'll be tough to include naturally in conversation. Let's see . . .

"And what makes this particular subject of the history of Russian philosophy from the tenth to eighteenth centuries so unique, Ms. Pennington, is how the bailiwick are so often referenced in . . . with unique symbolism . . . to . . ."

No. Moving on.

2. Bailiwick: the sphere in which one has superior knowledge or authority: a special domain.

Now there's something I can work with. Super knowledge. Authority. Let's see . . .

I'm just scrolling down to see some examples of *bailiwick* in a sentence to make sure I've properly grasped it when Lyla pops her earbuds out of her ears and stands. "C'mon, Sav. I wanna get there before all the doughnuts are gone."

My body says, *Good point—I only like the chocolate frosted ones*, while my mind stays steady.

Above Lyla's head, a utilitarian clock hangs on the wall. Nine fifty. And I still need to read through these examples and be sure I've got it.

"You go on ahead," I'm at the cusp of responding when Lyla says, "Not to mention, the new boss is back and will probably be watching for the stragglers so he can cut them."

I drop my hand off the mouse and stand up so abruptly my knee knocks painfully on the corner of the desk. "Okay," I agree and catch sight of my face in the decorative mirror above Lyla's workstation. My dark hair is a mess. The pale-gray sweater I put on today looks bulky and shapeless. And is that—I peer into the mirror more closely. *Is that a grotesque pimple right above my lip no female in this publishing house had the decency to inform me of?*

So much for sisters-in-arms! I cry out in my head, grabbing for my purse.

It's all that sugar. All that stupid sugar I've consumed in the form of Twizzlers and ice cream and Diet Coke till the wee hours of the morning to keep me awake while I try desperately to figure out how to fix my manuscript.

I pull out a tube of concealer and start dotting at the spot.

A small crease forms in the middle of Lyla's perfectly spotless forehead, and she crosses her arms.

"I've just got to . . . freshen up," I say, putting more dots beneath both eyes. And I can't miss those two dark shadows on each temple. And my forehead—I grimace at my reflection and begin dotting every area like my face is a polka-dot rug.

"Easy, Sav," Lyla says, observing my actions with the same

expression of horror one would make watching someone eat a dozen hot dogs at a county fair.

I rub at them all vigorously until it's all blended in.

Oh no.

Now I look like some pale, lifeless, overworked ballerina who *still* somehow has bags under her eyes. Why can't I be rid of them?

"We've got to *go*," Lyla says impatiently, checking her watch. "Why do you care all of a sudden anyway?"

"It's a competitive house," I retort, starting to slap my cheeks. "There's a lot of pressure to be professional."

"Well, you're really nailing it," Lyla says, eyeing me as I repeatedly smack my cheeks.

But sure enough, two little rosy spots start to form. "There," I say, standing back and admiring myself. "See? It worked."

Lyla nods. "Yes. Throw away the blush, ladies. Savannah Cade has solved all our makeup problems of the twenty-first century."

"Okay," I say, breezing past Lyla. "Hurry up, then," I add in my most professional tone. "We don't want to be late."

I've walked halfway down the hall by the time Lyla chimes in beside me, "Hey, Ms. Professional. You forgot your laptop."

I wince, looking down at my empty hands, and march back with as much dignity as I can.

Wednesday-morning Pennington Pen meetings are always held in the Lilac Room. There are a few reasons for this. It's one of the bigger rooms we have, plus it's one of the few technologically advanced spaces in the old building. And the walls are thick—which we need, because you wouldn't believe how heated conversations can get over color-code teal level #2C4952 versus virtually identical teal level #7CADA2 on a cover design.

There are eight members of the Pennington Pen division.

Two rather personality-lacking acquisition editors, Rob Orren and Yossi Jacobs, and myself. One editorial director, Giselle Shaw, who apparently snagged a job as a young editorial assistant back in college via her good looks and Daddy's checkbook. One marketing manager, Clyve Prinz, who is sixty-five and has yet to nail down the purpose of a Google calendar. One publicist, Marge Dippolito, whose ability to get our titles into some truly incredible prints has led a number of us to wonder if she's not working some sort of shady, back-alley business. One graphic designer and digital marketing wiz, Lyla, ironically the most talented and least enthused of the lot of us.

And now, Will.

I haven't seen Will since our last meeting on that beer-stained, cowboy boot–scratched floor. He wasn't at LOA the following morning, and word spread that he had left for New York—on business, presumably, although nobody knew for certain. All we knew was that decisions had once again fallen into Giselle's hands, thus explaining why I, specifically, had been pinpointed for the task of reorganizing every piece of paper in the filing cabinets dating back to 1970, and why the coffee breakroom had a shiny new pink espresso machine.

"Let's get to it, everyone. Settle in."

Lyla and I hurry into the room, and I set my stack of papers and laptop down on one of the remaining seats at the oval-shaped table. Lyla, meanwhile, drops her bag in the seat beside mine and veers for the doughnuts. Ms. Pennington stands at the head of the table, her pen tapping impatiently at the lot of us. Her blue eyes are piercing, her permanent frown is firmly in place, and her blazing red pantsuit is impeccable.

Her frown deepens as her eyes dart to the utilitarian-style

clock, a match to the others that adorn every room in the building. She pauses.

Lyla slides into her seat with a doughnut in each hand.

We wait.

And as the second hand strikes the top of the hour, Ms. Pennington drops her eyes to us. "Let us begin. Yossi, we'll start with you. Did you get the ASMI report back from Rogers?"

Yossi, who despite twelve years in the company jumps every time at the sound of his name, grabs for his papers. "Well, Pam has been very busy this week, what with traveling here from Louisiana for the conference—"

"You'll have to cut to the point, Yossi. I have another meeting—"

"Uh, no," Yossi stammers, taking off his glasses and rubbing them furiously against his tweed coat pocket. "She did say she'd send it to me by next week, though, and—"

"Failed to receive report," Ms. Pennington interjects, giving a short nod to Brittney, seated closest. Brittney, the delicate twenty-three-year-old assistant who spends every day trailing after Ms. Pennington with a notebook and pen, begins scribbling feverishly. The poor woman writes everything by hand because Ms. Pennington is so traditional. Pennington loves all old things—wallpaper, handwriting . . . It took ages for her to grudgingly agree to computers, and that, I hear, didn't even happen until the early nineties.

"Rob. Tell me about"—she glances down at her paper—"the developmental edits for Sonya. Has she received them, and how did she take it?"

And as Rob begins his own winding, skittish answer to her question, I take a moment to survey the room. Snow is drifting down outside the two windows facing the small yard beyond, and a cardinal sits on a nearby branch. Inside, the table is one giant mass of laptops and coffee cups, doughnuts and papers. And two seats to my left, at the foot of the table, is Will.

I feel a slight jump in my stomach and blink quickly back toward Ms. Pennington, not daring to let my eyes linger on anything but her. Rachel, our former marketing manager, was caught distracted by that cardinal out the window not too long ago and was fired on the spot for insubordination.

But as the questions and answers fire around the table, while I keep my eyes glued to Ms. Pennington, my mind wanders off to other matters.

Why does Will look so tired? There's a red rim around his eyes, looking like mine do after too many hours staring at a computer with not enough sleep. He's wearing glasses today, subtle copper-colored rectangular frames that make him look even more intimidating in his white button-up and navy-blue tie. Intimidating . . . and . . . well, sleek. Let's just call him sleek.

Does he always wear glasses? Or are those the blue-light glasses Lyla has been badgering me about buying? Honestly, I do not care.

"Savannah, did you finish that manuscript by Smith? What were your thoughts?"

I blink to attention.

"Yes. Smith." I shift in my chair, looking for my notes. "Smith's manuscript was . . . impressive," I say, pushing my stacks of papers aside in the hunt for Smith's proposal. "His perspective on the way George Bird Grinnell, America's environmental pioneer, led the way with such . . . such . . ." I hesitate, scouring my mind for the word. Ah. This is what I get for being so behind

I didn't get a chance to prepare my statement back at my desk. "Well, it was definitely his bailiwick," I say at last. "It's insightful. Smith really is"—I think quickly, trying to recall the words—"a leading authority in his field. I'd like to pursue taking his project to acquisitions."

"Fine," Ms. Pennington says, clearly not impressed by my word choices this week as she has been in previous ones, but not unimpressed either—and in our world, that's pretty good. She looks down at her paper to move on, but then, as though remembering something, suddenly lifts her head. "Oh, and Savannah."

"Yes?" I say quickly, only halfway through an exhale of relief.

"Giselle tells me you were spotted drinking coffee with Claire Donovan from Baird Books on Saturday. Please explain."

The room stops. Every muscle in my being pauses.

"Oh," I say in surprise, feeling a surge of both shock and revulsion toward Giselle. "Yes, that. Well . . ." *Quick, Savannah. Think. What were you doing sitting with an editor at LOA? During work hours? With an editor of romance? Why . . .*

I feel the panic within me rising as any plausible response falls short. All eyes are on me, including those of Giselle, who's sitting coolly in her chair, a simpering smile thinly veiled as she holds her silver tumbler to her lips.

"I asked her to."

Everyone at the table turns to Will in surprise, including me.

Ms. Pennington raises a brow. "You did, William? Why?"

Yes, William. What on earth can you possibly say now?

Will's expression doesn't so much as flicker, and his words don't miss a beat. "Claire Donovan is one of the most respected editors in the industry, one with whom I've had the pleasure of acquaintance for several years. She is nearing the end of her tenure, and I wanted to get her thoughts on a potential project before the opportunity slipped by. But as I ended up occupied at our appointed meeting time, I sent Savannah in my stead with my apologies."

Ms. Pennington's eyes narrow.

Will looks coolly back.

"A meeting with Claire," she says.

"Yes."

Somewhere in the distance, I hear a pencil snap.

"As you are well aware, Will, Pennington thrives on being a stable foundation in the nonfiction and literary fiction sector—"

"Given the financial reports of the past twelve months, one might disagree on both the terms *stable* and *foundation* here—"

Everyone's eyes bounce back to Ms. Pennington. "We have a loyal following—"

"Who are leaving in flocks for competitive publishers—"

"And decades of accomplishments lining our walls—"

"The dusty clippings from the eighties. Yes. I've seen them."

"And most important, we have no intention of *prostituting* ourselves out with flighty *paperbacks* one drops into one's shopping cart while perusing the aisle for *Cheetos*—"

All heads snap to Will. "Which is well and good, just so long as you inform everyone here to start looking for employment elsewhere as soon as possible."

"*It will never happen.*" Ms. Pennington's voice is so fierce it's shaky, and she stares across the table at her son so long I find myself counting to thirty before anyone moves.

Eventually, Ms. Pennington straightens. When she speaks, her voice has regained control. "For some of those here who may have forgotten, Pennington Publishing began in 1969 under my hand as a place to curate only the most distinguished

literature worthy of publication. Its mission and purpose will remain steadfast as it charges into both the new year and the years
to come. Now, if you'll all excuse me . . ." She nods to Brittney,
who shuts her notebook and stands. "I have another meeting."

Ms. Pennington sweeps out of the room, tailed by Brittney,
and we sit in utter silence while they parade past.

Nobody. Nobody in the whole world besides her own son
could've gotten away with what he just said.

Like everyone else at the table, I'm trying to process everything that just happened, every word that was just revealed. But
also at the forefront of my mind is the growing warm recognition of a single fact: he stood up for me.

For some unknown reason, Will Pennington took the blow
for me. Although, is it really called "taking the blow" when you
do what he just did? No. It was more like he entered the ring
for me, dodged every fist thrown at him like a master, and then
reared back, giving clean strikes, until his opponent toppled. Or,
in this case, found a handy excuse and got out of the room as
quickly as possible.

A cobra. That's what he is. Will Pennington, the cobra.

And all at once the room explodes with questions.

"Are we about to lose our jobs?" Clyve asks.

"Just how much financial trouble is Pennington in?" Marge
throws in before Will has the chance to respond.

"Why hasn't Ms. Pennington told us?" Rob interjects, looking bewildered by the chaos around him. "Is she going to cut our
division after all?"

But instead of answering, Will smoothly stands up and
addresses the room. "I want an update on your assigned tasks discussed in this meeting by this evening. Email me your responses,

cc'ing the entire Pen team, and we can discuss there. As for the sensitive matters discussed in this meeting, rest assured that when I have more information regarding the situation, I will inform you. Let's adjourn."

With feeble attempts at a few more unanswered questions, everyone eventually disperses into the hallway. Lyla, the only one who gave such a satisfactory answer to every one of Ms. Pennington's probing questions that she walked away with no assignments, takes my arm.

"What do you think that was about?" she says casually, as if we overheard two strangers arguing in a coffee shop and not a threat of losing our jobs. "You think the whole place is going under?"

I play back the conversation as we turn the corner and move toward the lobby stairs. It certainly was bizarre. I mean, we know there has been financial trouble; we have seen several cuts the past year. But nothing so serious that it seemed the entire company as a whole was threatened. Because it's normal with publishers this size. This is the struggle most smaller industries face these days. This is the conversation you just have to get used to when you work in this environment.

Right?

Right?

We reach our floor, and I feel the familiar temptation to tread on. To keep going. For a second I waver, my foot hovering on the following step, trying to be strong. I should get back to work. *Clearly*, with everything I just heard, I should get straight back to my computer desk and start typing away.

But . . .

"I'm just going to use the bathroom real quick," I say and remove my arm from Lyla's grasp.

She hesitates, raises an eyebrow, and checks her watch. "Really, Sav, you need to get that checked out."

"I know," I affirm, nodding fervently, pulling my feet toward the next set of stairs. "I'm going to make a doctor's appointment soon," I continue, taking steps upward.

"Tomorrow!" she calls after me. "I mean it!" And I give a thumbs-up before disappearing around the corner.

Scurrying through two more hallways and two more flights of stairs, I finally reach the ARC room and yank open the door. The whole way there I fight the rising anxiety that accompanies me every time I search the room.

What if nobody has touched it?

I'm on day three of forty-four and have tried to cut out that character, and sure enough, it's caused a total mess of the whole manuscript, and I can't make heads or tails of what to do with the ice-skating scene now. And should I even try to redeem chapter 8? And don't even get me *started* on the completely stilted dialogue I'm now seeing between my main man and leading lady—

I halt, one foot inside the tiny room.

Stare at the manuscript on the center of the rug.

Particularly the new handwriting in thick black ink on the green Post-It note lying on top of the stack. I take a step closer.

Dear Mystery Editor ~~and Intruder into My Most Secret Precious Oasis of a Room~~,

    If you are reading this . . .

    Help.

Rule 1: Stay on point.

Chapter 9

I pace slowly across the rug as I stare at the manuscript in my hands.

The first forty-two pages are marked up all along the sides—my mystery editor having gone back and doubled, even, the comments on those first sixteen pages where he had critiqued before. In some places text has been sliced through for so long whole paragraphs are missing. At two points in particular he wrote a word and underlined it along with not one, not two, but three exclamation points.

I say "he" because of three clues that, when put together, have confirmed my suspicions.

1. *The pen.* The pen used carries a thick black ink to it, almost expensive looking in the way the ink lands on the page. It's not a thin-tipped pink Sharpie, like Lyla likes to use. It's not a good enough clue on its own, given I myself like to use a black pen on occasion, but it's something, at least.

2. *The concise choice of words.* Now, I'm no expert, but according to one book I edited a while ago, *Communication Between the Sexes*, I distinctly recall the statistic that, on average, women use twenty thousand words a day— roughly three times more than men. And while the margins of each page are covered in comments, they tend to be short and to the point—to a fault. Never, *ever*, have I seen one compliment. It's like the job is to point out errors, and so he is pointing out errors. Any fluffy compliment is only wasted time.

3. He told me about his girlfriend. Well, ex.

No man in his right mind would say this. If I had said this to my ex-girlfriend when we first met, she would've run.

My index finger stops on the comment, and I pause and look at the passage in question. It's my leading man's first words as he stands in the pickup line at the coffee shop and realizes he's accidentally picked up Cecilia's cup. I reread the passage:

Renaldo lifted the coffee cup to his lips and enjoyed the smooth, bitter taste of caffeine soothing his weary throat. Ah. Double Americano with just a touch of pumpkin spice. Exactly how he liked it. But as he lowered the cup and moved for the door, something caught his eye. The writing on the cup.

Cecilia.

The word was written in large, flowing script across the coffee cup, and yet . . . He took another sip. This was his drink. His particular drink. He'd recognize it anywhere.

"Mmm."

He heard the woman murmuring contentedly as she took her own first sip. A young, beautiful woman with untamed curly hair and sparkling hazel eyes to match. And then he saw his own name, *Renaldo*, printed on her cup.

His eyes lit up. "Well, well, well," he said, closing the remaining inches between them until their shoulders touched. He smiled down at her, the young, beautiful fawn. "Looks like my lucky day."

He sounds like a serial killer.

Furthermore, what two people stand there murmuring delightedly about their drinks in the pickup line at a coffee shop? Illogical.

And for the love of all, pick different names. This is not an opera. You can have Renaldo. You can have Cecilia. You cannot have both.

And while my first reaction, which I seem incapable of helping in the face of any and all criticism, is indignation, the second—a bit surprisingly—is a little smile. I reread the passage, seeing it from his fresh angle, and all I can think is, *Oh my gosh, he's right.*

Renaldo does sound like a serial killer.

I read halfway down the page and can't help tittering as Renaldo continues, "I've been looking for someone . . . someone exactly like you. Come to my car. I want to show you something."

And all I can think is, *Cecilia, get outta there!*

I pause momentarily with the manuscript in my hand as the snow drifts quietly past the stained-glass window, seeing for the first time what my chapter is. Laughing as I feel the anxiety from the past three days ebbing away. Laughing as I feel, for the first time, a sense of hope.

He's going to help me.

I'm not going to have to do this alone.

When the chuckles stop, I grab my phone from a stack of books serving as a sort of nightstand to the beanbag and snap pictures of the comments in the margins for working through tonight. I don't dare risk taking the manuscript home in case he decides to pop up here later and find more things to comment about. More issues to address. More problems to note.

It's almost lunchtime, nearly time to leave, but I can't help grabbing a pen from the top of the stack I carried to the meeting this morning. Quickly I write below his memo: *And what fantastic pickup line did you use on your ex-girlfriend to win her heart, then? Because I've got nothing.*

I jot a few other notes below his in the margins, until at last the pressure to move back downstairs is too great, and I know it is time to leave. At this point, I wouldn't be surprised to find Lyla on the phone with the doctor, arranging to kidnap me and drag me to their office herself.

I feel myself smiling—a foreign expression for my face given these last few days—as I walk back down to my floor.

But when I reach my office door, Lyla is nowhere to be seen.

Instead, it's Ferris who is standing beside my desk.

Oh. Right. Is it that time already?

With two fingers tapping on the wood, he's peering at the picture frames on my desk, deep in his own thoughts. There's something in his eyes as he looks at the one of Olivia and me. It's the one we took at my college graduation.

I remember that day clearly. One of our better moments, both of our arms clasped tightly around the other's waist, bright-eyed grins as Dad said something playful about his beautiful, brilliant girls and snapped the photo. Ferris had his own college graduation that day, as I remember. He missed mine but met up with me later that evening out with friends. And in doing so, like so many other times through our lives, both he and Olivia were ships sailing in the night. How many hundreds, thousands, of times I've wondered, *How much sooner would we have broken it off had they really gotten to know each other at an earlier point?*

Had he joined us during the family beach trip my senior year?

Had he come that Easter when his family traveled to Oklahoma and he almost stayed with us?

Exactly how much heartache and time would've been spared, for both of us, had they really gotten to know their soul mates earlier?

I imagine, from the look on his face, he is wondering the same thing now.

He must've heard me, because he turns around. His former expression erases, and in its place his face lifts into a smile. If I hadn't been so certain about what I'd seen before, I'd believe the light in his mahogany eyes. His gentle soul. So quick to try to shield me from unnecessary reminders of the love I had lost and he had gained.

These are the moments when forgiving him is both easier . . . and harder.

"Ready to go, Sav?"

I push the thought away, fight off the swelling in my chest as I watch him standing that way with his hands in both coat pockets, collar popped up, expression just so. I nod. "Where's Olivia?"

"In the car," he says. "You'll want a coat. It's starting to come down."

I set down my laptop and stack of papers on the desk and, as I do so, fight the sudden urge to start organizing. How did I not notice before? My desk is an absolute mess. Multiple pens are scattered just about everywhere except actually inside my pen jar. I have a pile of books sitting precariously on one ledge and three old, half-drunk coffee mugs littering the area around half a dozen picture frames of family and friends.

No wonder he left me for her.

Olivia would never leave her life so cluttered.

"You can go on ahead, and I'll meet you down there," I say, anxious to get him away from the embarrassment of my work-space. "I have to finish up something really quick anyway."

Ferris makes a face. "Don't be silly. I don't mind waiting."

So instead of jumping into a pretend task and only elongating his stay, I shrug into my black coat and reach swiftly toward the hook behind the door for my scarf.

I'm just stepping out into the hallway, fumbling to get my phone into my coat pocket while winding the scarf around my neck, when I nearly collide with Will—and his mug of coffee. We're like magnets of the same pole, and just as his chest comes within two inches of mine, we repel ourselves so far back I knock into Ferris, and Will, along with his coffee mug, bumps into the opposite wall.

Ferris, thankfully, has a quick reaction and grabs beneath my arms before I can do any damage.

But, for a moment, I can't help myself. It's been so long since

I've felt Ferris's hands, since I've been surrounded by the scent of musk and citrus coming off his cologne, since I've been so close to his face. For a second I'm lost.

But in the next, I pull myself out of it and return to stable ground.

"Sorry, Ferris. Thanks," I say, pulling myself off his chest. My scarf is wound around me now like some sort of torture device. In fact, it's actually doing a fairly good job of choking me. My fingers get to work unwinding it, and as I do so I look over to Will. Coffee has splattered all over his hand, I notice, and he's moving his mug from one hand to another to quietly shake the remaining droplets off.

"I'm so sorry, Will," I say, not really certain whether he or I was to blame.

"Hazards of these narrow halls," he replies. But then he's shifting his preoccupied gaze from his hand and the still dripping mug to us, and I notice that it stops not at my face but on my middle. And his frown deepens.

It's only then that I look down and realize Ferris still has his hands around my waist.

"Everyone all right?" Ferris says, seeming a bit dazed himself by all that just happened.

I take a step to the side, and he slides his hands away, putting them smoothly into his coat pockets.

"Fine," I say and immediately feel like the halls really are as narrow as a cardboard box.

I can't define it exactly, but I sense an overwhelming desire not to be standing here at this moment. But it's not just because of Ferris, I'm realizing quietly. It's not just about feeling dangerously close to exposure with the way my face and my hot, flushed cheeks are betraying me in this moment. My cheeks aren't flaming merely because of the secret thoughts about Ferris I sometimes can't help but harbor. It's something else too. Will is a factor. And I realize I particularly don't like that *he* is the one seeing me and my reaction to Ferris in this hallway. I care that *he* is in this situation and wish he hadn't been the one to see it.

Why is that?

It's not, I know deep in my soul, just because he is my boss.

A long, awkward moment passes. "Anyway . . . this is Will Pennington, our new publisher for Pennington Pen," I say, holding out a hand as if I'm showcasing a new painting. "Will, this is . . ." For but a moment I find myself hesitating, stumbling to explain. This is the first time I've ever had to introduce him, I'm realizing suddenly, not as my boyfriend. "Ferris." I amend this quickly with, "My sister's fiancé."

Will's eyes give a subtle flash of surprise, and I can tell that he's reassessing the situation under new light.

"Nice to meet you," Ferris says automatically, as though he hadn't caught any of that and didn't care to. "Well, we should be off, then, Savvy. We've only got an hour."

"'Savvy'?" Will repeats, his brow crinkling. "Is that . . . your preferred name? Because I can—"

"No," I say hastily, my voice almost cracking. "It's just a family nickname. No need to start spreading that around."

"Ah." There's the subtlest whisper of a smile on Will's lips, and I know he has read through the lines. "I see. Well. You enjoy your lunch at . . ."

"The blood bank," I reply.

"Ah," Will repeats, the smile growing. "The blood bank. How nice."

I can practically read through his response, hearing the words he edited out: *"Yes, Savvy, you enjoy your date with your sister's fiancé at the blood bank, because everything about this conversation makes complete sense."*

I feel Ferris's hand on my waist again, making to nudge us along, but this time I don't fall under the spell of his touch. Nor do I move on as he's intending. I stay rooted.

"It's a family thing," I say swiftly. "My mom, dad, sister—we all make a date to donate every eight weeks. You know. Get in some quality time while we do something in the community." I see by Will's expression I've made very little ground and feel compelled to add in a lighthearted tone, "Some families make lunch dates together. The Cade family makes blood dates. Anyway, I'd better be going. I'll be sure to get that report to you by six. And . . . I really do think Smith's manuscript has real promise."

"Yes, well, that's your bailiwick, so we'll be leaning on you," Will replies. Although his tone is all business, I see a slight twitch to his lips.

I feel a blush starting to creep up my neck and loosen my scarf in hopes of concealing it. Before I can think of anything else to say, Will nods in the general direction of us both and turns on his heel.

It's only halfway down the hall that Ferris mutters, *"Bailiwick?* Good grief, Savvy, what sort of pretentious prig uses *bailiwick* in conversation? No wonder these people stress you out."

"Oh, and look at this one, dear. I know we've been thinking gold china all this time, but wouldn't some decorative cream plates look so lovely with the peony centerpieces?"

I'm lying back in the farthest chair to the left of a long row, seeing my mother in my periphery trying to clumsily hand off her laptop full of Excel sheets to Olivia in the chair beside her. My eyes aren't focused on them, though, but on the nurse standing over me, pressing her finger at the largest greenish-blue vein at the crook of my elbow. My hand balls up while my forearm prickles.

No matter how many times I give blood, I still have anxiety.

"Now remember, my veins are deceivingly small," I blurt out, just as I do every single time I go to the blood clinic. "People always say they look good but then have to use a—"

"Butterfly needle. I know, dear." The nurse with her hair pulled into a slick ponytail smiles at me as though she's heard this a thousand times. Which, to be frank, may be the case. But even so, the memory of that one time it took three nurses three torturous attempts on each arm, and the continued phrase, "The vein's going to blow . . . It's going to blow . . . Oh *no*, it blew," is too etched in my mind for me to ever forget.

The nurse pats my arm. "You'll be just fine. Just keep giving the ball a squeeze every ten seconds, and I'll be right back."

I give the foamy red ball in my hand a big squeeze and start the clock in my head.

One . . . Two . . . Three . . .

Unlike for my mother, father, sister, and Ferris lounging in their chairs beside me, looking more like they are suntanning at the beach, giving blood has never been easy for me. My blood pressure is chronically low. Half the time I come here, the staff make me eat crackers and drink a Coke before I can even start, just in case. And my blood, when they can actually get it, so stubbornly refuses to come out of my body it always takes twice as long. Then, of course, there is the ever-present reminder of that one time I passed out afterward.

Not that any of these things stops me from donating. No, I'm a Cade. We just arrange carpool.

"How are you feeling over there, Savvy?" my father calls out across the room. He's sitting in a Hawaiian shirt, which he does on every blood day as his own joke, pumping his own ball with one hand while holding a Coke can in the other.

Just then the nurse returns to my side, and my anxiety skyrockets. I smile and manage a thumbs-up with my opposite hand, and my dad lifts his Coke can to cheer me.

"Hey, Sav."

I'm staring at the enormous needle hovering over my skin as Ferris speaks.

"Savvy, look at me."

I drag my eyes away and force myself to look at him, my chest thudding. Ferris's eyes are soft, full of life. *Unlike me, who is slowly becoming a corpse.* "Remember that time we hosted that murder-mystery Christmas party? Everything went wrong just before it started. The chicken Parmesan burned, and the printer ran out of ink for those character cards you needed to give everyone, and we had that stupid fight over my costume?"

"You were *supposed* to be Santa, Ferris," I say, squinting to avoid looking at the hovering needle. "You promised me you'd be Santa. It was kind of a key role."

His smile widens. "What was it you yelled at me just as the pot boiled over?"

I think back to that night just after college and smile a little as the words come to mind. Begrudgingly, I say them aloud. "'If you can't dress up like a holly jolly Santa on the brink of a killing spree, I don't even know what we're doing here.'"

I feel the painful prick in my arm. Squeeze my eyes shut.

A moment later, I hear medical tape being ripped off its roll. I open my eyes. "There now," the nurse says, securing the strip of tape over the needle in my arm.

I exhale for what I'm certain is the first time in a minute and turn back to Ferris. Already I can feel the color coming back to my cheeks, which is ironic as blood is also now dripping into the moving scale on the floor beside me.

To my surprise, though, Ferris's expression has changed. His eyes are intense, thoughtful as they meet mine. "Whatever happened to those friends?"

"Oh," I say, taken aback slightly at the turn in conversation. I try to remember who exactly had even come. There were six of us. I remember that clearly because of the character list for the party: one narcissistic Santa, one burnt-out Mrs. Claus, one Rudolf in a midlife crisis, one jealous Dasher, one mischievous elf, and one lonely snowman facing unrequited love with Mrs. Claus. I know Farrah and Michael were one of the couples, because back then we were inseparable. "I don't know. I guess we all just . . . moved apart."

"It's so strange how that happens," he muses. "One minute you do everything together and the next . . ." He shrugs.

I give the ball a long squeeze. It is odd how that happens sometimes. Farrah and I even still live in Nashville. After graduation we kept up for a while, but then work started to fill up our days, and we both started making friends with our new jobs, and within the year we were texting each other, saying we really *had* to have coffee soon, loading our texts with heart emojis, but never really pursuing anything. "I guess we just made different friends. I started hanging out with Lyla more. You got close to those guys from your work. I think we just find 'our people' as we go along in life." I pluck a phrase Lyla likes to say for the moment. "Eventually we meet our kindred spirits."

But Ferris doesn't look convinced by my words, or like he even mildly agrees with them. Instead he's thoughtful, almost brooding, and I watch him, waiting for him to pull together his thoughts and respond. For some reason, he cares.

"Look at this, Ferris." Olivia snaps her fingers in the air. "Mom says we can save ten cents per square foot on the table-cloth if we rent from Enchanted Experiences."

So, instead of me hearing what he has to say, Ferris eventually gets wrapped up in the wedding conversation as the three of them pass the laptop back and forth. I watch the Hallmark movie on the television stationed on the wall opposite for a while, squeezing my big red ball while trying to gather what's going on onscreen through lipreading since the volume is so low. But eventually not even the tall blond woman and her candle-shop problems can hold my attention, and my mind wanders.

After all, I have my own mystery to solve. Just *who* is the mystery editor?

The thought has popped up a few times over the past several days, but always when I'm so busy rushing here and there, doing this or that, that I haven't had a spare moment to dwell on it. Now, though, stuck in this chair attached to the wobbling blood machine, is the perfect time.

Could it be Yossi?

Nooo. He's so afraid of doing anything to Ms. Pennington's disliking he jumps at his own shadow. If he ever opened that filing cabinet, he'd stare at it silently for about half a second, slam the whole thing shut, and never look back again—even if the whole room was glowing.

Rob?

No. He's much too . . . pleasant. And long-winded. He'd never put such gut-jabbing criticisms on paper. He's such a people pleaser we have a time getting him to give any real critique for any of his authors. All his authors think they're geniuses because he'll go through a whole manuscript leaving only a few tiny comments here and there like, "Well, not to press, but under the normal standards of the English language, it is customary to use a punctuation point at the end of a sentence. In fact, the first recording of a punctuation point, derived from the Latin *punctus*, was in the middle of the sixteenth century, when . . ." When all he needed to say was, "Missing period."

Clyve? No. Clyve handles the marketing just fine but can't make heads or tails of things like "narrative arc."

Well, that covers everyone at the Pen imprint. It must be someone at Trophy or Arch or Scribe. Unless . . .

For some unknown reason, my stomach flips, the thought alone making me feel a little bit dizzy.

"You're coming along," the nurse says reassuringly, observing my blood bag as she walks by.

"Thank you," I say, still feeling the world spin a little. "But could I get another Coke by chance?"

Her expression turns to sympathy. "Sure thing. Are you starting to feel dizzy, honey?"

At the words, Ferris's attention breaks from the handful of

graphs in his hands, with their corresponding pictures of flower bouquets. "You doing okay, Savvy?"

"Yes," I say quickly. "Just . . . I thought it might be a good idea."

The nurse nods. "Of course. Let's get you some sugar just in case. I'll grab some crackers too," she adds and drifts off toward the mini fridge across the room.

My cheeks tingle as I feel Ferris's gaze on me. I hate to be the perennial problem patient.

A buzzer on the machine goes off at the farthest end, and Dad raises his own Coke like he just won a horse race. "That's me!" he calls.

Ten seconds later, Mom's buzzes. "Oh darn," she says. "I was so close this time."

Leave it to my family to make this into some sort of game.

Fifteen minutes later, and I'm nowhere close to done.

"I told you to stop drinking all that caffeine," Olivia says to me as the nurse checks my bag and comments on how the blood is slowing down. "You drink all that coffee and expect your blood not to turn into molasses—"

"She had one cup, Olivia," Ferris says in my defense. "I doubt it made any difference."

"That's not what my research says," Olivia retorts. "I read that caffeine not only blocks your neuroreceptors for adenosine, it has a half-life of three hours, and—"

"I read five," Dad chimes in.

"Oh, I'm sure it was three, Dad," Olivia says. "I'm positive."

"You're talking about the article in the *Washington Post* from 2017?" Dad asks. "Because I could almost gamble on the number five."

And while everyone else in the family engages in a research-driven discussion on blood coagulation, my mind slips back into the single idea pervading my thoughts.

Will Pennington.

Oh my goodness, Will Pennington.

He's blunt.

He's no-nonsense.

He's incredibly intimidating.

The timing works out, really. He's freshly back from New York City just around the time I get this surprise. But . . . is he really *that* rude? Really?

How is it possible to know, when nobody you know actually *knows* him aside from his own mother (and you'd never ask her in a million years)?

I sit on the thought for a solid minute, and then the lightbulb turns on.

Of course.

What better person to ask about how he edits than one of his own authors?

With one arm trapped on the armrest, I tilt my hip and reach into my pocket for my phone. My fingers, not used to doing the typing, fumble the name Trace Green into Amazon's search bar.

It's a little industry trick I learned when I started two years ago. Almost every book includes acknowledgments, and while for the typical reader this is just a page to be skipped over, for the nosy author, agent, or editor, it's gold.

I tap until the acknowledgments page of Green's most recent book pops up, then skim the page for Will's name. Green's publicity team. Green's fabulous literary agent. Green's second cousin's boating companion's brother, for all his inspiration. Green's wife, three kids, and two puppies.

Hope ebbs as I read line after line without any mention of William. The farther I go down the list, the more space the people mentioned occupy in Green's heart. I'm just about to give up entirely after the mention of Green's Lord and Savior, Jesus Christ, when my eyes fall on the name. I slow down. Read.

And to Will Pennington, my longsuffering listener, relentless encourager, the one without whom I could do none of this, thank you. You are not only the greatest editor I could ask for but the most selfless, generous human being I aspire to live up to. The next round's on me, friend.

Will Pennington. Longsuffering listener.

Relentless . . . encourager.

Not just *a*, but *the* most generous, selfless human being. On the earth.

Wow. I was pretty pleased when one of my authors called me "smart," and Will over here is basically getting the Nobel Peace Prize.

And how exactly would I define my mystery editor?

Hmm.

I swipe to my photos and tap on the latest picture I took today of a comment.

If you use "suddenly" one more time, I'm going to die from overexposure. Cut. The. Adverbs.

Yeah.

"Selfless, generous human being" isn't the vibe coming to mind.

The machine beside me buzzes, and I look up.

"Well, lookee there, Sav," Ferris says, pausing in his move to stand up, the newest blood-donor T-shirt in one hand. "You finished before Olivia."

Dad—who has been preoccupied trying to decide whether to take a large or extra-large T-shirt declaring *Keep Calm and Give Blood*—turns as he sees the nurse coming up to my side and switching off the machine. Olivia, with her half-drunk Nalgene of water in one hand, frowns from her chair.

"How *wonderful*," Mom exclaims. She and Dad are gazing at me as though I just declared I'd been made publisher of Pennington. I would roll my eyes but for the real sense of glowing pride hidden deep inside.

Ferris grins. Even he looks proud. "Well. I guess it looks like you were doing something right after all."

Chapter 10

*A*nd if Pennington is going to be the type of institution that throws out empty promises without actual performance, then my client and I will not be able to stand idly by . . ."

"Yes, Diann," I say over my shoulder. "But if you recall, we were able to get Annabelle's work included in both the *Gardens and More* and *Ladies Tea Society* magazines just last month."

I'm listening as I stand at the window centered between my desk and Lyla's, watching the scene below through faded, fringed lace curtains. The historic street is covered with equally old and beautiful Victorians, all with wide porches and gabled roofs, baby-blue porch ceilings and bay windows. But it's not the beauty of the elaborate gingerbread trim on the whimsical yellow house across the street I'm distracted by at the moment. It's Will. With his hand ever so gently resting on the back of Ms. Pennington's coat as he walks her down the cracked sidewalk off the street and opens the door of her car for her to slip in.

I smile to myself as I watch the car turn on and him stand there silently, hands in his pockets, waiting as she drives off for some meeting or other.

Suddenly there's a tug on my shirt and I swivel my head to look down, brought back to the present as my author's literary agent continues her monologue on speakerphone.

Lyla, from her seat, mouths, "I need your opinion."

"Let's not be coy about it, Savannah," Diann continues. "We both know Annabelle's release was included in a mere roundup, and both of those publications have a tenth of the subscriber list of *Landscape and Leisure*. But Oswald Makers, on the other hand, was *featured* in . . ."

Oswald. Poor sweet Oswald never has a clue how much drama his success causes us. Our publicist, Marge, sends out all our titles to the same relevant magazines and publications. It's not *our* fault that the editors always snatch up Oswald's newest titles and only occasionally want to include anyone else's. And if I had a dollar for every time my authors' literary agents got on the phone bright and early the morning after whatever publication released . . .

"I would be happy to ask Marge to email you the list of magazines she is sending Annabelle's latest out to," I say, while across from me Lyla clicks between two graphics and points.

I shrug. From my vantage point, they look identical. "They're the same," I mouth back, which clearly, from her expression, was the absolute wrong thing to say. Her blue eyes get a bit of fire in them as she jabs one long pink fingernail at the text of one graphic, clicks over, then jabs her finger at the other.

"The point is when my client decided to make the move from Sutnam Press, we were under the impression Pennington believed strongly in the potential of Annabelle's manuscripts. But instead of fulfilled promises, all we have seen the last few months has been favoritism for particular clients—"

"I don't know," I mouth as Lyla jabs her finger from one identical graphic to another faster.

"—two rounds of edits with far too many unreasonable asks for changes—"

"The left," I throw out, seeing that Lyla is on the brink of exploding.

"—cover design that was *far* below the quality we expected—"

Lyla, who was at maniac Energizer Bunny level two seconds prior, halts. Her eyes go from manic to scarily calm in the matter of a second. She holds out her hand for the phone.

Oh no.

I don't dare not hand it over.

"Ms. Brightside, hi." Lyla snatches the phone from me, jabs one fingernail on the key to turn off the speakerphone, and cradles it against her ear while swiveling in her own chair toward the wall. Her fingernails begin clapping furiously as she types on the keyboard about three hundred words per minute. "This is Lyla in Marketing and Design. Yes, I'm looking over the cover I created for Annabelle at this moment. If you'll look at the cover-test results we gathered compared with Annabelle's last cover with Sutnam—which was actually a stock photo also seen on amateur-level business cards and cosplay blogs with five visitors per month—you'll see that . . ."

I leave Lyla to her scary rant and swivel back in my chair. I've finished most of my duties for the week, aside from the ever-present backlog of proposals and queries filling up my in-box. With one quick glance back to Lyla—who is clearly going to be occupied for a few minutes, and almost undoubtedly face some remedial meeting with the boss this afternoon—I rise.

Time for another visit to the ARC room.

I furtively pick up my purse, which is heavy, given it's holding a fourteen-inch laptop these days, and pull the strap over my shoulder.

"No, no, I'm not *implying* you're a sham of an agent exploiting the goodwill of your clients, Diann," Lyla continues and I slide out into the hall. "What I'm *saying* is you're a sham of an agent exploiting the goodwill . . ."

One minute and twenty-two seconds of short pleasantries and slinking through halls, and I push the door open to my little hideaway. My heart thuds a bit louder as I hear the old metal filing cabinet squeak and give way at my push. I only left here four hours ago, but my book is all I've been able to think about these days. A week solid of passing notes back and forth through the manuscript, sometimes two or three times a day. It's fairly remarkable, too, that so far I haven't raised any suspicions or spotted any clues that would raise suspicions of my own. But then, everyone does tend to hole up in their own offices during the day, slipping in and out for the occasional meeting and coffee break but otherwise left fairly to themselves. As far as I know, only Lyla has raised a brow at me, but that's because she's my officemate. And as far as she's concerned, I'm on antibiotics for my "special problem."

My eyes are already searching the Post-It on top for his writing. For the newest log. And sure enough, I spot it.

You're up.

And exhale.

We have a system.

The ARC room is mine from eight to ten, noon to two, four to the end of the workday. He can take the rest, and neither of us can show up or leave within ten minutes of our designated times. It was about four days into this writing back and forth that the topic came up. It was lunchtime, and I had just run up to the room, a bowl of potato salad in one hand, nothing but wild hopes and dreams in the other, and was opening the door to the ARC room when I saw all the lights were on. Faintly I heard the squeal of the filing cabinet at the far end, and without waiting to see any figure pop out from the corner, I darted for the hall. Needless to say, my next note was on the topic, laying out a set of rules.

I don't know why exactly he went along with it.

Maybe because he, too, wanted to remain anonymous in this little exchange of words, as I do, considering I'm writing, as Ms. Pennington likes to say, "material on par with stuffing cotton balls in one's mouth" during work hours, at a publishing house that cares so much about serving upmarket fiction it actually has in its mission statement the goal to "overwhelm the population with quality stories, so as to delete from society that which is replete with twaddle." There is an asterisk beside that sentence and a footnote at the bottom of last year's yearly summit stating: "Specifically remarking upon thrillers, magical realism, mysteries, historical fiction, westerns, dramas and—above all— romance in all forms."

Or maybe he didn't want to reveal his identity in case I turn on him and get him in trouble, considering that while nothing is stated in any rulebook (obviously), every time I come here it feels a little like jumping over caution tape.

Or maybe because he wanted to set clear boundaries on when the room was his, because like me, he feels like it's his own little oasis.

Or maybe, just maybe, he, too, found the whole thing to be a bit of extra fun—like the joy of slipping notes back and forth in middle school. It wasn't about the words that were actually snuck back and forth back then that made passing notes special; nobody really cared to know "What did you eat for lunch?" and "I ate a turkey sandwich. U?" It was the method that was fun. The knowledge that you passed off a note, however trite it might be, and it was bound to be returned with an addition or two just for you in just a few minutes.

I don't know if he feels that way about our notes.

But I sure do.

And the things we learn from each other in our correspondence aren't really revolutionary either, although it certainly feels that way.

Things just come out as we jot our comments over a scene. Personal facts. Stories. He reads voraciously—far beyond the requirements of the job. Went on vacations as a kid to some old, beaten-down cottage off the coast of Rhode Island. Was bullied for a chunk of time in middle school before he hit a growth spurt.

And each little story, each little fact, feels like a *zing*. A little nugget. A gold star.

Already I'm flipping through the pages of the manuscript as I move to the beanbag. At a glance I can see he's addressed a couple of notes on character development in chapter 7 (evidently pushing a puppy off the couch is a real red flag for character likability), which I'm looking forward to addressing later this evening. But today's *zing* comes with the newest addition on page 65.

Yesterday he left the oh-so-gently stated comment about my character's first date: The fact that your character calls this "the best night of her life" over stale rolls at a 2-star restaurant is more ironic than Ms. Pennington's ever-present belief that "Medieval poetry is the way of the future." I responded by asking him what his genius idea was for a first date, and while he overlooked any response on the topic this morning, he seems to have circled back to it. And for a first, the answer is so lengthy he's added a Post-It note to the side to make room.

> **The perfect date depends on the people involved. If she enjoys fine food, then I'd take her to the Catbird Seat. If she enjoys music, then I'd take her to the Schermerhorn Symphony Center. The perfect date doesn't have anything to do with me. It's entirely about finding a setting that highlights who she is and seeking to learn about each other within that amenable atmosphere.**

I roll my eyes at this answer and click my pencil until the lead peeks out. This is *exactly* the kind of thing I am trying to avoid in my book. Every protagonist in the romances I read seems to be an undervalued, secret child prodigy who bakes award-winning apple pies, surprises everyone (including herself) with fluency in three languages, has a library full of classical literature she knows by heart, and volunteers at the homeless shelter in her spare time. No female lead is normal. They're all ruby-lipped Victoria's Secret–level models with the talent of a hundred lives combined just waiting to be swept into the arms of their heroes.

Yes, but what about dates with average human beings? I

write. I think back. *What about with girls who spend every day working in a job they aren't stellar at? Who live off oatmeal-square cereal as it's the only thing they can afford? Who spend most evenings either going to some charity event their family has coordinated, watching some movie sandwiched between their sister and sister's fiancé, or slaving away in my room writing this stupid book that apparently is so flawed nobody will ever read it?*

I stop, staring at my own words, then flip my pencil around.

I can't write that. It's much too personal.

And besides, I've even made the critical error of switching from the hypothetical "their" to a most definitive "my."

It's unprofessional.

It's cringy, even.

But then, as I hold the eraser of the pencil over the words, I hesitate. Because a part of me does want to know: *What about me?*

What would somebody think of a person like me? Who, out there in the world, would think *I* was special enough to make the heroine in their story?

Or am I to be only the protagonist of my own?

I hesitate for another long moment and then flip the page. I'm going to leave it. Leave it and see what he says.

I work through the rest of the notes, taking pictures of the comments I need to address in my manuscript that evening, replying to comments and adding questions of my own.

I'll have you know I actually owned a cat named Whiskers when I was a kid, and yes, he really did bark like a dog and was immune to catnip. That's a real thing.

*Well, if her ears are allergic to earrings, like mine,
then I really do think it'll be a nice touch for him to
notice and . . .*

*No. I'll concede that being able to season
your own pots is a good skill, but honestly, it's not
something to brag about . . .*

By the time I've finished, I've learned a few more things about
my mystery editor. He's tall, not supremely so, but enough to
know offhand a few places to buy smart suits with extra length.
He is actually dyslexic, a surprising issue that very few know
about. And he doesn't think my manuscript is hopeless.

I know because at the bottom of chapter 7 there are new
words.

This is good. Do more of this.

The first positive comment. The first positive comment amid
a slew of critiques.

I feel myself smiling as I lean back in the chair, sunlight streaming through the window highlighting a thousand dusty particles
dancing around me. The light has changed, I realize, looking up
from my page to the wall opposite, where about two dozen simple
wooden frames hang, each showcasing an autographed title page
of a book. It glints on the glass so roughly I blink, the room that
bright haze just before the world goes cool and dark at the end
of another day. I stand and realize my knees are achy.

How long have I been up here?

I check my watch. Four fifty-two p.m.

Then my steps. 8588.

I hurry through the ARC room, hesitating at the door to the hallway as I try to remember if I shut the filing cabinet door in my haste. I'm fairly certain I did, but as I turn back just to be sure, doorknob in hand, I stop dead.

Sam from Contracts has stopped and is looking at me with a startled expression as if he, too, is caught in a trap.

"Sam." I let go of the doorknob. "Hi. How are . . . you?"

Sam smooths his tie and flashes a smile. "Good. Good." There's a beat of silence as we both look at each other.

Sam?

I never noticed how tall he was before. I can't help but glance down at the hem of his trousers. Six feet? Six one? Does six one qualify someone as needing to order special lengths?

But surely not.

Not *Sam*. Giselle's ex, *Sam*.

Aside from one lackluster dinner date with Sam my first week on the job two years ago, I can't think of a single other instance when we've spoken alone. The date had proven we were so incredibly ill matched for one another that we spent a solid twenty minutes talking about the weather just waiting for the bill to arrive. Ever since, we have both mutually skirted around each other. Keeping things professional. Giving the polite nod in greeting here and there, discussing in one group setting or another a contract when necessary, but never anything more.

After all, while he's nice-looking enough, I never felt that spark for him.

He never really felt that spark for me.

We were just two single people of similar age, with reason-ably similar interests, who thought it was worth a shot to see where that door led.

Which, for the record, was nowhere, unless you wanted to count it leading to a fractured relationship with the resentful, ex-girlfriend boss.

No, that date only opened to a cinderblock wall.

Right?

"Well . . . I'd better get . . . that . . . book," he says, edging around me.

"Oh yes. Good plan," I say, although in reality I have less than no clue as to what he's referring to. I move out of his way, jutting my own thumb backward while trying not to trip on my heels. "I'd better get back downstairs too. For . . . dinner with Lyla . . ."

He nods fervently, as though he agrees this is absolutely riveting and essential information, and turns around. The second he is out of sight I stride down the hall.

Sam. Sam?

I can't help but feel a wave of disappointment, although I don't really understand why. So . . . so what if Sam is my mystery editor? That wouldn't change anything. He's . . . helping me with a project just as well. His points are valid. I'm finally able to work through my manuscript. This is a win-win here. I haven't lost anything.

But if that's so, why do I feel like something's lost? The magic deflating slowly like an expired balloon?

It doesn't matter, I tell myself firmly. And besides, it's too early to tell.

Right. Because our lawyer Sam routinely has to go up to check out advance copies of books for his contracts.

Sure.

Again, not that it matters.

At all.

Chapter 11

*T*ablets and bars. They are a *stellar* combination.

I lower my new (blue-light, completely nonprescription) glasses over the bridge of my nose to give a critical look at Lyla onstage. It's a bit challenging to see her here, though, all the way in the back behind the cluster of tall, bald men who look like they've all had too much to drink.

C'mon now, I want to say to the man one table over. *This view is pathetic. Of all the spots in this bar, you pick this one?*

The music is painfully loud, as is apparently the requirement for all places playing live music anywhere. But the room is at least on the classier end of the joints where Lyla normally has her gigs. Honestly, when we (I say "we" because Lyla, her husband, Garrett, and I are basically one unit in all things Lyla-let's-get-you-to-become-a-country-star) got the call last Thursday that the Polar Star was inviting her to come play, we all about lost it.

I mean, this is a fair skip and jump from the greasy floor-boards of O'Mainnin's and Stateline.

This is the Polar Star.

The bouncers wear matching polos. The air smells like smoked brie and cigars. And most important, scouts attend regularly.

My phone starts ringing on my lap as Lyla starts her third song.

Game time.

I pick it up with the frazzled, busy attitude of one hating everything about this moment. "What?" I say into the receiver, loudly. "I'm busy."

Somewhere on the opposite side of the room, Lyla's husband mumbles something into his phone. It's so loud that I can't hear what he's saying. But that doesn't matter. We've done this so many times, I know the lines. "Well, I don't care what Jerry wants. I'm occupied."

I pause for roughly four beats and look at Lyla critically. "I'm not sure, but I may be onto a new lead."

Out of the corner of my eye, I see the nearest man angle his chin my direction. His eyes skirt down me, taking me in: female, dark-brown hair in overworked bun, simple pearl studs, black sweater, boring shoes, alone, tapping occasionally on my tablet.

In an office I'd hardly look out of the ordinary, but here? Surrounded by middle- and high-class groups looking for a night on the town? I stick out like a sore thumb.

A posh, intellectual, savvy sore thumb who clearly can predict the best and brightest in the biz.

In other words, the competition.

I tap on my tablet with the phone cradled on my shoulder while Lyla sits on the barstool and sings her heart out. Maybe it's the lighting or the venue, but tonight she truly does look and sound better than usual. The spotlight on her long, curling blond hair glinting perfectly against the backdrop of a black wainscoted wall. Her voice crystal clear, feminine, yet hinting of power and soul as she strums the song I remember her writing late one evening at university.

I tap a few nonsensical words on the tablet with my sternest I-am-important frown—LEMONADE PICKLES DAIRY FARM—and see the man raising his posture slightly and craning to see the words. Looking for some clue as to who I am, no doubt. What I think. How important my opinion is.

Lyla's voice begins to tip up into a long, eight-beat note, the penultimate moment of her ballad, and I lift my gaze as if surprised. As the note lingers, my long-held bored expression slowly cracks. As if I've spent years watching nobodies, hoping to find that lost treasure, weary and exhausted as I work this lonely road. And then, suddenly, I've found it. My fingers slowly drop from the tablet as if I'm not even aware of them, as if they are doing what they are meant to do on their own: find and press against my chest. My heart. Because this woman onstage is it. She is the *one*.

Honestly. I should've become an actress.

Lyla ends the song and applause begins, just as I snap to attention on the phone. "Peter," I say, scrambling for my tablet and hastily rising. "I've found her. I don't care if we're booked up. Let's just pray she doesn't have an agent yet." I take a step toward her and then pause. "What do you mean you want to hear her first? Peter, we've got to *snatch* her up before somebody else will. I can't *wait* until you hear her—"

I pause.

"Well, of course I'm right. I was right about my last lead, wasn't I?"

I pause and let fury cloud my face. "Yes, but don't you dare make me recall the moment you lost us Dierks Bentley because you thought you had time to take a *bathroom break*." I dart my head around and, in the swift glance, see Garrett working his own corner, using the same script.

This is the part where I squeeze my eyes shut, look furious, and respond with, "Fine. I'll meet you outside, but you'd better hurry."

The plan is to follow the call with me grabbing my things, rushing outside looking terribly important, then dropping the charade and popping in next door to scroll through Pinterest before sneaking back ten minutes later to try the routine on somebody else.

For the record, we've been fairly successful.

In six months we've gotten three lurkers after her show, two approachers who gave her their card, and one who seemed incredibly eager but, when push came to shove, never called her back. It's only a matter of time, though. These are just the bites before the big catch.

But just as I squeeze my eyes, right as I'm on the verge of giving my showstopping finale, a voice pops up beside me.

A strong voice. Masculine. And one, I realize with instant trepidation, I know. "That's a pretty low blow to bring up Bentley."

My eyes open, and I find myself face-to-face with Will Pennington. He's lost some of the business-y exterior, wearing a simple taupe crew-neck sweater, dark jeans. But perhaps what's most relaxed about him is the amused expression in his eyes. The slight smile raising his lips. How much has he heard?

I can't help but cringe as I think about what I look like

now—an absolute tablet-carrying, booking agent–imposter nutcase.

The man in the black across from me pauses. He is halfway into rising from his seat, too, possibly off at this very moment to make a go at Lyla during the pause between songs.

Shoot.

I can see the hesitancy in the man's face, like my response in this very moment will tip the scales one way or another.

My eyes dart to his attire, making a final assessment. All-black, but not the typical, corporate all-black I've seen a hundred times before. No, this guy has a light beard. Black sweatshirt with bleach-white cords hanging down on both sides. Sneakers that look so new and unassuming they must cost hundreds. Eager eyes. Sleek black business card already in one hand. Classy font with fussy numbers in gold writing.

He looks new. Not new as in, "Hey, I just started this company yesterday in my basement," but new as in, "I'm the little guy working in a totally overwhelming, posh agency, and I'd better bring in some big fish or I'm out of here."

New and lowly in big and flashy. The perfect combination.

Shoot. There's no choice here. Not when this very moment could be the one we look back on as the moment that changed everything.

"Peter!" I cry out. "You're so . . . quick!" I swivel to face Lyla, now on her fourth song. "What do you think? Didn't I tell you?"

I keep my eyes on Lyla as if I'm glued to her performance, when the reality is I'm much too terrified to watch his reaction.

But if he only *knew* how long Lyla had worked for this.

Marketing and design is her skill set.

Music is her soul.

For as long as I can remember, this has been her passion,

and she's never wavered. I've always admired her for that. For knowing what she wanted and passionately going after it, no holds barred. No matter what other people think. No matter what hardships come her way. Even on those terrible days when she showed up and sang for no one. She kept at it. I understand that. I empathize with that. I get that.

Will's expression is stern as he gazes up at Lyla, and I can't tell if it's because he's playing the part of studious agent or because he's about to tell us we're both incredibly immature and don't deserve to be representatives of Pennington Publishing.

And the longer he stares, the more formidable his expression feels.

It's because he's realizing there's something wrong with us.

Her because she's really trying to become a country star in this town and me, well . . . me because I spend my evenings in the back of bars, trying to lure agents into giving her a contract.

"Remarkable talent. Iconic beauty that sets her apart from the others. Do you think she's written this song as well?"

I swivel back and, to my surprise, see Will gazing at Lyla as if entranced. He's so convincing that for just a blink I think he might be serious.

"Yes!" I wave my hand out, much too enthusiastically. "Yes, she writes all her own songs!" I catch myself. "I recall she said so when she introduced one of them . . . at the beginning . . . at some point."

"Well, then, let's make haste," Will says. "What are we waiting for?"

"Nothing!" I cry, and then catch myself. "And by nothing, I mean we can't meet her yet. Because . . ." I stumble. What is my excuse now? He's here, after all.

Will's brows rise. "Because?" he says after a pause.

"Of course . . . we have to go outside first and call . . . Oswald! Oswald has to clear all decisions first as head of the agency."

Will's lips twitch. "Oswald," he repeats. "Of course. With a lead like this, Oswald will have to approve. Well, then, let's be off—" He ushers me with his hand. There's a question in his eyes, as though he's unsure if this is the next step in his role. "Right?"

"Right," I say, nodding, and lead the way outside.

And sure enough, as we leave the room I glance back to see the man already off his seat, rushing like a darting, eager fawn for the stage.

The moment I burst onto the sidewalk, I'm laughing. I swivel around and see Will behind me, grinning as well.

Meanwhile, the two bouncers stand on either side of the door, looking decidedly unamused.

"Thank you," I begin to say, just as he says, "What on earth was that?"

My laughter comes to its slow end and I grin up at him. For a moment, he looks entirely boy-like. Not like a boss by whom I'm intimidated much of the time, but like the boy next door. The one you grow up playing tricks with and throwing rocks across the creek with.

I hesitate and then go for it.

"Come with me, if you want. I'll fill you in."

And for just a moment, I feel the bubble I'm riding on drift downward as I see a crease form along his forehead.

I'm not sure what he's thinking about, but it's clear he's hesitating. Why?

I feel a growing sense of panic.

Am I asking my boss out?

Does he think I'm asking him out?

Does he not want to come because he's aware he's my boss?

Does he think I'm hitting on him? Oh my gosh, *am* I hitting on him?

But before my thoughts can travel down that road into a new set of questions, the expression on his face dissipates.

And in its stead comes a resolutely carefree smile. "Lead the way."

I pick the least grimy option of the five establishments surrounding me, and we make our way for the doors. The bar is oddly hot, given the cold January air on the neon-lit street outside. People swarm under at least a hundred industrial lightbulbs hanging from wires, and somewhere off in the corner another band plays. We order and slide onto two stools lining the exposed-brick wall bordering a pool table.

Will looks at me expectantly the moment we sit down. "So? Is this . . . what you do for fun, then? Impersonate booking agents on the weekends?"

"If you must know, yes," I reply over the speakers and people and general sense of managed chaos. "It's one of my prime hobbies these days. Gives me something to do in the evenings."

I grin and take a sip of my beer.

"I see," he says, eyeing me with mock critique. "So your social life in its natural state is as riveting as mine."

"You can always join me. I've already seen your work tonight. I can tell we'd make a good team."

Shoot. I'm doing it again.

I want to throw my hands out, insisting that I'm not trying to hit on him, but then realize, of course, that would only succeed in confirming those suspicions. Instead I sit here, forcing (and failing at) a nonchalant smile while pretending to be suddenly quite interested in a woman's purse as she passes by our table. Sequins. *Riveting*.

But when he speaks, it's on an entirely different topic. As if he just took the words I said and slid them neatly off the table. "So, our marketing manager and graphic designer wants to be a country star."

"Yes," I say, nodding eagerly, more than happy to jump to this new topic. "Yes, I think the cat is officially out of the bag. What tipped you off?"

"Well, aside from her actually singing onstage, which was the big clue, of course—"

"Of course," I repeat.

"—I'd have to say it was the Dolly Parton hair, bedazzled belt buckle she wears to staff meetings, and framed photograph on her desk of her singing with her guitar with the words in pink puffy paint, 'The Next Taylor Swift.'"

"Ah. Yeah," I say, leaning against the wall. "I may be partly responsible, then. I made that frame for her back in college." My smile carries a wince, recalling how cool and chic I thought I was back then for the metallic-gold spray-painted frame with about a thousand shakes of glitter when in reality it was (and still is) hideous. But Lyla declared she adored it and, honest to goodness, has kept it on one desk or another since.

"You're a good friend," Will says.

I laugh. "If you think demoting the beauty of someone else's world with hideous homemade gifts they feel compelled to keep means I'm a good friend, then yes, I agree."

He grins patiently, as though acknowledging my joke but wanting to stay on point. "Not just for the frame." He waves a hand around the bar. "For what you're doing here. For every-thing. Few would go out on a limb like this for their friends, simply in hopes they become a rock star."

His expression is one of sincerity, and feeling the sudden discomfort that comes from a direct compliment, I smile. "It's *country* star," I correct. "Country star or nothing. I do have my limits."

"Of course. My apologies. Country."

His expression is bright—merry, even—as he grins at me. The change from his work posture to off-duty posture is astound-ing. His forearm resting casually on the table. Eyes dancing as we play our little games.

You could almost believe he was two different people. Will—the guy who hangs out with you after work, cracking jokes, squeezing out stories. And William Pennington—the man in the impeccable gray suit who strides down the halls like he's in the middle of Manhattan surrounded by slow tourists and has somewhere to be.

I have been to at least six meetings this week with him and he has yet to smile. In any of them.

"Do you like your job?" The words pop out of my mouth before I can catch them. "This new one, I mean."

Immediately, his relaxed face tightens.

"I'm just wondering because," I add quickly, "I imagine there's a lot of pressure. You know, being at the top. Tough eco-nomic times. All that."

You shouldn't have brought it up, Sav. Clearly the man doesn't want to be reminded. I'm terrible. I'm like that stranger in the grocery store who asks you if you feel bad because you look terrible.

"I'm not at the top," he says.

"Oh, right," I say. The last thing I want to do is quibble over definitions of exactly what "at the top" means. "Sure. So, it's not that bad, then, I hope. I was just wondering. Anyway."

I look down at my boring black shoes and brace myself against the sudden shift of position. One moment I felt, I don't know, attractive and fun. Now I feel like a child in a school uniform talking to her teacher.

"I didn't say you were wrong," he says after a pause. "Just that I'm not at the top. And that, actually, is the problem."

Wow. So he's going with honesty. If he wasn't sitting here looking at me with such a modest and frank expression, if I was instead looking at his words alone on a transcript, I'd say he was incredibly prideful, leaning toward egotistical. After all, who admits candidly that the problem is that he's not the CEO of the company? As if his personal ambition was rightfully wounded by such a "problem" as being second in command. As he explains to me, a lowly assistant acquisitions editor. Talk about the first of First World problems.

But there is something about his expression that hints I'm not reading his words correctly, and I am just about to open my mouth and ask for clarification when he raises his brows at me and says, "Why? What do I look like at work to you?"

"Oh . . ." I let out a nervous laugh because that is the *farthest* thing I want to discuss. And how exactly would that go over? *Well, Will, since you ask. You look and act as rigid as a pin needle, with a scary razor tip. You are terrifying, 100 percent business, and, frankly, 99 percent of the time, look miserable.*

The week after our impromptu meeting at the Painted Pony, he'd hardly met my eye. It was like the meeting had never even happened. All he did was give out orders, work behind a closed door ten hours a day, mysteriously leave for days at a time, and, one scary afternoon, fire Clyve. (Who, let's be honest, was the marketing manager but had yet to understand a computer. It was time.)

But even so, the main word that comes to mind is *scary*.

"Efficient," I say at last, settling on the least offensive, possibly complimentary term possible. "You seem efficient."

"Efficient," he says slowly.

"Mm-hmm," I murmur between pressed lips, not daring to give anything more.

He gives me one long, dubious look and then, to my surprise, laughs. It's the first time I've heard it. A heady sound, full and rich. It's such a nice sound that it's a real pity to the world he doesn't laugh more often. Even the two women behind us who turn seem to think so.

I lean forward a little, smiling brighter.

Not territorially, of course. There's nothing to own here. Nothing to claim.

Just . . . a little movement.

"You know, Savannah," Will says, not seeming to notice, "you'd do just fine in New York. But how about we just . . . leave the office at the office." His eyes land on a dartboard on the opposite wall and a couple, having thrown the last dart, moving toward the exit. "How about a game? Or . . . are you needed back at the Polar Star for an encore?"

The reality is I am wanted back at the restaurant. Although, really, I did a pretty good job tonight with that one man. With any luck, that agent has already slipped Lyla his calling card by now.

And anyway, it's probably healthy for me to do something else socially for once.

Lyla, for her part, would be proud. She's always saying I need to get out more, doing things particularly outside the realm of sitting somewhere doing something with Ferris and Olivia.

"This is usually the part where I make a scene waving a contract over my head trying to get Lyla to sign, but it can wait," I say, sliding off my chair. "Darts it is."

As we weave through the crowd, I realize I never asked him if he had to get back to his own group at the restaurant. He didn't come alone, surely. He's not one of those guys who rounds out his Friday nights alone at some upscale bar, right?

I risk a glance at him, suddenly feeling a swell of pity.

Gosh.

How did I not see it all this time?

He has just moved back from the City. Left his whole life up there after being dumped by his publisher. Come here after having been gone a lifetime. Only to discover all of his old friends are gone. People have moved on. Moved away. Gotten married and had babies and left him, just when he's returned home, utterly desolate and shaken and in need of old chums to fill the void. And now here he is.

On a Friday night.

Alone.

It's terrible, really.

All this time he's walked around acting so independent and unconcerned and so . . . so . . . in charge, when in reality none of us at Pennington Pub really see him beyond being "the new scary boss."

I feel a sense of duty welling up inside me.

It's the Cade way after all: to *be* the change we wish to see in the world.

Great opportunities to help people seldom come, but small ones surround us every day.

We rise by lifting others.

All that.

With my head full of platitudes, I feel my energy lift as I walk beside him to the dartboard.

I feel quite charitable, in fact.

I mean, this isn't quite up to the share-my-latest-good-deed-at-the-family-table-over-dinner level, and it's not tax-deductible (as my parents always ask), but it is close.

I grab three gold and weary darts off the board and step back to the nearly rubbed-off red strip painted on the floor. I give Will a bright smile.

"After you," he says, ushering with his hand. "You ever play before?"

"A bit," I respond, raising the dart and squinting at the board for a practice throw. I toss and it lands on the beige nine.

"Care to make it interesting?" he asks as I move aside and he takes my place.

I eye him. Measure him up. "Maybe. How?" My eyes brighten as an idea forms. "If I win, I get executive-level voting power during the next pub meeting."

He tilts his head with an incredulous brow. "You want to wager becoming the boss. Over a game of darts."

"No," I say, raising a finger. "I want to become boss over *winning* a game of darts. There's a difference."

He laughs and throws a dart. It lands squarely on the red eighteen. "I was thinking more along the lines of whoever loses buys fries. But how about this?" He pauses. "Loser has to answer a question."

"A game of Truth or Dare? Are we in middle school?"

"There'll be conditions," he adds.

"Like what?" I say. And even with the thought of it, I feel my energy zinging, giving me a high. The atmosphere around us is loud, buoyant. Music is playing from at least three directions. The clamor of plates and glasses is everywhere.

All of this is the same as when I was stuck with Tom at the Painted Pony Saloon, and yet here with Will the floor doesn't look so much beer-stained as richly vintaged with the wear of a hundred thousand friends gathering over the years. The sound isn't throbbingly loud so much as vibrant and alive. Even the cluster beside me doesn't look so much brazenly drunk as just very, very friendly.

Well, except for that guy who just stumbled off his stool. A little more awkward than friendly.

"We each get three vetoes. And, of course, we will keep this on a professional level."

Professional. Of course.

"So basically like the icebreaker 'get to know you' game Yossi tried to get us to play during our last retreat."

"But with fries," he adds, raising a finger. "I'll be a good boss and throw in a basket of fries."

I frown. "Yossi tried that tactic, too, but with doughnuts."

But despite myself, I can't help cracking a smile as he heads for the bar.

A few minutes later, he returns with a basket in hand. "Ladies first," he says.

I stand at the line. "I'm beginning to feel like I've gotten swindled into working on a weekend," I mumble, gazing at the board.

I throw my first three and come to a total of 32.

He throws his, and the total comes to 40.

"So," he says, pulling the darts off the board. "Why do you want executive voting power at pub board next week? What's your angle?"

"No angle. It's just . . ." I shrug. "Rob is going to push for the Weaver proposal, and Giselle is going to sway the group toward that influencer singing group, and they're both bad calls."

"Because you want Smith," Will says matter-of-factly.

"No, I've reread his proposal and done a little more digging, and I'm losing my enthusiasm for him. I'll still take him to the meeting, but between you and me, I'm not sold."

Will gives another one of those rare laughs and throws a dart. Then another. "That's quite the candid statement."

I smile a little as I watch him throw his third. "Well . . ." I shrug, warming up to the realization that I do always say too much to him. And he never seems to mind. "I'll still do my best to sell him in there, but let's just say if I end up convincing you all, I'll have also convinced myself."

"Then what's wrong with the Weaver project or the singing group? If you aren't gunning for your own author, what's your opinion on them?"

"Well, Rob may think Weaver has all the potential in the world, but I'm nearly positive his social media platform is bolstered by paid bots on his Instagram." I pause as I move into position before the board, then cast a look back. "I mean, honestly, Will. His area is taxidermy. Where are these two hundred thousand passionate followers of taxidermy? Where? And as for the singing group . . ." I shrug. "They may technically be celebrities, but they're still pretty low on the totem pole. Mostly, though, the issue is the manuscript. It lacks originality, passion, and purpose. They never have a clearly defined goal, they never captured my interest, and frankly, they're not famous enough to have us assume people will buy it based off their brand alone. They're not a household name, which means sales would have to actually rely on good *content*. Which it doesn't have."

I throw a dart, and it lands on a beige 15.

"Wow. A spitfire response from such a fair face," he says.

My cheeks tingle at the compliment. Right? Was that sincere? "Well, it's the truth. And I don't get paid to give fluff."

"And can you take it like you give it?"

There's a playfulness in the question, but even so, I'm slightly stilled. It does sound quite critical, doesn't it? I never had thought of myself as harsh before, but isn't this just the way my mystery editor would say it too? But then, there's the difference. I would never say any of this directly to those authors. I'd pack it deep, *deep* within a thick layer of compliments.

"No," I admit. "I get wounded easily. It's a flaw, really. One shot and I act like a wounded doe, limping around for a week. Anyway," I say, throwing another dart, "we were talking about the proposed projects."

"So you don't trust Giselle's judgment?" he says, crossing his arms as he waits for his turn. "She does have several stellar clients."

"Sure," I say, taking aim and putting the board in my line of sight. "Because she always dumps the worst authors on us and takes the best for herself. Last year I discovered two authors from the slush pile, wooed them, got them through pub board, and the second everyone got on board she slid her name into the contracts and bumped me out."

It's not until after I throw my third, watch it land on the triple twenty, and turn with a gleeful grin that I realize Will is no longer looking as relaxed as I am. No. He's frowning now, suddenly looking quite a bit taller, shoulders broader, as he gazes at me with arms still crossed over his chest. In fact, he doesn't seem to look like he saw my winning shot at all.

"Which contracts?" he says.

I stiffen.

But his gaze is penetrating, and I've learned enough in the last two weeks never to dance around a reply. "Dutton and Seuss."

I can't be sure, but I feel like the lighting must have shifted. It's the only way to explain how his eyes are starting to take on that iceberg-blue fire. "What about Harry Sullivan? Surely he would've put a stop to that. He was her boss."

I clench my jaw. "Well . . . if you haven't noticed, Giselle is fairly intimidating."

And then I realize. He really *hasn't* noticed. He's so scary himself, he hasn't had a clue.

"Does my mother know about this?" he says.

"Your mom?" I can't help but reply. "Your mom is her biggest fan. Nobody would dare tell on her."

Except me, apparently, I think, biting my lip. The one who just revealed this information oh so candidly to her son.

"The mismanagement of this company is overwhelming," he says, spitting out the words more to himself than to me.

For a moment I feel a swell of pity for him. Coming home with no other options, discovering his mother's empire she built from the sweat of her brow under not just financial crisis but intense management duress. Being hit with waves of new problems every day, some of which his own mother is to blame for, while also dealing with the confusion of their mingled professional and personal relationship. It certainly would be a shock.

"Well, it's not all that bad," I say. "We've made it this far, after all."

"By the skin of our teeth," he says without emotion.

He looks so frustrated, I pity him.

"And the people who do remain are—for the most part—loyal and talented. We may not be Sterling, of course, but the people at Pennington do love their jobs. We're even, in our own odd sort of way, like a family." I smile good-humoredly. "Even with Giselle being the classic wicked stepsister. We're going to come out of this. You'll see."

His expression shifts as I talk—an expression that for some reason makes my spine start to tingle. The fury in his eyes isn't totally dissipated; it's more like embers now, glowing in the background. They're clearly going to be burning for a long time. But there's now a sort of thoughtfulness in his eyes, too, as he gazes into my own.

Somewhere in the distance "Big Green Tractor" starts to play. Out of the corner of my eye I see a couple of people shuffling closer, eyeing the dartboard enviously.

"Well," I say after a long pause. "I think we may need a new game."

There's another long pause, and we both just look at each other, trying to sort out how the next moment will go. It seems like we're standing on a scale, trying to decide in the middle of a millisecond our next move. On the one hand something feels decidedly off—me chatting with the boss, sharing secrets. Talking too much. But on the other hand . . . the more tempting hand . . . it's nice here. Cozy.

We both hear a phone ringing from his pocket, and after some hesitation, Will pulls it out. He looks at the name on the screen for a moment, then at me. "I probably should get going," he says.

"Me too," I agree—all too readily. I gather my things.

As we move back onto the street, I feel the ambience shifting, the evening festivities coming to a close despite the continued party around us. Will shoves both hands into his pockets.

Almost like we're in high school and he's walking me home. *But why?*

The thoughts continue, pestering me as we head back to the Polar Star. What exactly made Will come here tonight, alone? Who exactly called him, telling him it was time to leave?

The buzzing on his phone was the reality check that he has a life behind a door I haven't been welcomed through yet. Perhaps will never be.

The thought disappoints me, silly as it is, and I scrabble to ignore it.

"So," I say, not even sure where the rest of my sentence is going to go. "I never got to ask you any questions."

"I suppose you didn't," he replies, nodding to the men on either side of the door as we brandish our IDs.

A part of me feels my spirits lift as I realize he's coming in behind me. He's coming *inside*, not parting ways at the sidewalk and drifting off into the stream of traffic.

Up the narrow stairs to the restaurant's main floor. He's not leaving. Yet.

And for the first moment of our acquaintance, I admit to myself, just a little, how aware I am of Will Pennington. He's scary, sure. Terribly intimidating when he stands at the podium, looking over the group of us with a sort of intense weariness that says, *What am I going to do with this lot?* But . . . he's playful too. Spontaneous. Fun. He clearly doesn't just live for work all the time.

He can't be but a few years older than me, but he's like a grownup, a real grownup who dresses the part, acts the part, *is* the part. Unlike me, who rents a room from my younger sister, chases after outlandish and unpredictable dreams like writing, and has a real fear that someone will discover I still have no clue how taxes work. I'm just a kid playing in an adult's body.

Will, on the other hand . . .

I glance back, see the way his wavy hair lifts carelessly to one side. A touch of hair product on it. Just enough to style, not enough to overwhelm.

He's truly . . . a *man.*

"So," I continue, holding the railing as I move up the stairs. "Do you like country music?"

It's the worst, the lamest, question in all the world, but it's all I can think of as I reach the top step.

"Hate it."

"There you are!"

I halt. Because there, standing right in front of us, is Giselle.

Chapter 12

"*O*h. Savannah." Giselle's lips pucker into a thoughtful, quite expensive-looking frown. "I didn't know you were coming to this little soiree."

Soiree, as a matter of fact, was my Word of the Day three weeks ago. Soirees are reserved for intimate gatherings. Upscale parties. Special get-togethers. She's used the term perfectly.

I don't have the heart or willpower to glance over at Will. I mean, I *just* said those things about her. I *just* ratted her out. I feel like I just discovered Will was playing on the opposite team all this time. All that time in the bar next door it felt like he was an untaken player, someone who hadn't been picked up yet for the team on either side. The red team: full of executives with all the power. Or the blue team: the rest of us at Pennington. The underdogs. The common man.

But he's the publisher of Pennington Pen. He's Ms. Pennington's own son. Of *course* he's one of them.

And Giselle, to drive the nail in the coffin, looks dazzling. Her short platinum hair looks so silky smooth she could be in a

Pantene commercial, and the silvery top beneath a sharp white blazer shimmers in the light to give just the right playful touch to this business affair.

Me, on the other hand . . . I feel my face wincing despite myself. I actually spent twenty minutes in front of the mirror this evening working to make my bun look like the product of an overworked genius of an agent who didn't care a wit about the world around her.

Quickly, I run my hand over the side of my bun.

"Oh," I say, as casually as I can muster. "No, we just bumped into each other."

"Ah." What little interest she had in me shifts back to Will. "Well, Will, we were starting to worry. I was just about to get Sam to check the restrooms to make sure you hadn't hit your head and weren't stranded somewhere." She gives a little laugh just as Sam pops up beside her, and my misery is complete.

Evidently I was shielded from view by Giselle, because the second Sam's eyes move from Will to me, he gives an almost imperceptible startle. "Savannah. Hello."

"Hi." There's something *extra* amiss in his tone. It's almost the stilted remember-that-first-terrible-date greeting he usually has. Almost. But no, at this moment there's no mistaking it's something more. Extra cautious. Extra nervous. The way his hands shift uncomfortably toward his pockets. Now his gaze moves pointedly to Will, almost as though he's guilty about something. Hiding something.

Just like he was outside the ARC room.

And again my thoughts give a flourishing, *Sam?* Could he really be my mystery man?

"Our food is here," Sam murmurs, in a tone that even for

Sam is over the top. Of course, he is the passive one in the on-off relationship that is Giselle-and-Sam. I mean, he'd have to be. If there were two people as aggressive as Giselle in the relationship, they'd kill each other. So, while I'm used to seeing the tail-between-his-legs attitude whenever the two are together, it's surprising seeing it even worse now.

"Finally," Giselle says. "I told you all we shouldn't have come here. This place not only looks like two tins of condemned veal but is just as slow as it is plug-ugly. Let's go sit."

But as she trots off, Sam following like a puppy, Will doesn't move.

When the world apparently shakes because somebody hasn't blindly followed her directions, she stops.

Turns.

"I'll be right there," Will says, not moving.

She plasters on a bright smile. "Great."

But then she doesn't move either.

The two of them smile expectantly at each other for a long, uncomfortable moment until, when it can't be any more evident that he is not going to walk with her to the booth no matter how long she silently grins at him, Giselle lifts her chin. "We'll just tell everyone you're coming . . . then."

"Good plan." Will gives a short nod, and when it's quite clear she's gone, he looks down at me. "Well. Savannah. Thank you for the interruption this evening. It was a most welcome one."

I want to say, *You, sir, were the one who originally interrupted me, remember?* But it seems trivial to point it out.

"Enjoy your . . . meeting," I say.

I also want to add, *And please,* please *don't repeat what I told you about Giselle to that group.* But that seems desperate, and won't make any difference anyway. If he wants to share with them what I said, he'll share.

So, with very little power over the situation, I smile as merrily as I can and give a little wave, trying very hard not to look like the girl who didn't make the softball team. "See you Monday."

He nods, but his eyes are already starting to cloud as he turns toward the booth that lies ahead.

Giselle has been demoted.

I can hardly believe my ears Monday morning as I stand on the tiled marble floor under the vast, quaking chandelier of the foyer. Word has buzzed through the building so quickly the whole place seems to hum.

Giselle. *The* Giselle. The one who's shown her glossy face here for ten years. The one who has had her eyes set on the publisher position the past two. One of Ms. Pennington's favorite pets (because Giselle is more skilled than anyone else here in the art of counterfeiting literary intelligence).

Numbly I take in the news surrounded by a dozen hushed—and in some cases giddy—conversations.

The second I turn the knob on my office door, I'm greeted with an explosion of energy from Lyla. "Did you hear?" she says, practically jumping from her chair and rushing at me like a puppy whose master has come home at the end of a long day. "Can you believe it?"

"Hardly," I say, bewildered.

Lyla shuts the door behind me. In fact, all the doors on the hall are shut today. The typical, unspoken rule is to have them open, allowing Ms. Pennington to keep an eye on us whenever she spontaneously, much like a warden, walks the halls. But today everyone on our hall is talking about the latest news.

Giselle the Giant has fallen.

And surely . . . *surely?* . . . not because of me.

"I saw her this morning carrying a box from her desk downstairs. To the *first floor.*" Lyla's eyes are positively mirthful. "Honestly, I'm surprised she didn't just quit. You know how she is. She'd probably rather be unemployed than lose her dignity by being demoted to the *first floor.* I say she'll find somewhere else and quit within the week."

"Where did she go?"

"Trophy. To be an *assistant.* I just can't believe it. Harry I could believe. Clyve made sense; his work was always subpar. But Giselle? I mean, she was out with the bigwigs just two nights ago! I saw them!"

And as if on cue, there's a knock on the door. We both jump, and in the next moment we're flying toward our desks and jabbing both of our computer mouses to make the screens come to life.

"Come in," I call out as nonchalantly as I can.

To my surprise, it's Will.

The ease in his eyes is gone. All remnant emotions from two nights ago, in fact, are gone, leaving only that same hard, exacting expression he wears from eight to six. Even his clothes look tighter and more uncomfortable with their perfectly pressed and sharp angles.

"Savannah. I was hoping for a quick word."

"Oh. Of course," I say.

Lyla's eyes practically become saucers as she watches me follow behind him into the hall. After all, why wouldn't they? Those have been the words of doom the past twelve months. Anyone receiving them got the inevitable boot.

Who knows? Maybe it's my turn.

I trail behind Will to the end of the hall, where a single door looms. Two people walking down from the opposite side stop as we pass, practically flattening themselves against the wallpaper with more giant-saucer eyes to let us by. Good grief. I have no doubt that rumors are already spreading. People are probably right now calling dibs for my desk space.

We step inside his office, and as we do so, I hear the door click shut behind me.

I've only been in this room a handful of times.

"Please grab a seat." He motions at one of the two modern-looking leather chairs on the other side of his desk.

As I take a seat, I glance around. The desk is the same auspiciously large, wearied pine as every other desk in the building bought in the 1970s, but everything else about the room is new. The red Persian rug peeking out from beneath the desk and stretching across half the length of the room. The black-walnut bookcase to one side, spilling out books both new and old. The wall behind Will, covered with two windows facing a large maple and its spindly winter limbs. On either side of the windows there used to be frames. Dozens of frames, highlighting a life spent in publishing, documenting nearly every accomplishment for the world, and Harry himself, to admire.

But there are no frames now behind Will's head. Just a fresh coat of cold gray paint, tinting toward blue in the morning light.

Will takes a breath. "I'm sure you must've heard."

He doesn't elaborate. After all, he has grown up inside these walls; he must know how fast word travels.

"I did," I say at last. "I must admit, I'm surprised."

He nods, not seeming to want, or need, to know more. "I just wanted you to know that I appreciate you speaking with me so candidly Friday evening. The more I can understand the myriad problems going on in this company, the easier it will be on everyone in the long run."

So that's what it was, then. My fears—no, I won't even let myself admit that in thought alone. My *suspicions* confirmed. He pulled me off to chat more about the company. That even explains the so-called "bet" to make things more interesting: play a game of darts and get all the dirt he can on what's really going on in the company. And I was just *so* willing to share every single thought in my head.

"I'm glad to hear it." My words are uplifting, and yet my tone is distant, polite. As polite as my rigid posture as I sit in this chair trying with all its might to force me to lean back.

"Tell me, what do you think of Yossi?"

"Yossi?" My antenna rises. Yossi has been with the company for ten years, and yes, while he may bore me to pieces every *single* meeting, he's a good man. Loyal to Pennington. Lover of books. Worthy of only good things. "Yossi is great."

"Is he really, though?" Will raises an eyebrow—the exact same way he did when he questioned my dart skills the other night. Only this time, it doesn't evoke quite the same emotion. This time, I stiffen. "He's been late to work three times."

Sure, he has a problem getting to work on time, but that's because the man is so eco-conscious he bikes to work. Sometimes he falls prey to the puddles. And sometimes he stays up all night reading, riveted by some new inspiration or other, and sleeps through his alarm. It's a true booklover's dilemma. But we're in a publishing house. These are the known, and surely accepted, consequences of hiring true-to-the-core readers for the job.

"And I've noticed he's not quite as on board as some others when it comes to working as a team."

Well, can you blame him? He was under Giselle's wing, and every time she ended up getting her hands on his manuscripts, she inevitably screwed something up, blamed it on him, or watched the manuscript receive praise and took credit that really belonged to him.

"Yossi has been nothing but a treasure to this company. He's truly one of a kind. Honestly, you should fire me before you fire him."

There. I said it. I told him the truth, and in doing so may have put myself on the line.

"Yes, but is he confident?" he continues without swerving. "Can he command a group?"

When did I become the Pennington snitch? When did I become the rat who skirted around the darkest corners with the higher-ups, whispering secrets that determined the lives of others? Every single time I've met with Will now, somebody has been fired or demoted or moved to another position. Sure, I'd be lying if I didn't say I appreciated it, but now Yossi?

Asking me for dirt on Yossi?

I can't do this. I can't be the company snitch who gets the reputation for whispering little injuries in the boss's ear whenever I'm frustrated.

I raise my chin. "I think these questions are better left to Yossi himself. I'm sorry, I have quite a bit of work to do. My expense reports are due today. I think I'd better see myself out."

Will, who's been so intensely asking me questions that he's

been leaning forward, his elbows on the desk, sits up in surprise. The intensity in his gaze lifts, as though he's seeing me for the first time.

"Yes," he says after a lengthy pause. He stands up, the polite distance back in his posture. "Yes, those reports are due today. Good thinking."

There's a wedge between us now. I feel it, and the way he moves toward the door to usher me out, there's no doubt he feels it too.

As I turn at the door, I see a new expression clouding his face, and for a moment I waver. Perhaps it's my imagination, but he looks almost . . . hurt. Like somehow in there he was finally being vulnerable, too, eager to have somebody else with whom to share his concerns. It must be lonely at the top.

Still.

I pause just before he opens the door and, risking several things at once, put a hand on the cuff of his button-up shirt. "Yossi is a good man and an asset," I say quietly. "What he lacks in punctuality he makes up in loyalty, goodwill, and a passion for the job that has already stood the test of time."

He's quiet, his expression unreadable, and I continue.

"I just hope you take some time to really get to know the employees under your wing before making hasty decisions."

A slight crease forms on his brow, and I don't know what he's thinking, but I certainly know my own thoughts. Will Pennington has been here two weeks, and in that span of time has fired Clyve, changed Tom's editor, and demoted Giselle. And now, here, he's considering making a grave mistake with Yossi. Maybe some of that has been called for, but the reality is he's charged into Pennington like a bull in a china shop.

"You think I made the wrong decision with Giselle?"

"No." Slowly, I shake my head. "I and the whole Pen team thank you for that, truly. I just . . . don't feel comfortable being the one to have influenced you in your decision. I'm just a lowly editor. You are the hotshot from New York who's boss. I'd hate to lead you astray by speaking out of turn."

His voice is low, quiet, as he responds. "I don't ask for many people's opinions, Savannah. But when I do, it's because I respect them and the lens through which they see the world. You may be, as you say, a lowly editor, but you also have insights into this company that I find admirable, and true." For a long moment Will looks at me, but when I don't budge, he gives a polite smile and turns the knob. "At any rate, I asked for your opinion on Yossi. I appreciate you giving it."

He opens the door.

⸻

I swing through the ARC room during lunchtime two weeks later and, to my surprise, open the door to a whole new world. It's a land—a whole fairyland—of lights. It really does feel like a fairyland too. I was expecting nothing fancy out of this typical gloomy February day, with the clouds a chalky gray and the forecast nothing but sleet and freezing rain. And then, *ta-da*. Instead of a dark, shadowy room lit by one hanging bulb, I find nine hundred lights twinkling in glory. The room glows.

And as I pick the manuscript off the stack of books lingering beside the beanbag chair, I can't help but feel my heart glowing as well.

My mystery editor added lights. For us.

Us.

That includes me.

As I go over his newest additions, my eyes can't help nearly shimmering with tears of mirth as I read, then reread, the expansive story written all down the page. Maybe it's the humiliating story about my mystery editor's worst blind date that does it. Maybe it's the ball of tension that's starting to release in the pit of my stomach since I passed the halfway mark on the manuscript. Or maybe it's the new string lights surrounding the little room, making the whole place glow.

Or maybe all three.

I take my pen and finish off the conversation we've had going back and forth for the past four days at the bottom of the page.

Okay, okay, I get it. I'll take out the blind-date scene.
But geez, that's pretty embarrassing, Mystery E.
Then I trust you can keep that little secret
between you and me.
Or use it in my next manuscript . . .
You wouldn't dare.
Wouldn't I?
Not if I'm editing it.
Does that mean you're up to the job? Mystery E.
henceforth and forevermore? This is getting a little
Phantom of the Opera-esque.
I always thought he got a bad rap. He built
Christine Daaé's career.
You like the show?
One of my favorites.

Fine, then. This book gets contracted, and I'm taking you to the show. My treat.

Make it on Broadway and you have a deal.

Broadway it is.

I smile to myself as my finger slides to the bottom of the page and I add: *By the way, these lights are beautiful.* Then I turn the page and laugh at his own note: These lights are the ambience this room needed.

Agreed! I reply, then move on down the page.

I've spent more and more time up here in the ARC room lately, and while I can justify in good conscience repeatedly leaving the second floor because I've been devoting so many hours to the job at night, the real trick has been managing to sneak away so much without suspicion. Thankfully, with everyone at Pennington having such a tangle of meetings with one person or another throughout the day, everyone seems to have assumed I'm off to talk with someone about something. As it turns out, as long as you're turning in quality-level work on time, there's a surprising lack of accountability for Pennington editors. And with Lyla and the way she falls so deeply into new projects you could practically eat from a dinner plate on her head without her noticing, it's been remarkably easy to escape and come back without notice.

There's another long paragraph at the bottom, and I pause. It's a moment where my lead lady has messed things up yet again and the best friend—the perfect, polished best friend—comes in to fix things up and save the day. My leading lady isn't perfect. Actually, to be perfectly honest, my leading lady isn't perfect *at all*. She's a mess, really. Incomplete. Untalented. Truly mediocre. She is neither the glossy girl living with a perpetual can light spotlighting her every move nor the ugly duckling in the back of the room who turns out to be a witty, suddenly-knockout-gorgeous-when-she-washes-her-hair type of female. No, she's just Cecilia. Fifteen pounds heavier than she was in college, and yet the chocolate muffins matter more to her than her weight. Funny, but never commanding a room with her wit. Enjoys movies and music and TV but couldn't read music if her life depended on it. Intelligent enough to get by but not intelligent enough to win awards or get promoted to anything big. She's just . . . Cecilia.

She's also, I'm realizing, just . . . me.

I've heard other authors say they write to explore their own problems. They write to work through what they're going through. It's a sort of therapy.

And here, looking at my own work through fresh eyes, I see. I've done it too.

The problem is, what has changed? Nothing. My life hasn't changed. I haven't finished this book with a eureka moment and grown. I've learned no lessons.

I'm still just me.

Where's my darn eureka?

I read through the rest of Mystery E.'s entries, defending my actions on some, taking pictures and making notes to adjust things on others. The positive notes are popping up more and more, I've noticed, especially as I've printed out new copies of my edited scenes to stack on top of the manuscript for him to see. He likes the way things are turning out. And, with growing certainty, I do too.

Honestly, I'm starting to both marvel at this new manuscript and feel a pinch of terror whenever I think of the condition of the manuscript I sent to Claire before. *This* is so much better. So much so that it's humiliating to think about what I sent before.

I reach the last of his notes and check the time. The room is luminous. The gray clouds swirl outside the purple- and green-tinted glass panes. This place feels so cozy I wish I could stay all day.

But it's time for our monthly pub meeting. Time to tap out from my turn in the magical room. Time to go.

Just before I do, though, I take out my pen and write a note in the margin of chapter 15.

So, Mystery Editor. Why are you helping me?

The question is simple, but still, I feel my heart race as I write it. I've wondered so many times as I've read his notes through the pages, but have never summoned up the bravery to ask.

Part of me has feared he would read my inquiry and think, *You know? Why* am *I helping her?* And then he'd drop me and leave me to my hopeless fate. But the longer we've gone along, giving it 100 percent over the hours, over the days, the more I feel like I'm not so alone while doing this. We are a team. Somehow, remarkably enough, I sense he wants this manuscript to succeed just as much as I do.

It doesn't make sense. But I really feel it.

Fifteen minutes later, I'm sitting in the Magnolia Room at the oval table as the room slowly fills. My feet are tapping the floor as I review the last of my notes, a tick Olivia has truly helped create. I'm at four thousand steps for the day, thanks to one drizzly walk to work, but for the third time this week, I'm still lagging behind.

Some new girl is sitting in Giselle's old seat, looking quiet and uncertain of herself as she sits beside Brittney, Ms. Pennington's PA. The new boss, no doubt. Although . . . that's a bit quick, isn't it? Certainly it'd take more than a couple of weeks to find any truly worthwhile replacement for her job. And why couldn't Will have hired from inside the publishing house? These are all just issues stacked on top of existing issues in a load that's building against him.

His demeanor has grown harsher over the past few days. People have been calling him a chip off the old block—which, to everyone except Ms. Pennington herself, is the opposite of a compliment. In the span of three days, Will has dropped the night janitor—poor Robby of over twenty-six years—down to part time and given all of us more cleaning responsibilities, taken away three people's company credit cards (that I know of), and cut the cord on the new espresso machine, replacing the station with grocery store–brand coffee.

And to be honest, I don't know how I feel about it all.

I don't blame people for getting their feathers ruffled; I nodded vigorously when Maggie declared during one lengthy tirade, *"If we're going to be living in 1984 conditions, you'd think they could at least let us keep our coffee!"* And I certainly fought on Yossi's behalf. But at the same time, whenever I see Will's exhausted face as I pass him in the hall or go past his door— always cracked open, always with the light on no matter how late in the day—I can't help feeling for him. He's the boss making the calls and yet he looks more miserable than the people he's letting go. On the bright side, at least Yossi is still here today.

Maybe I made an impact after all, I think. *Maybe part of the reason he's still sitting here today is because of what I said to Will. And no one will ever know.*

Lyla scurries to my side and bends toward my ear. "I just got a *call*!"

"Rob, close the door, please," Will says, and the feel of the room shifts as the meeting begins.

Even from this distance, I can see Will's tense face as Ms. Pennington stands just as he himself starts to rise. She moves a foot to the left to command the head of the table. "Okay, everyone," she says, her voice higher than usual. "Let's begin."

Ms. Pennington is like that. Always wanting to be in the middle of things, knowing *everything* that is going on. Micro-managing. And while that may have worked to a degree with Harry, the last publisher of the Pen division, who always acted less like a boss and more like a microphone for Ms. Pennington's will, it's clearly a point of tension now that Will is running Pen. As we all feel and see. Every day.

"From whom?" I manage to whisper to Lyla.

"Frank Stenneti Entertainment! FSE!" Lyla whispers back as though it should have been obvious. It's been fourteen days since she played at the Polar Star, and since then we've had a dozen meetings, one issue with the warehouse for shipments, one livid agent conversation, three blasé agent conversations, and two suck-up-to-agent conversations. That night is about as far from my mind as the load of wet laundry forgotten in my washer the past three days.

"Quit dawdling, everyone," Ms. Pennington continues.

"No one is dawdling," Will says quietly. "Everyone's clearly seated and ready."

Both Lyla's and my attention snaps to Will. I have the urge to press my lips together to keep from saying, "Ooooooh," like kids do when watching a fight forming in the halls.

Now that I look at him, he does look even more taut than usual today, like he's on the back end of a really long argument that didn't go well. Who knows? Maybe they've already been going at it behind closed doors.

Ms. Pennington, looking sharp in her red suit, pretends not to hear him.

"Yossi," she says, "I haven't seen an updated proposal. I was expecting that in my in-box two days ago."

"As I'll remind you from our previous conversation," says Will before Yossi can speak, "you haven't received it because he sent it to me—his publisher—and I rejected it. The proposal wasn't worth pursuing."

At this, I see Ms. Pennington's jaw clench. There's an ire in her icy blue eyes as she meets his matching ones. "The concept was riveting."

"It was outdated. The public's attention is not on the great harmonica players of the nineteenth century."

"Then we *draw* their attention to the topic. That is our duty. We create a culture. We enrich society."

"Yes, but how well has that worked the past fiscal year?"

The only sound in the room is Brittney's pen scraping furiously on the paper as she writes down the conversation. None of us dare breathe.

Finally, after several long moments have passed, Ms. Pennington tilts her chin. "I've just remembered an urgent email I need to attend to. I'll leave you all to things here and will be looking for a report from Mr. Pennington this evening."

And in one smooth move, Ms. Pennington somehow manages to slide through the crowded group surrounding the table and standing against the walls, Brittney with pen and pad following closely behind.

All of our eyes now shift to Will, waiting for what comes next.

Will stands. His face is emotionless, as though in his mind the conversation was prudently handled and it's time to move on to the next line item on the docket. Instead of looking like his thoughts are churning with shouts of *I can't believe I just spoke to my mother like that! I must amend myself immediately!* like I would, he's calm. Eerily calm.

"Hello, everyone. Thank you, especially the sales team, for coming in and joining us today from your travels. We appreciate you."

The men and women lining the walls give frozen smiles.

"Now, first off, you'll notice we have a new face here today. Allow me to introduce Moira." He gestures at the new woman at the table. "Our newest intern."

New. Intern.

A new, unpaid intern.

Oh.

"She's just begun spring term of her junior year at Belmont, so she will be joining us mostly in the afternoons and using most of her time filling in to meet the needs of the editorial staff. But I also want to see that she gets her feet wet with all the departments so that she can learn about the workings of the publishing industry. I can assure you she will be a great benefit to all of us here, and at the same time I hope we can benefit her with great work experience as well. So please, be sure to give her a warm welcome after the meeting."

He gives Moira a nod. Moira, the poor girl, looks like a popsicle stick with a smiley face. What a first day on the job.

"Second, I want to be the first to inform you all of Yossi's promotion to editorial director."

At this, I nearly knock over my coffee.

"Yossi, as you all are aware," continues Will, "has been an asset to Pennington Publishing since the beginning. What he lacks, I hear, in . . . punctuality"—at this, Will at last lets a wry smile slip onto his face, and a few chuckles go around the room— "he makes up for in loyalty, goodwill, and a passion for the job that has already stood the test of time."

I feel my breath halt as Will's eyes meet mine.

He wasn't planning to fire him.

He was listening to my advice. In fact, he's using my *exact* words that I said to him. *How?* is the question running through my mind. How is it possible that Will Pennington, son of the CEO of Pennington Publishing, cares enough about my words to lean on them for his decisions?

Who am I? Nothing but a lowly assistant acquisitions editor at the bottom rung in a company full of experts. I wasn't offended when I wasn't included in that upper-level meeting at the Polar Star. In fact, the thought never crossed my mind. Why? Because I am Savannah Cade. Not my mother, Laurie Cade, not my grandmother, Hazel Cade, not even my great-grandfather, Geoffrey Cade, caught out of his hospital bed after having his arm amputated in the first world war fixing the creaky bed. Just . . . me.

So what is it he sees in me that he finds worth trusting?

I'm not sure, but what I see in his eyes now, the telepathic message I feel sent through the airwaves to me at this very moment, tells me one thing: he does. For whatever odd, crazy reason, he respects my opinion. Respects me.

The shock of the realization lingers with me through the rest of the meeting, the afterglow of the rare sensation making a home inside my chest. I've never been respected before. Not really. Not with my family. Not with Ferris. Not with Giselle. Maybe, just maybe, this'll be the start of something good.

The meeting goes more smoothly than ever. Surprisingly, it isn't the sales team that turns down my proposed author but Will himself halfway through as he interrupts to say, "I'm unconvinced. Let's move on." It's crisp. To others it looks most certainly cutting. But given I told him as much myself that night during darts, I don't take it personally.

I stand at the coffee maker in the corner after the meeting is over. It's late, the meeting having gone on much longer than usual, and a feeling of euphoria is fading out of the room as I pour myself a cup of coffee. It was a rare moment of team bonding back there. Yossi certainly surprised us all with that pep talk about the power of words and our work, and the ruddiness is still on my face as the steaming liquid fills my cup.

I take a sip, and the fact that it tastes like burnt cheap grounds can't even dampen my mood.

"How is it?" Will sidles up to me and reaches for a paper cup off the stack. He looks good. Certainly less stressed than the person we saw two hours ago going toe to toe with his CEO . . . and mother.

"Do you want honesty?" I say, turning to lean against the counter of the station with a small grin.

"If that's okay with you. Yes."

I catch the way he's looking at me as he speaks and take in

the words. He's silently asking for something else. Referring back to our conversation in his office when I subtly asked to step away. He wants to know, it seems, if I'm okay with stepping back in.

My smile deepens, giving the answer in full by expression alone. But just to be clear, I say, "That's perfectly okay with me." I pause, then add, "Your coffee sucks."

His eyes momentarily widen, and then he picks up the coffee-pot. "Is that so? I'll have you know these are the finest coffee grounds three-fifty a bag can buy."

I watch with amusement as he takes a sip, then holds the coffee in his mouth before taking an inordinately long period of time to swallow.

"Missing that espresso machine now, aren't we?" I tease.

He drops his cup into the trash can, and the coffee splashes along the plastic lining on the way down. "Fine. I concede. I'll bring back the espresso machine. No absurdly priced espresso beans from Fazatti's, though. And no syrup station."

"Bulk espresso beans from the Bean Station," I counter, "and we'll contribute our own syrups to share among the group."

Will eyes me for a long moment, then puts out his hand. "You drive a hard bargain."

"Happy to represent the group," I reply, shaking firmly.

"The Pennington spokesperson," Will says, smiling as his hand holds mine. "You know, I may just take you up on that offer."

"I'm sure we'll have plenty to talk about," I reply. And in more ways than one, I mean it. The idea sends electricity through my veins, all the way down the palm of my hand sitting warmly in his.

It's funny. You never quite realize that you have expectations for how someone's hand will feel. It's not like I had consciously ever wondered before. I just expected it to be smooth, probably because a part of me also expects that his life up north was full of gripping portfolios and opening sleek taxi cabs instead of operating heavy machinery. Why would his hand be calloused, the muscles beneath his palm strong, when his life is one of facts and numbers? And yet . . . I bite the inside bottom of my lip, forcing myself to stop thinking about it. I don't actually have the heart to let go, but I at least force myself to stop looking at his strong hand all but enveloping mine.

"So, how did things turn out for Lyla the other evening?" Will says, breaking his grip at last.

I take a breath. Put my hand quickly at my side.

"Pretty good. She got a call from that agent after all." There's a pause, and I add quickly, "Not that she's planning to leave Pennington. She loves it here."

"Yes, so I've gathered," he says, his eyes moving pointedly to where Lyla stands in a cluster of coworkers, looking bored out of her mind. Her AirPods peek out clearly from her ears.

When he sees my wide eyes he adds, "Don't worry. I've already come to realize she's an eccentric best left to her own devices." He pauses. "Well, most of the time. We may need to take away her phone privileges."

I laugh. "You've been getting complaints about her?"

"Half of my calls are about her." He shrugs. "But she's the most talented person in this publishing house, and I'm including myself in that statement. I'm not going to lose her over a temper. Besides, everything she says is dead on, and if I'm honest, part of me likes to see her tell it to them like it truly is."

My grin widens. "That's not very publisher of you, Will Pennington."

His eyes twinkle. "Then I trust you can keep that little secret between you and me."

And I do tuck that little secret away.

Deep away in my thoughts all the way on my freezing walk home.

All the way up the three flights of stairs.

All the way to my door.

The thought—the whole conversation, in fact—takes up residence full time, setting out a love seat in the living room of my mind. Will Pennington sidling up to me, not anyone else, after the meeting adjourns. Will Pennington's playful smile. Will Pennington's resilient, authoritative air when he makes decisions for the greater good. Will Pennington's banter.

And his words.

I walk through the living room in a rosy haze, laptop bag over my shoulder, feeling light as a feather despite the blocks and blocks of trudging through freezing rain. I leave damp footprints as I step along the hallway toward my room, and I hear Ferris and Olivia talking in faint, disagreeable tones as they sit at the kitchen table, poring over some wedding document.

Everything feels okay. Better than okay.

Why? Because with a sense of growing certainty, I sit on my bed and slip out the manuscript I gathered into my laptop bag just before the doors locked for the evening. As I flip through the pages, I stop on page 149 and see the words. The same words I remembered the moment Will spoke to me after the meeting: Then I trust you can keep that little secret between you and me.

Here in bold black ink.

It has to be him. Will Pennington.

It has to be.

Chapter 13

I t's not him.

I hardly believe my eyes as I walk into the ARC room two days later.

It has been two days since Will left.

And here, in our secret room, I discover a candle sitting in the middle of the floor.

And worse, lit.

The candle gives off a strong smell of gardenia. I inhale deeply, and while I should be smiling, while part of me wants to be thrilled, the emotion doesn't come. The string lights are on, giving the room a romantic glow. And yet I know for a fact Will Pennington is approximately 885 miles away this very minute on yet another business trip to the City.

So. It's not him.

It's not him.

It takes a while to digest that thought.

Will Pennington is not the mystery editor.

Which means somebody else is my mystery editor.

Who has added a beautiful array of string lights around the room.

And lit a candle.

And gone to great lengths to support me as I pursue this project.

And is witty and charming and strong and . . . *wonderful*.

And may be Sam.

Sam.

I chew on that thought until a gust of wind clatters the old sparrow glass and brings me back.

Sam.

Sam isn't so bad. I did like him enough that first week to go on a date with him. And sure, that date didn't go well enough to pursue another one, but that could be for any number of reasons.

Maybe he's too shy to show who he really is. To reveal on a first date the man I've been seeing on the pages these past few weeks. Who knows? Maybe Giselle terrified him so much he got used to repressing who he really is in favor of keeping the peace, and has gotten stuck there, talking about weather and groceries and nothing of actual substance. Nothing with *passion*.

But *this* Sam, I think, flipping over the next page of the manuscript and skimming the words. This Sam is a treasure. This Sam, if it truly is Sam, is someone I should certainly want to know more.

I see a new comment and pause. The question I left for him the other day, the one I've checked for a response to a dozen times, finally has one.

Beneath my question, *Why are you helping me?* are the words: Because I believe in this story. I believe in Cecilia. Cecilia is real. Flawed. Human and yet, still, one of a kind. You have written a story that gives readers hope that they, too, despite all their own blemishes, can and should be valued the same way. This is a story the world needs to hear.

I read and reread the paragraph a dozen times.

He loves my story. He believes in Cecilia. Likes her. Gets her.

And if he values Cecilia, he values . . .

No. I can't make assumptions.

I stand up, and with it, my resolution is clear.

Sam or not, I am falling for my mystery man.

Chapter 14

There are flowers on my desk.

Big, floppy pink flowers spiraling out in a dozen directions, supported by bright-green leaves and baby's breath. The room smells like I've walked into a Bath & Body Works.

It's just before lunch, and I'm returning to my desk after dropping by Yossi's office to talk about Charles Henry, the new acquisition I gained after Giselle's departure to the first floor (where she still files her nails during work hours). The flowers weren't here thirty minutes ago. And yet here they are now. Waiting patiently for me.

On Valentine's Day.

I take a tentative step toward them while trying to manage my expectations. I have no boyfriend. My mother and father, for all their merits, are too busy handling a catering event at the nonprofit downtown today to send me a pity bouquet given my single status and my sister's looming wedding date. So that leaves . . .

I dare not think it.

I just reach for the card.

I open the gold-sheen envelope and, with nearly shaking fingers, pull out the card. The message is typed beneath the header of *Enchanted Florist*, and reads: *And tonight I'll fall asleep with you in my heart.*

I stare at the words.

So honest. So raw.

He's just come out and said it. Taken the leap.

And I realize we're jumping ahead to a new level in all this. The level where we're openly putting aside the games and bravely asking the question: What do you think—not about scenes and characters and settings . . . but about us?

I feel my face flushing and wish with all my heart in this moment Lyla was here to talk this over with instead of taking the day off to work an event at the Dolly Parton–inspired rooftop bar for Valentine's Day.

But as she's not, I guess I'd have to say . . . yes.

I'm ready to take a step forward.

Although I chatted around and found out Sam and Giselle broke it off a couple of months ago, there is still risk involved. To openly accept a date with Sam again would be considered mutiny. Giselle might not be my boss anymore, but she is still scary.

Clever scary when she wants to be.

The worst kind.

The poisons-your-yogurt-in-the-community-kitchen worst kind.

I'm just sitting at my desk, spinning the card in my hand as I think through all the ways she could make my life anywhere from unpleasant to no longer existent, when a knock at the open door startles me.

I turn.

"Ferris. Hi," I say, sweeping the card into a drawer and shutting it.

"Hello," he says, smiling broadly. He steps inside as his eyes move over the flowers on my desk. "So . . . Happy Valentine's Day."

"You too," I reply quickly, standing so that I'm in front of the flowers. I don't know why, but I feel the need to conceal them from him, to get them out of the forefront of conversation as much as possible. For one thing, I have no desire to explain my mystery situation. For another . . . Why, exactly?

"Savannah. Ah." Will halts in the doorway, a stack of papers in his hands. He pauses, gives Ferris a polite smile. "Hello again."

"Hello." Ferris gives a polite smile back.

There's a pregnant pause, Ferris looking at Will, Will frowning slightly at Ferris. Me standing in front of the flowers that, for no valid reason, I feel compelled to hide.

At last, when it seems clear Will isn't going to move, Ferris turns to me. "So, Savvy. I was just . . . going to see . . ."—his eyes momentarily dart to Will—"if you might be available for lunch."

"Oh," I say in surprise. "I thought you were going couch shopping with Olivia today."

"Yes . . . Yes, I was . . . But she has to work. I was hoping you could help me instead."

Couch shopping. Well, it's not on the top of my list as far as fun Valentine's Day activities go, but it would be a welcome substitute for my soggy chicken salad sandwich waiting for me in the breakroom.

I'm just opening my mouth when Will jumps in. "Actually, *Savannah*"—he says my full first name with a bit of emphasis—"I have to go down to the courthouse just now to get some paper-work notarized. I was hoping you'd come with me. Seeing as you are now the official spokesperson for the Pennington people."

The smallest twitch of a smile lifts his cheeks as he speaks, and Ferris looks uncertainly from me to him. "Oh, official, is it?" I say. "I didn't realize it had been approved."

I turn to Ferris, realizing a bit belatedly that I've abandoned my post at the flowers and am shrugging on my coat. "Sorry, Ferris," I say, though I don't quite sound sorry at all. "I'm going to have to raincheck. But you know how Olivia is. Just make it as functional and gray as possible, and you've got yourself a winner."

"Right. Sure." He stuffs his hands in his pockets, looking so startled and, quite frankly, rejected that for a moment I wonder if I should change plans. But to go on a car ride with Will . . . To talk over plans about ways to help the company with Will . . . Well, it's too good of an opportunity to pass up. Not to mention, who knows what interesting things I'll learn about him? He's still somewhat of an office enigma. Jumping into our lives out of the blue. Jumping out just as quietly on his mysterious trips. Never revealing much of his personal life. Who knows what I'll learn on a car ride with him?

Such as the little golden nugget I'm standing here learning five minutes later, for example.

That *this* is Will's car.

I'm quite sure I never actually took the time to think of what exactly I expected he would drive, but I know for a fact I never would've come up with this.

Will pulls open the door of the old red Chevy for me. It gives a defiant creak.

"Thank you," I say, taken aback not only by the formal

manners but also by the truck in general. It looks like it's from the eighties. There's a sizable dent on the front right corner of the hood. And the beige cloth interior looks like it's been stomped on about twenty thousand times. But aside from all the wear and tear, the cab interior is spotless, not a crumb or loose paper to be seen. It smells faintly of cedar and grease. It's cozy, like one of those Alaskan cabins in the woods.

He shuts his door and turns the ignition.

"I gotta say," I comment the second the engine starts to rumble. "I didn't expect you to drive a car like this."

"Thought I was more of a Lexus man, did you?" he says, sounding unsurprised.

"Well, yes. After all, look at you. You don't exactly dress like a lumberjack."

"My job doesn't afford me the opportunity to dress like a lumberjack." He grins and turns onto the main road. There's a pause before he adds, "This truck was my father's."

There's something in the way he says it. *Was.* Not *is.*

"I inherited it last year," he continues.

Ah. And there it is.

"I'm so sorry," I say, and feel it. Truly.

"Thank you." Will nods, his eyes fixed on the road.

I know little of Ms. Pennington's personal life except that she divorced her husband twenty years ago and has been alone ever since. I knew nothing about the man she had once been married to, just that she'd had one husband in the course of her life and one son—some bigshot named William who worked in the publishing industry in the big city.

"Anyway, he loved his truck. And was always practical about his needs. I like to think I will keep on learning that from him."

I glance over to the dash. The RPM gauge on the left-hand side is covered by a Polaroid that looks thirty years old. A poorly exposed picture of an infant perched on a wooden high chair in front of a little round birthday cake, hands and cheeks covered in icing as his big blue eyes look into the camera. There's a number on the cake, a baby-blue *1*, and a man with a toothy grin has one arm draped over the boy as he stands on one side, a woman—no question, from the striking blue eyes, a younger Ms. Pennington—on the other.

"Was he very different from . . . your mom?" It feels awkward asking your boss about his personal life, especially in a truck like this. Maybe if I were riding along in some sleek, personality-less BMW I'd feel different. We'd chat mildly about sales numbers and the weather. But in this? Sitting on well-worn fabric with the scent of cedar and nostalgia all around? It feels impossible. It feels as personal and unavoidable as if I've walked into his own bedroom.

"In many ways, yes. In other ways, not really. Mom is . . . old-fashioned. She clings to the yesteryears like it's her duty, regardless of the situation at hand. Dad was like that too. Had more old antique farm tools in his barn than he—or I, now—knew what to do with."

"So where are they now?"

"At the moment? Still at the farm. Along with every other piece of junk I inherited." He smiles lightly. "I have four coffee-pots to choose from for the morning commute. Because clearly that's what every person needs on his countertop."

I pause. "So you've moved into his house? Full of his things?"

"For now, yes."

I look out the window, surprised at his answer. Never in my life would I have imagined Will Pennington to be the kind of man who went from posh NYC living to some farmhouse out in the country. In fact, more than once on my downtown walks, I've looked up at some high-rise condo building full of glass windows and exposed brick and glittering chandeliers and wondered if it was his. I don't know why, exactly. I just assumed.

"So, let me get this straight," I say. "You don't live in an apartment downtown."

An amused question forms in his eyes as I ask, but he shakes his head.

"You don't have some sort of waiter hanging out in the lobby ready to take your clothes to the dry cleaners."

His grins slightly as he again shakes his head. "They're con-cierges. And no."

"Why did I think you would?" I say aloud, honestly a bit puzzled.

"Because you think I'm elitist, from the sound of it," he says, stifling a chuckle as he makes a turn.

"No, because you came from the City," I say, resolved. "In my mind, everyone who works in publishing in the City must be the most glamorous person alive. Eats sushi every night."

"Well, we are a sushi-loving people," he concedes.

"Goes to the newest posh jazz club to drink fifteen-dollar margaritas."

"Oxford commas, actually," he corrects. "And they're more like twenty-three with tip."

"See? Glamorous."

We sit in silence at the light for a few moments, flurries dusting the windshield.

"Actually, I like the change. I love the City, but my heart was always here. Besides, Mom needed me."

I raise a brow. "Your mother? But . . . didn't they . . ."

He seems to have expected my follow-up question. "They broke things off years ago but then . . . never truly followed through."

My incredulous brow rises farther. "You mean they . . . what? Had different houses but stayed together?"

Will shrugs. "I guess they just never really let go."

I sit back in my seat, picturing it. The couple who were so different on paper—he with his multiplying coffeepots, she with her love of old books and dictator-like demand for obedience—unable to ever fully cross the other off the list. Unable to fully and truly take the other's name off the electric bill. To blot them from their address book. And instead to find themselves in the evenings suddenly in the driveway of the other's home.

It was sweet, in its own way. Sweet and sad.

Will takes another turn. "She doesn't let on, but Dad's death has been hard on her."

I smile softly. So he's also here for his mother. To be with her in her time of grieving. "I'm glad you can be there for her."

"Me too."

The light turns, and the cars start moving. Will hits the gas, and we continue to chug along.

"So," I say, more to relieve us of the quiet than from actual interest in the conversation topic. "I believe you wanted to talk about ideas for the company."

"Do you mind my asking, why was Ferris really here this morning?"

Ferris? What?

For a moment I'm too stunned to reply.

"To go couch shopping," I say eventually, as though the answer is obvious.

"Yes, so he said. But did he state his actual reason for coming?"

I wrinkle my brow. I am intelligent enough to gather his insinuation, and I don't like where the path of this conversation is leading. "He's marrying my sister in four weeks. They want a couch for their new living room."

There's a long silence—so long, in fact, I spot the courthouse coming into view through the flurry-dappled windshield.

"Savannah. I'd like to ask you a few questions, not as your employer, but as . . ." He hesitates. "As your friend. You are welcome to say no, of course. But if you don't mind indulging me for a moment, I'd appreciate it."

He sounds so sincere, with such good intention, that I can't help giving in.

"Of course you can," I say. "Ask away."

He jumps right in. "How long exactly did the two of you date?"

"About . . . eight years."

He gives such a startled look, I amend with, "On and off. Sometimes off for years."

"Are you serious? That man dated you for eight years. And now is engaged . . ." He looks like he can't even bring himself to finish the sentence, so I do it for him.

"To my sister. Yes."

"And how long did he date your sister before they got engaged?"

"Three months," I reply, well aware of how this sounds. "Now engaged for nine."

There is such a lengthy silence this time that I go ahead and cut to the chase. "I know how it must look from the outside, but they are in love," I explain, repeating the mantra the family has said a thousand times.

"And he left you for her," he says, his face taking on one of those terribly intimidating expressions he gives when he's about to fire someone, "but comes back to ask you to go couch shopping for his future bride. Your sister."

"I know how this sounds. But this is how my family works. We are loyal to each other to the end. It's kind of our family mission statement."

Will pulls into the last, lonely empty parking spot at the corner of the courthouse. He puts the gearshift in Park, hesitates for the blink of an eye, then turns to face me.

"And that's where I wonder if I should correct you, Savannah. You may be loyal, but it doesn't sound as if the rest of your family is loyal to you."

He sounds so harsh, as if editing my life.

But despite his words, and the way he is frank in a manner that no one—not even Lyla—has ever been, I feel myself crack a little beneath them.

The strength and conviction in them. The unwavering support of my side. It's been so long now that I've been trained to ignore those words and beliefs myself that I've forgotten the emotions are still there. The words bring up such a reaction that I know I must still be hurt, so very hurt, by all that's happened. Not just the loss of Ferris. Perhaps not even the loss of Ferris at all. But the sense of loneliness. Betrayal. And the requirement to put on a brave face and repeat my rehearsed lines through it all.

Always.

I open my mouth to say my usual "You know how it goes. 'The heart wants what it wants.'" But then I feel my breath stall. It'd be pointless anyway. He wouldn't believe it.

"Well, I do harbor a secret hope it rains on their wedding day." I say the words and then clap my hand over my mouth.

Will looks unsurprised. In fact, he smiles a little. "And the venue gets soaked?"

"Floods," I continue with a smirk as I drop my hand. "Floods so hard that the guests can't make it over the tiny, ornate bridge to the wedding venue. And every photograph is so foggy you can't see the people. And all the curls fall from Olivia's hair. And all those stupid, *stupid* flowers the family has talked about non-stop the past nine months get carried off into the wind."

We grin at each other.

"But . . . ," I say, sobering.

"Yes?"

"But the better part of me hopes that after all that misery they do get their private moment to say their I-do's and go on to have a nice life together. I really do."

His temple creases with a smile. "I know you do. For what it's worth, you are a good sister and a remarkably thoughtful human being. You deserve the same kind of happiness you wish to bestow on them."

I feel myself warm at his words, from the tips of my toes to the tips of my ears.

"Even so," he adds, "I don't think they'll make it to the altar."

My smile falls. "What?"

He levels his gaze. "Savannah. The man tries to take you couch shopping. He picks you up to go give blood. *He brings you flowers on Valentine's Day.* Do you really think that is typical brother-in-law behavior?"

He opens his door, letting the conversation transition to a natural end, neither needing nor wanting a response. But he's not right, I want to say as I sit there in the cab of the suddenly silent truck. Those flowers weren't from him at all. They were from Sam. But then . . . I don't want to share that fact either.

"That's not fair," I respond, throwing open my door, refusing to give up. "How do you know I don't have a boyfriend?"

"Do you have a boyfriend?" he says from across the bed of the truck, although, in asking, he acts as though he already knows the answer is no.

What is this?

Do I *look* like a girl who just can't have a boyfriend? Is there really something so obvious about me that would lead him to believe, *Savannah Cade. Ah, yes. She never dates.*

"Well, no," I say a bit begrudgingly. I shut the door, and it slams with surprising force.

We walk in through the back side of the building and stop at the elevator halfway down the hall. The black-and-white tile floor looks scuffed from an endless flow of traffic, the old halls still carrying that ever-present scent of bleach water and bills. Is the courthouse always this crowded? A number of people I notice are stopping to read the map of the building along one wall, and we join a cluster of at least ten people beside the elevator.

"Anyway," I say, tilting my chin upward as we squeeze in with the group and Will hits the button for the second floor, "I have a suggestion for staff meetings."

"Yes?" he prompts, holding his binder of papers in front of

him. Beside him, a handsy couple start going to town. My eyes widen, and I quickly avert my gaze.

But they're not alone, I realize. A woman to my left grabs a bald man by his ruddy cheeks and pulls him in. What on earth is going on?

I can't help it. I catch Will's face, which looks as uncomfortable and surprised as my own, and let out a noiseless giggle.

The couple beside him change positions with their hands, and the woman's elbow knocks into the back of Will's head.

"So," Will says, squeezing his arms as close to his chest as possible to avoid touching the couple. "Staff meetings."

"Right," I say, my eyes mirthful. "So. Everyone on salary"—I spot a roving elbow and dodge it before it rams my face—"needs to get Friday afternoons"—oh dear, the couple beside him has started slow dancing—"off in the summer."

The number two lights up, and the doors open.

We spill into the hall.

Only this floor is just as crowded. Paper hearts are strung across the ceiling all the way down the hall. Music is playing through speakers. And there is a string of couples leading all the way to one particular door at the end of the hall.

Are those rose petals on the floor?

"As you were saying . . . ," Will says, clearly trying to pretend he has not walked us into this madness.

"Yes," I continue, moving aside to let a woman and the long white train of her wedding dress pass. "As I was saying . . . everybody else in the industry does it. We should too. Denying us the choice just makes us feel like a baby company clearly not up to par with the publishers in the big leagues. It'll boost our self-respect."

"And give everyone the chance to catch Friday matinees," he counters, clearly unamused as he pushes a string heart from his face. When I just reply with a look, he adds, "I've never understood that industry norm. It's just an excuse for New Yorkers to beat the traffic on their weekends out of town."

"Well, whether the rule was made for vacationing in the Hamptons or not, we deserve it. We are just as qualified, just as hardworking, and after the year we've all had, I can't think of a better proposition to lift everyone's spirits."

I can see he's mulling it over.

"You don't think productivity would be affected?"

I smile, sensing a victory ahead. "I guarantee it won't."

We take three more steps forward in line. Then another two, before he finally puts out a hand. "If—and that's a big *if*—everyone can do the same load of work in four-and-a-half-day weeks, then I'll agree to afternoons off from June 1 to the final week in August. But I'm going to monitor production, and I won't hesitate to pull back if the company starts to suffer."

I grab his hand and shake so swiftly it startles him. "Deal."

A man separates momentarily from a rather firm squeeze his fiancée is giving him and points at our handshake. "See, Delilah? That's all we need to do. Shake hands on it and be done."

The woman, presumably Delilah, shakes her head from her perch by his side, her arms wrapped around him like a koala gripping its tree. "No, Danny. For the thousandth time, we make this official or I'm out. And taking the TV."

Ah. True love.

I go over a few more items with Will, and while none of the others garner such quick agreement, I make fair headway regarding limited parking spots, the weird smell in the women's bathroom, the illogical and potentially harmful nature of creating ARC spines that don't reflect the same color and nature of the final product—particularly given that 95 percent of the time the books are spine out in the bookstores—and the thermostat that is perpetually five degrees too low.

Finally, after at least one dozen brides have left the county clerk's office clinging to their newly betrothed—or, in one case, watching one woman stalk out alone, dumping her bouquet in the hall trash can as her would-be spouse chases after her—we arrive at room 206. At last.

"Should I . . . ?" I hesitate, feeling suddenly uncomfortable about going in. But between standing in the back of the room watching him get papers notarized and standing out in the marriage madhouse subjected to an incredible overexposure of public affection and tulle, my preference is written across my face.

"Sure," he says, "This should just take a minute."

So, together, we step inside.

It's an unassuming office. A single window with dusty blinds slit open to reveal a row of windows on the back side of another building. But where there were scattered petal droppings in the hall outside, in here it looks like a florist exploded in the dead of night. Rose petals cover the walkway between the doorway and the man's desk like a red sea. Bouquets of fake roses sit on every available table space. The clerk across from us wears a single carnation corsage on the front of his old beige button-up.

He registers us coming in and stands, not really looking at us directly but at the stack of papers on his desk. "Stand here, please."

"Uh, right," Will says and shuffles uncertainly forward,

raising his papers. Being always the squeaky-clean kid I am, I follow without question. "So—"

"Hold your questions to the end." The man clears his throat. Then with one bony finger he hits the Play button on an ancient cassette player on the table. Suddenly, an organ booms "The Wedding March" through the speaker.

I feel instant hysteria rising in my chest, sort of like acid reflux that sizzles against the rib cage. I press my lips tightly together as I glance over at Will. One look, however, only makes it worse. His usual cool persona has instantly collapsed, and his neck above his trim-fitting suit coat looks like it's been out in the sun for twelve hours without sunscreen. In Bermuda.

"Dearly beloved," the clerk says, reading from a paper on his desk, "at this time of"—he checks his watch—"1:14 p.m. on Tuesday, February 14, 2021, we are pleased to gather this fine gentleman . . ." He raises his eyes and gives Will a meaningful look.

"Uh, William Pennington, but I think we have a misunderstanding. This is the clerk's office, yes?"

"That's correct. To gather this gentleman, William Pennington, with this young lady . . ." He pauses and this time turns to look at me properly for the first time.

By this time I've got two bright spots on my cheeks.

I'm just opening my mouth, my mind undecided on whether to give my name and let the ruse go on a little longer, when Will throws an arm out. "*Sir*, I'm here to get these notarized."

"We will notarize your marriage certificate at the end. Please, if you haven't noticed, there are quite a few couples we have to get through. So if you don't mind to just follow my directions—"

"We are *not* here to get married!" Will booms. And as though he needs to emphasize the point, he takes a gigantic step away from me.

At this point I can't help but throw my hands over my lips to keep from going into hysterics over the entire situation. The clerk swivels his gaze to me and, clearly misunderstanding my posture as being on the cusp of collapsing into tears, swallows hard.

He blinks, and his expression shifts to one of compassion.

He clears his throat. Opens a drawer and pulls out a pamphlet. "Actually, we have a room today for these little 'moments.' If you could just go down to 212, you'll find a safe space to talk it over, and then"—he slants a meaningful look at me—"depending on how things go, you may get back in line if you wish. We recommend perusing this packet as well," he adds, pushing it into my hands. I look down to an enormous stock photo of a ticking clock, with the words above: *WHY WAIT?*

Pressing my lips very, *very* hard together so as not to disrespect him by laughing at his kind offer, I pull my face into the most respectably peaceful expression I can manage and nod in gratitude.

"I'll just wait in the hall," I manage to all but whisper, my chest starting to burn with pent-up laughter.

Which I let out the second I shut the door and am back in the hall.

And for another several minutes I stand there outside the door, amid the lovestruck horde, grinning as I replay Will's face in my mind. At last, Will opens the door, papers in hand.

The moment he does, his blue eyes lock on mine.

And we start to laugh.

Couples all around us break from their little romantic holds on one another to eye us curiously, a few even giving a hearty clap.

"I can't . . . even . . . ," Will begins after our laughter settles into mutual grins. He shakes his head. "I don't even know what to say. I just . . . apologize. I'm so sorry for that."

"For what?" I say, grinning deeper to impress upon him how unoffended I am. "Lesson learned: Never visit the courthouse on Valentine's Day. Ever."

"Unless one wants to get married."

"Naturally."

He smiles at me as though grateful I'm not making this into a situation. In the distance a bell dings, and he glances down the hallway as the elevator opens and more couples spill out. He looks back down at me. "What do you say we go out the front? Avoid any more elevator situations?"

"Good idea," I say, then watch him from the corner of my eye. "So . . . just to be clear before we move on, I'd like to raise the point that you took a *Titanic*-size step away from me in hopes of disassociating yourself back there. Now, an objection? Sure. A tiny step to make your point? Fair. But really, was that giant leap necessary? I didn't think I was *that* awful of an option as far as clerk-office weddings go."

"Not you," Will responds as he glances at a couple passing us, of whom the woman seems to believe wedding dresses should be made entirely of black leather. "Just chalk it up to a particularly bad experience."

"What—did you accidentally get married in Vegas?"

"Make it a priest at a Presbyterian church and very nearly."

I nod. "Ah. So you have a little wedding-altar PTSD. Interesting."

"She was just the wrong decision at the right time."

I raise my brow but don't press as we move down one flight of stairs, taking us to the front doors. Already I feel I have walked into a treasure trove of information I hadn't been expecting. It feels imprudent to ask for any more. "Well, I'll take care not to tease you any more with the sight of tulle."

"Or doves," he adds, smiling as he pushes open one of the double doors. "I struggle with the sight of doves."

"Fine. And doves," I say. "Although, is this an issue of just doves or birds altogether, because I imagine it would be quite difficult to walk around . . ."

My words trail off as we step onto the top of the wide concrete steps descending from the front of the old building. The clouds have at last joined together and decided to collectively dump all the precipitation they have in one grand and glorious event. The wind has stilled for the event, leaving the thickest, clumpiest flurries I have ever seen to dive toward the ground. Covering lampposts. And bicycle stands. And blanketing the ground as far as the eye can see.

I grin and raise my chin toward the sky, because truly, in a moment like this you can't not grin.

Thick snowflakes grip my lashes and dot my face as I look back down. And when I open my eyes, blinking furiously and wiping my eyes, I see Will's face. He's not looking up at the sky. Nor is he looking at the snow-covered ground. He's looking . . . at the people.

The curious . . . people.

Down the center of the stairs just below us, there is a tunnel with a mass of people on either side. Several are shaking poster boards with hearts on them. Others are throwing rice at a couple—who are clasping hands and running through. Everyone cheers.

As the couple ahead of us reach the concrete sidewalk, the mass turns their expectant, jubilant faces on us.

Will pauses. Looks at the notarized paper that, I now realize, looks very much like a marriage certificate.

Then at me.

His blue eyes hold a mirthful question.

In response, I smile. "Well, at least there are no doves."

And without waiting a second longer, he clasps my hand and lifts his paper victoriously into the air. As we descend the steps, someone who clearly *loves* love shakes her poster with a high-pitched whoop. Rice pelts our faces alongside flurries, so much I wince and close my eyes half the time.

It's euphoric.

And I can't help noticing, despite the chaos all around, Will's hand as it clasps mine.

Suddenly, it makes sense, the toughness of his hand. Suddenly, I can imagine him in that old yellowed-linoleum kitchen, reaching for one of his four coffeepots each morning. Looking out at the snow in his childhood backyard. Musing about his hardworking father, perhaps with some regrets, perhaps with some fond memories, about life and death and their interwoven path. About mistakes, bad and good, that lead us onward.

He holds my hand all the way until we reach the sidewalk, and at last, after we pass a building and move out of view, he lets go.

He exhales. Grins down at me.

"They were just so hopeful," he says apologetically.

"Agreed," I reply, smiling up at him. "We couldn't let them down."

He's quite close to me just now, I realize. Several inches closer than the amount of space the average conversational situation calls for. Close enough that I faintly smell the cedar and grease coming off his person, not just his truck.

My hand feels instantly cold without his, and I long for the warmth and companionship of his grip to return.

There's something in his eyes as the flakes fall between us. A faint question. A thought bubble hovering over his head. But whatever it is about, it doesn't pop and he doesn't speak.

Instead, he grins again and shifts on his heel toward the parking lot.

Meanwhile I, trying very hard to ignore the disappointment, stuff my hand in my coat.

And as the dust of the previous thirty minutes settles, we walk along the snow-covered sidewalk, stamping footprints onto the freshly laid path. Both quiet. I mean, what does one say after pretending to marry her boss?

At the truck, he opens the squeaky, creaking door for me, and for a moment I can't help wishing he is the man behind the manuscript. That he is the one I'm too sucked into now to even entertain anyone else. I *like* Will.

I may as well admit it openly, even if it's just to myself.

But I can't deny that the real person I spend my days and nights thinking of, the one whose conversations constantly run through my head, the one who's gotten to know me from the inside out, who has supported me, criticized me, fought to understand me, heard my stories—good and bad—and given his own in return, who is the one I wake up every morning excited to talk to and go to bed every night wishing for more from, is my mystery man. And nothing, not even clasping my hand and running through a tunnel of love-addicted fans, can change that.

It's time to face my editor.

Chapter 15

This is, without a doubt, the worst kiss in the history of mankind. Have you ever actually kissed someone before?

I prickle and write hotly beneath his words from my beanbag chair.

I'll have you know I've kissed plenty of people.
PLENTY. I live with mistletoe over my head.

Okay, that isn't *quite* true. Unless we're counting my parents, who still kiss me on the cheek more often than is culturally appropriate.

Still, this is *the* climactic scene. It's *the* kiss. *The* kiss in a romance that ends with a happily-ever-after kiss.

To say I struggled through writing the grand-finale kiss scene is like saying the neurologist is a fine doctor except for that moment he does any actual surgery. In frustration, I give up and head back to my office.

An hour later, I return to find a new note.

These people are acting like they're made of card-board. Where are their hands? They are at their sides like eighth graders at a middle school dance.

He's never underlined before. Used exclamation points, sure. Plenty. A couple of all-cap words, most definitely. But here, there is not one but three underlines beneath the words. I can practically see him in my mind slashing away with his pen beneath the glow of string lights and the smell of gardenia. We've given up blowing out the candle these days. We come here so often, it's basically supervised all day long.

I bristle and scribble beneath his note. *So I forgot their hands. You can use your imagination. Readers do that, you know. Fill in the blanks themselves.*

His return comes promptly before lunch.

The reader isn't going to be using their imagina-tion here because they'll be so annoyed that she somehow draws in one second and then steps away in the next. You spent eight sentences describing the tree they stand under and give absolutely no description to their actual kiss. They are acting like they hate each other. They act like they hate kissing.

I throw my hands up in the air and write the first words that come to mind. The truth.

Well, fine. I admit it. I hate kissing. It's disgusting. It's unhygienic. It's a bizarre cultural phenomenon. Do you even know how many germs are in someone's mouth? Six billion. SIX. BILLION. And how exactly, while we're at it, am I supposed to describe tongues playing hockey with each other in a mass of saliva? Is that really what you want? If I were to be completely honest, I'd say the whole world should give up on it altogether. We should all just give jolly soft hugs to one another. That actually makes sense. And keeps you from spreading mono.

I return from lunch to find his answer.

Holly. I know this is really your pen name, but I feel the need to press the point by calling you by name. Be it any name at all. So, Holly. Have you really chosen to write romance when you don't actually believe in one of its biggest tenets? The attraction between two people is imperative. If this is how you feel, you should consider a new genre.

I hesitate, then respond.

They ARE attracted to each other! They just . . . prefer holding hands. And anyway, romance isn't just about attraction. It's about companionship. You don't see old married couples who've been through two world wars and five babies together making out on a bench when they're ninety and think to yourself, Now THAT'S what it's all about.

You see the way they hold hands, the way they serve each other scrambled eggs on plates they got on their wedding day, the way they shuffle through the paper in the mornings together without needing to fill the space with empty conversation. Because they are happy. Just happy. Together. That is why I want to write romance. I've seen enough insta-meet romances at conferences and in supermarkets. Books that presume instant attraction magically leads to a lifetime of happiness. But I know what really happens after the last page.

My chest tightens but I keep on.

I know what it's like to be left because a man gets captivated by someone prettier, someone more graceful, someone who dazzles the room. So please, don't try to convince me to change genres because I can't capture a kiss. What I want to see in all this, what I want to share, is a story about two normal people, with both hiccups and highlights, who share a lifetime of companionship over eggs and wedding plates.

When my pen finally stops, I lean back in the beanbag and stare at my words. I sound too passionate. Too emotional.

Too . . . unhinged.

And what's this all about, really?

A scene. Just a little scene. And for a long minute I think about crumpling the whole page up, throwing it in the trash, and never bringing up the scene again. But I don't.

I leave it.

Because . . . well . . . it's the real me.

And if there's any hope of anything happening for us beyond the margins of my manuscript, I need him to see the real me, flaws and all.

I drop my pen and, forcing myself to stop thinking, to stop hesitating, walk out the door.

When I return that afternoon, he hasn't responded.

But when I return at the end of the day, I find his words.

Chapter 16

I'm sorry. I was speaking tongue in cheek, but my remarks didn't translate well on the page. For what it's worth, you have met your goals in this story, and already exceeded them. I'm proud of you.

As for the scene, though, and to stay on point, if you are going to have a kissing scene, you need them to kiss like normal human beings. Have you ever considered that . . . you don't like to write about a kiss because you've never actually experienced a good kiss?

I stare. The man took my ardently felt monologue, gave it a polite pat on the head, and told it to go play while the adults stayed on task. And the task is my pathetic ability to write a kissing scene. Which has turned into an oddly sensitive personal subject on *my* history and ability to kiss.

Fine, I write. *Since today is all about my romantic ventures, apparently, no. My former boyfriend was my first, and last, kiss, and to be completely honest here, I always thought doing laundry would be a better way to spend time. So there. Perhaps, since you're so "good" at it, you should just write the scene for me.*

I tap the period so hard with my pen it splotches and drop the manuscript on the stack of books beside the chair. Roughly I blow out the candle. Turn off the string lights. And make my way for the door.

So. Sam has had wonderful make-out sessions with glossy Giselle. That's *fine*. That actually makes sense, really, given I can't imagine any other reason he would've stayed with her on and off all these years. Giselle. Passionate with her words, passionate kisser.

Isn't. That. Just. Great.

My mood follows me all the way home. Somewhere in the back of my mind, the reminder that I'm *finally* at the finale of my manuscript tries to push its way to the forefront and cheer me up, but despite how hard it rallies, the encouragement only lasts a moment before another brooding thought forms.

Sam has kissed Giselle. Probably a thousand times.

I fumble with my keys to the front door.

Oh, but remember! You're going to make your deadline after all!

He's probably addicted to her siren-like ways. Can't help himself falling for her over and over again for this very reason. Maybe that's how she does it, in fact. On their off seasons, she corners him in some very unsuspecting way and grabs him by the collar, making him yield to her with her silky locks that fall perfectly over one eye and raspberry lip gloss.

Just three more days until you send it in! You've done it!

And no matter what happens between us, she'll always be lurking in the corners, ready to steal him back.

"Savvy, you okay?"

I look up to find I've been standing in the middle of the living room, a disgusted expression creeping over my face.

"You look like you might be ill." Olivia, per usual, cycles on her Peloton, her finger holding a page in place.

"Fine," I say, rearranging my face into an easy smile. "Fine. Just . . . thinking about a conversation at work."

"Oh, good," she says, looking genuinely relieved. "I couldn't have you missing out on the fundraising banquet."

In another context, one could construe the words as a sincere sentiment. Like a sister saying, *Oh, I'm so relieved you feel well. After all, you are my sister and best friend, and I'd hate to go to any fun event without you.* But I know better. I know what she's really thinking.

The Steps-4-Life fundraising banquet happens at the end of every February. It serves as both a motivational moment for Olivia to step onstage and rally everyone into finishing their step-a-thon challenge strong and—with little silver bowls set at the center of each table—a place for the wealthy and fit to give back to the community and keep the program going. My job is kind of like the senator's family's job. We stand behind her during her speech, smiling and looking pretty.

"And don't forget we're wearing warrior blue," she adds.

I frown. "I told you, Olivia. I don't have anything in 'warrior blue.' And I don't have time"—*or money*, I think to myself—"to go shopping. Can't I just wear the red dress you had me get last year? I've only worn that one once." Last year. For this same dull event.

Olivia's frown deepens into one of disgust. "Red isn't in the palette, Savvy. The theme colors are warrior blue and victory white. And we *have* to match. You'll be onstage for pictures. Don't you *want* to look nice in the pictures?"

She cycles faster, concerns over the color of my fabric revving her up. "And I'd be *happy* to let you borrow one of my dresses. It's just . . ."

She trails off, and I finish for her. "I know. You're a size 2, and I'm an elephant." I turn toward the hallway.

"You wouldn't have to *feel* that way if you just let me help you!" she cries out from behind me, over her own speeding, spider-web legs.

For the rest of the evening I finish up some edits for one of my authors and then work through my own manuscript on my computer, reading and rereading with the most critical eye I've ever had on it. And yet, by the time I click off the lamp and crawl into bed, I feel certain. Finally certain.

My manuscript *is* ready.

All except the final scene.

The next morning, I drop by the ARC room before the coffee is even brewing in the breakroom, and the halls are fresh and polished with the lemony scent of Pine-Sol. I don't know if I am actually expecting anything miraculous to have happened overnight, but still, the desire to know if my mystery editor has responded is too strong to let me wait.

**I won't write the scene for you. But . . . maybe I
can help.**

I'm pretty sure at that moment I look like a praying mantis. A praying mantis with enormous eyes bugged out of her
head.

He can . . . help.

Me.

To write a kissing scene.

It's not the words exactly that I'm so focused on but the three
periods in the middle. *But dot dot dot maybe I can help.*

My cheeks begin to grow hot. My forefinger and thumb get
a bit slippery as they hold the page.

And how . . . exactly . . . does he want to help?

Surely he doesn't mean . . .

There's no way . . .

Absolutely not.

I put the tip of my pen to my lip. Hesitate over how exactly
to word my response.

Yes, I'd love that!

I scratch out the words as quickly as I write them. No need
to sound desperate. Also, who does that? It's like screaming, *Kiss
me! I want you to kiss me!* in someone's face just before they kiss
you. Awful.

*So . . . what do you mean? Like . . . you want to kiss me?
Like we're in second grade?*

Ah! The moment I write my attempt at lighthearted sarcasm I feel an overwhelming surge of embarrassment and cross it out so frantically I rip a corner of the page.

Finally, after much pacing around the room, I find my reply.

I can use all the help I can get. What do you have in mind?

There. And before I can convince myself to blot it out again, I leave.

Chapter 17

I'd like to take you to dinner.

That's it. He's thinking dinner. I exhale as I read the neatly written words on the bottom of the page, my head still prickling. Of course he wasn't thinking *kiss-in-a-dark-room-for-educational-purposes.*

That was an absurd notion, Savannah.

Insane.

He's thinking dinner. Dinner at a nice restaurant where we finally meet face-to-face and discuss scenes for publishing purposes. Like reasonable adults.

But as I flip the page, I see he has written something else.

To clarify, a date. I'd like to take you on a date.

My heart skyrockets for about three seconds, and for a solid minute I don't move. He wants to take me on a date. A first date.

Like one of those dates we've discussed all along the margins in reference to other people and other situations. Except this time, it's me. He doesn't want to take some girl named Chelsea to the Catbird Seat to talk about how her gluten-free lifestyle changed her life. He wants to talk to me. Romantically. Because he'd like to *date* me.

I feel elated, as though I'm floating.

And yet . . . the end has come. The magic of this little room . . . about to end. He's ready to leave the tree house full of songs and games and embark on the real thing. He's moved to the ground and is beckoning me to come down at last.

I feel a little as though Peter Pan has grown up, and I'm not quite ready.

But we're partners in this. And the game can't go on when one half of the team decides to quit. I scribble, *Would love to. When?*

And from there, the conversation bounces back and forth throughout the afternoon.

Tonight. 7 pm.
I can't at 7 pm. I have a fundraising banquet at 5. How about 8 . . . 30? 8:30?
Deal. See you at 8:30. Meet here?
Perfect.

So. I'm meeting my mystery man for a dinner date.

Sam. I'm meeting Sam for a date.

The thought surrounds me as I walk down the hall toward a meeting, emotions filling me to the brim.

It's not really so much the I'm-meeting-my-mystery-man-for-a-dinner-date part that's troubling. I long to meet this man. He's become a part of my thoughts every waking (and sometimes sleeping) hour of the day. He is brilliant. Witty. Blunt, yes, but in a way I've come to respect. And more than anything, someone I've come to wish was my companion everywhere.

Everywhere I go, everything I do, I find myself wishing he was here.

Watching Olivia and Ferris that night they tried to simultaneously jog in place *while* making soup *while* sealing invitations to their wedding. Oh, he'd think it was hilarious.

Sitting at the Tin Can with Lyla and watching the live band in the corner. Didn't that guitar player look just like Brad Paisley? It was uncanny.

Standing in the courthouse hallway, seeing the loads of brides and grooms in line.

Well, actually, I didn't think about him then. Not that afternoon.

But other than that, the other 95 percent of the time, my editor is perpetually in my thoughts.

The only *slight* problem is that I have a hard time connecting the intellectual, witty, companionable editor who so deliciously keeps me on my toes with . . . Sam. Sam, whose hobbies include being on the board of trustees at the YMCA and Rotary International. Sam, who took a week's vacation last year to go to Branson, Missouri.

Branson, Missouri.

So, for the most part, I don't.

I just pretend they are two completely separate entities.

But now? Now . . . I'll have to face the facts. The fact that he is actually an incredibly fascinating human being who also happens to enjoy Funny Farm Dinner Feud shows. And talks for long periods of time about QuickBooks.

I'm the first in the room for a titling meeting—quite early, in fact—and catching a glimpse of my watch, I dump my stack of papers and computer on the table and start pacing. I'm only at 3600 for the day, pitifully low, and I'd try to make up for some of it after work on the way home except that the fundraising banquet is tonight. I drove so I could leave straight from work, dash home to throw on a two-sizes-too-small "warrior blue" dress after all, and fight traffic all the way downtown for the banquet. And if last year is a signifier of what's to come, I'll want to get in all the steps I can now so Olivia doesn't pull me forward to be her "living example" again of how "we may feel like all hope is lost, but the truth is we just need to surround ourselves with positive influences who can motivate us toward becoming our better selves" (aka her).

My pace quickens and the length of my steps shortens until I look like a waddling penguin in a hurry.

There's a shuffling noise, and I look over to see Sam just stepping through the doorway.

He halts.

Then looks like he's walked in on me naked.

"Sam," I say, halting immediately as my embarrassment grows. "Sorry . . . I'm in the middle of a step-a-thon race and . . . well . . ." I trail off awkwardly, realizing I don't know how to finish my sentence.

Or paragraph.

Or conversation as a whole.

This is the first time we've really been face-to-face, alone.

We have been avoiding each other the past few weeks. I suppose he feels just like me, more willing to open up on paper than when someone else is looking straight into your eyes. After all, it's so *easy* to be honest on paper, like when—

My face blanches as I remember, looking into his eyes.

Like when I admitted to that little toe-fungus issue I had not so long ago. How at the time, I was defending the character's bath caddy and shower shoes in the gym and finished with the words, *And that's why you always use shoes in the shower. You never know what germs may be lurking about.*

To which he had responded: I meant the whole unnecessary scene. Much as I appreciate a lesson in personal hygiene, the scene itself is the problem. She runs into him at the gym. We don't need to know that afterward she showers while giving herself a lecture about athlete's foot.

Oh, how *embarrassing.*

I mean, I know I shared these things, but I assumed I would just meet him and feel all risen above it, like I would just shrug and laugh a bit and feel like all of those awkward little secrets and personal stories would just bring us closer. Now, looking into his darting eyes, I know.

They didn't.

"Good for you," he says, raising a jerky hand to wave my comment off. He's still standing in the doorway. "I was just speaking with Nanette about the issue of limited mobility during work hours. I'd love to find a solution that would encourage movement."

Speaking of moving, I notice he still hasn't.

And then I notice something else, and my eyes flicker down to the bundle of items in his arms.

Two coffee mugs. Forest-green ones, with gold cursive writing across them saying . . . I squint, but his arms shift and the font is suddenly concealed. Coffee mugs, plus a bag of espresso, and . . . are his eyes darting toward the community-shared syrups in the back of the room?

Is he planning to *steal* the community syrups?

"Anyway," he continues, catching my eyes and then twisting his wrist to see his watch. "I just realized I've forgotten something. You—carry on," he says, then gives me a stiff smile.

"Thanks. I . . . will. And . . . I'll see you later?" I venture, dipping a toe into the waters of honesty.

He nods vigorously. Immediately. So quickly I couldn't even finish my sentence. "Absolutely. And good luck with those steps."

"Thanks." But I'm talking to an empty room, because he's already gone.

Our secret room has gained a coffee machine.

I smell the coffee beans the second I step into the space.

Hot, brewing coffee gurgling in a small two-person coffeepot in the corner on top of a stack of books. And two forest-green coffee mugs set neatly on the floor beside it. The words clear now in the glow of the string lights.

You Light says the first in flowering gold script.

Up My Life finishes the second.

A little coffee station. With no syrup, I can't help noting with a smile.

I step over to the mugs and pick one up, turning it in my hand. Hanging illustratively on the words are string lights.

Well, it's a little cliché, but despite it, I can't helping feeling a little glow inside myself.

Sam may not be the best face-to-face, but he is truly one of a kind. I've never felt so pursued.

This . . . all of this . . . I've never been involved in anything so romantic.

I take the coffeepot and pour myself some despite the fact that I'm more of a coffee-and-cream girl and despite the fact that it's five o'clock and I need to leave.

And, wanting to take a little of the moment with me, and to make a symbolic step forward for us, I clasp the mug firmly in my hand as I go.

Taking the mug with me.

Into the world.

It tastes a bit bitter, I think, but I swallow a huge mouthful anyway as I follow the deep, swirling staircase of the old mansion down and meet Lyla in the foyer.

The entryway is crowded, a bustling group buttoning coats and wrapping scarves around necks, trying to leave for the day, and as I slip my coat over one arm, I see Sam making his way down the stairs.

From across the room I catch his eye and, in a moment of bravery, raise my mug to him. *To tonight,* I think in my head and take another acidic sip.

His eyes bulge. Actually bulge.

His foot falters on the last step, and he stumbles forward until crashing squarely into the back of Will.

I stifle a laugh, undeterred now by how different the man in front of me acts from the real Sam I know beneath. I am determined now to see this out, one way or another. And I will raise my mug, and expectations, to the long-awaited meeting ahead. Nothing can stop me. Nothing can deter me from this determined feeling of elation at meeting at long last. Nothing.

For better or worse, to tonight.

Chapter 18

*U*nless this devil of a dress kills me first.

And, more specific, the way the hem of this dress makes my thighs bulge under the can lights.

In a banquet hall of several hundred people.

I pull at the unrelenting fabric of the "warrior blue" dress sliding up my thigh to unreasonable levels. Thirty minutes into a very stubborn dispute, Olivia eventually got her way on having me wear the horrible, cap-sleeved dress from her college graduation. I put up a fight, but the battle was lost after Mom and Dad, both marching in place on the living room rug in quaking pearl earrings and jostling necktie (supporting Olivia in getting some extra steps in before the banquet), took her side.

Mom shuffled her champagne-sequined handbag from one hand to another, looked at me, and said, "Honey, you look beautiful. And really, what's there to worry about? Nobody will be looking at you onstage anyway."

So here I stand, *not* in a flattering floor-length dress with one shoulder clipped by a beguiling gold feature, like my red one last year. Instead, I'm showcasing a knee-length, two-sizes-too-small spandex number from the nineties with cap sleeves and my rear end sticking out like two buns in a hot oven. My skin looks pale and sickly beneath the spotlight.

Olivia, on the other hand, holds the microphone with one incredibly toned arm, looking like a model straight out of a magazine.

My parents stand to my left, nodding enthusiastically with each of her words.

Ferris is to my right looking . . . well . . . looking quite green.

His eyes are glued on Olivia as she speaks, but instead of nodding at the parts of the speech where we've all been told to, he's just staring. Staring. And brooding. So intently there's a decent chance he doesn't even hear her.

Wow.

I've had my turn with first-time jitters up here, but he looks like he's about to lose it.

"*Anyone* can say they have a dream," Olivia says, sweeping one arm over the crowd. "People fill up their in-boxes and heads with dozens of goals and dreams. But you know what makes you different from most people?" Her hand, in a rather startling move, slams on the podium with each of her following words. "Actually. Doing. Something. About. It. That's where you are different. That's where all of you who've made the effort to come out tonight, to show you really mean business, shine. And we are in February, people. The year has just begun. So make this your year. Not only to reach your step goals and health goals but to start making real, tangible achievements in every area of your life. It all starts here. Just joining us tonight is step one of a *fantastic* journey."

A round of applause moves through the room, and my

mother, father, and I lift our hands in supportive clapping. There was actually a drill for clapping. Appropriately enthusiastic but not too attention grabbing.

Ferris doesn't clap.

At this point I break "protocol" and turn my head. "Ferris," I whisper.

He doesn't move.

"Ferris," I whisper again as the clapping starts to dim.

I nudge his side and he jolts as though forced out of a dream.

"You okay?" I mouth.

And his eyes, once they've locked on mine, don't move. His stare is fixed on me now.

I give him an overbright smile, baring all my teeth as if to say, *See? This is what we do when we have stage fright. We just look straight ahead and smile*, and then turn my attention back to Olivia.

But he's not doing it. He's not changing his position.

It's time for another group nod, and I give it my biggest and brightest.

And I'm just settling into another round of nodding and clapping when I feel a tug on my elbow. Ferris is holding on to my arm.

"I need to talk with you," he says.

My eyes widen. "Now?" I hiss. "We're a little busy."

"Now," he says, and he's not even whispering! He's just standing here onstage with loads of people watching us, holding on to my elbow and talking like we're in the middle of a coffee shop.

Olivia has even noticed, and halfway into her raise-arm-in-triumph paragraph, her eyes slide over to give us an incredulous *What-the-heck-are-you-two-doing?* glance.

I open my mouth, momentarily stranded between two bad options: turn my gaze toward Olivia and pretend Ferris is not trying to pull me off the stage or accept it and actually *walk* offstage in the middle of her speech.

Well, in light of the available choices, I take the one I'd rather be doing anyway. "C'mon," I whisper and shuffle with tiny sideways, penguin-like steps toward the velvety blue curtains at the back of the stage.

The second I'm out of the public eye, I turn around. Or maybe Ferris turns me around. I'm not quite sure which. Either way, I'm acutely aware of his hands now gripping my elbows.

"I've made a terrible mistake," he says, his words coming in a rush.

I raise my brow, although warning flares are starting to shoot off in the corner of my mind. "Ferris, if this is about your stage fright, don't worry. You can just take a stand about it—"

"It's not about stage fright. I *wish* this was about something as simple as stage fright." And suddenly he's letting go and pulling back, raking one hand desperately through his hair. He takes a pacing step one direction, then back.

He's in real distress. The flares in my mind are getting bigger and brighter. I haven't seen him this way since . . . well . . . since the last time he came back to me after we broke up in college.

Oh no.

No, no, no, no, no.

I cross my arms over my chest, the tight blue fabric stretching to its limit beneath my rib cage. He *can't* be doing this. He absolutely *can't*. It's not possible. I'm boring, average, underachieving Savannah, and he's already chosen Olivia.

Perfect, shiny, gorgeous, super-successful Olivia.

My *sister*.

Who's planning to marry him in two weeks.

"Ferris?" My voice is more high pitched than I intended. Brassy.

When he stops and looks at me, any shadow of a doubt is gone.

"I'm so sorry." His words are husky. Not in a sensual way, though. Not like last time when he came crawling back to my door. Back then, the come-hither tone was inescapable. I knew I was going to forgive him the second I opened the door and saw his sorrowful puppy dog eyes. The way he leaned against the doorway as if he owned it.

But tonight? Tonight he sounds like a man on the edge of a panic attack. "I don't know what happened," he says, shaking his head. "You and I—we had just had that stupid argument—I can't even remember what it was about—"

"Because we had them all the time," I say quietly.

"Yes." Ferris nods his head. "Yes. Yes, we did, didn't we? We were *passionate*."

It strikes me that he's saying it like it's a positive thing. That the frequent arguments we had were a sign of something good. But we weren't like those hot-blooded couples in the movies who yell and scream and throw plates and end up kissing passionately on top of broken pottery. No, as I remember, our arguments only made me feel cold, unheard, alone.

He's dragging his hands over his face now, as if truly on the edge of despair. "I don't know what to say to make it up to you."

He's mumbling more to himself than to me, I realize, like he's been trying to work this out for some time.

"Don't say anything," I say.

And suddenly he drops his hands from his eyes and looks me full in the face. He grabs my wrists and, in the strongest, most level voice I've ever heard from him, says, "Savannah, I don't deserve you."

"I'm not—" I begin.

"*Please,*" he continues. "Please, just hear me out. Please."

I give him one long look. Now that I notice, behind the fine tuxedo suit and the perfectly gelled hair, I see honey-brown eyes rimmed in red as though he hasn't slept in days. I see desperation. Genuine, heartfelt desperation. And it tugs at my heart.

"Somebody is going to see us," I whisper, starting to untwist my hands from his.

"Let them," he answers with an unwavering tone. "Let them. I don't care. I can't play these games anymore."

"*I* care." I tug my hands free. "You are marrying my sister in *two weeks.*"

"I can't." At this, his voice cracks, and his gaze veers off toward the curtain and Olivia beyond. "I can't marry her."

"But you are *so* perfect together," I remind him. "Like you always say, 'Cupid shot his arrow.'"

"No, Dolos shot his arrow and set me on the path to misery," he says, his voice hard. "Do you know what it's like to be with her? Do you have any *idea* what it's really like to be with her, Savannah?"

"I mean," I say, taken aback, "she can be a bit overbearing—"

"*Overbearing?*" Ferris laughs. "Overbearing was months ago. I dream about the days of overbearing. Now my life is nothing but logging what I eat, how many tasks I get accomplished before noon, how many steps I take. How many *steps* I take! Do you *know* the last time I had actual food in a restaurant? Do you know how long it's been since I've eaten *steak*? And the *wedding*!" He throws his arms up in the air. "On and on and on about the *stupid* wedding! Do you know how many *bakeries* I've been to in the past nine months?"

His voice is rising, taking on an I've-lost-my-mental-stability tone. People backstage are starting to look, and, to my surprise, he really doesn't seem to notice or care.

"Six?" I venture.

"*Thirty-two.* Thirty-*bloody*-two."

He's looking at the floor, but then his gaze shoots up as if he remembers where he's at and the aim of his message. "But *you*." He takes a step toward me. "You were a *treasure*. Letting you go, Savannah, was the biggest mistake of my life."

There's silence, and then he moves in closer, his voice lowering as his chin tips down toward me. "Let's get out of here. Now. We can go anywhere. Do anything. Shoot, we can fly all the way to Vegas right now and get married. Just please, *please* forgive me for what I've done. And I *promise* . . . I'll spend the rest of my life making it up to you."

I stare at him. Vaguely I hear the hum of activity beyond the curtain and the clinking of glasses. But mostly I'm looking into his eyes. His desperate, tired, eager eyes locked onto mine.

Ferris wants to leave Olivia.

Ferris is sorry for leaving me.

Ferris wants . . . to marry me.

Right now.

And my head feels like a ship full of various packages has exploded, and I'm trying to sort through the wreckage, discovering new and overwhelming emotions and memories at each turn.

But as I do so, one single point does come to mind. And it lingers.

In this moment, I'm getting everything I've dreamed of.

In one succinct moment, all the secret hopes and dreams I've held over the past year are happening all at once. Olivia is going to get her heart crushed, just as mine was. Olivia, for once, has been rejected, despite her perfectly sculpted jawline, despite her unrelenting tenacity, despite her Energizer Bunny lifestyle and row of neatly framed accomplishments. And I . . . *could* . . . be back with Ferris.

Marry . . . Ferris.

Finally get my own happily-ever-after.

How long have I dreamed, even in the quietest way, of marrying him? A third of my lifetime.

And yet.

More than anything else, the biggest thought in my head— the strangest part of it all—is the words of Will Pennington. Not Sam, my mystery editor. Will.

And the words he said while he looked into my eyes outside the courthouse: *"You deserve the same kind of happiness you wish to bestow on them."*

And he's right.

And that isn't Ferris. It was, for a long time, the dream of Ferris. The longed-for idea of what we *could* be. But it was never him. Never truly.

It's Will.

The follow-up thought strikes quickly: *But of course it is. How could you have ever thought otherwise?*

It has been him all along. For all that my mystery editor— Sam—has going for him, there's just something missing every time I meet him face-to-face that cannot be forced into being. No matter how I try, I can't force the spark to exist when it's not there. No matter how much it pains me to accept that fact.

I take a step back and, in doing so, see the question in Ferris's eyes.

He really did think I'd come back to him, didn't he? The thought makes the heat rise in my cheeks.

"I had no idea you felt this way, Ferris," I say, brushing my dress off as if I'm brushing off the conversation. "I'm sorry to hear this."

His eyes widen in disbelief. "Of course you did, Savvy. With all the coffees and the little chats. With all the flowers. You knew—"

"Yes, well, that's the problem, then, Ferris. It's a little hard to tell you're trying to hit on me when you're bringing both me and your fiancée coffees in the morning and flowers on behalf of the pair of you at night."

He stops. "They've never been from her. They've always been from me. Just me."

There's something in the way he says "they" that stops me. I pause. Raise a finger. "You sent me more than one bouquet?"

"Twice!" he exclaims. "Twice, just in the last month! I know it was a bit of a risk sneaking them into your room and office, but I had to do it." He rakes another wild hand through his hair. "I *had* to show you I care. That it's been driving me insane to be without you—"

I realize he's reaching for my hands again. And as though there's a slowly moving copperhead slithering my way, I jump back.

As I do, my eyes catch the sight of a particular shade of warrior blue behind him.

Olivia's face is horror stricken, her long, slender fingers at her lips. Her eyes shimmer, and despite it all, I feel my big-sisterly defenses rise.

"I'm sorry, Ferris," I say, my jaw flexing. "My sister is here, and I need to attend to her. I wish you luck wherever your slimy backside lands."

And without hesitating a moment longer, I move aside and reach for my sister, who has, at last, broken her six-year hiatus from crying and dissolved into tears.

Chapter 19

ou'd think it was impossible for someone to use so many four- and five-syllable words to say the same thing.

"Yes," I say, nodding as I come into the room. "He's horrible."

"Horrible doesn't cut it," Olivia says, rubbing a tissue fairly violently beneath her nose. "He's the most substandard, abominable, ignominious, *louche* man to ever walk this planet."

She shakes a tissued hand impatiently at me, and I hand her a pint of ice cream. Another one.

I stand in the doorway and check my phone. Eight thirteen p.m. For two hours I've been plying Olivia with tissues, ice cream, cheese, and boxes of oatmeal squares, dry. I think I've broken her. One encouraging comment about how she could use a little "break" from her diet and this happened. *This.*

But eight thirteen isn't so bad. If I can squeeze out now, I might just have enough time to meet Sam. If I hurry.

I take a step toward the hall. "I think I'll run to the store real quick. I can pick up some things for the morning. Would you like that, Olivia? Some of that nice yogurt you enjoy?"

Olivia scowls from her floor nest, her silky blue dress in a puddle around her feet. The back of the bodice is halfway unzipped. There's a litter of empty cartons around her feet. And the level of mascara that has run down her face and dried . . . Well, she looks like a cover for an eighties rock CD. For once in our lives, if we were in a lineup at a school dance, I'd be the one picked.

Well, I take that back. I suppose I can now say twice.

"What did I do wrong?" Olivia says, breaking off a block of cheese with her teeth. "How did it go wrong?"

I give a sympathetic shrug. "Sometimes we pick the wrong people, Olivia. We live and learn."

"No," she chokes out, swerving her raccoon eyes at me. "Really, Savvy. What did I do wrong? I don't want your empathy. I don't want frothy, girls'-sleepover-style answers. I want to know what I did. I want quantifiable *data*."

"Well, you can start with that," I retort a little tersely. "You can start with not being so snappy at everyone for everything. And you can *stop* calling me Savvy, because you know I don't like it."

"That's good," she says, reaching for the legal pad on her bedside table. And here she goes. Another list. She clicks a pen and starts writing. "Snappy. I can be less snappy."

Fine. Well, as long as we're on the subject . . .

"And less demanding," I add.

She nods in stride, as though we're talking about something as objective and impersonal as the latest stock-market numbers and not all her pitfalls. But it's an enjoyable experience, telling her all the ways she drives me crazy and having her, for once, take it all in. Like a flash sale where I decide to run in and grab everything I can, I throw out every issue with her I can think of while the doors are still open.

And sure enough, she studiously writes it all down.

And for several minutes, it feels like I'm experiencing that impossible moment when you wish on a loose eyelash and then blow it away, and your wish actually comes true.

But after about ten minutes, the euphoria starts to wear off. She looks so sincere and earnest, I can't help slowing down. I take a step toward her. Cautiously take the legal pad from her while she writes.

She looks up.

"Are you happy, Olivia?"

For a moment she gives me an incredulous look.

"I don't mean right now. I mean, in general. Are you happy?"

She looks around her room, looking to give it real thought.

"Because I don't know about you," I say, "but I've lived under your roof for a while now, and I've seen the cost of what success really is. It doesn't seem so bad at first. From a distance, when I lived with Lyla, all I heard about were your new promotions, your published papers, your marathons, nonprofit creations, and admissions into doctorate programs. But from up close, I see how hard you push yourself to do everything. Not just everything, but everything at *once*. Lunges while cooking for the elderly, while listening to audiobooks in French. Biking while wedding planning, while calling it a 'date.' Ferris couldn't live under that kind of pressure. And maybe you might consider slowing down and really asking yourself if *you* can either. If you can happily."

"Can I . . ." I can see Olivia's hand is itching for the legal pad, and no doubt by Monday morning, if I don't manage to really get this across to her, there'll be a stack of self-help books a ceiling high waiting for her beside her Peloton.

"You've tried to persuade me to take up your lifestyle for a while," I continue. "Why don't you let me persuade you to live mine for a little bit and see how it goes?"

Several moments pass in silence. As if the very idea is too stunning for words.

"So . . . if I tried living like *you*—"

"I'd watch that attitude," I interject.

"Then," she continues, shifting tone, "what would you recommend I do? Now?"

"I think you should finish your ice cream and then take a nice long nap," I say. "And on Monday morning, first thing, I think you should make an appointment for the Float Spot."

Two tubs of ice cream later, I've finally deposited Olivia into bed and dashed off for Pennington Pub. I'm late. Quite late.

But given the circumstances, it couldn't be helped.

And of course he will understand.

He'll have to.

Any mature adult would.

Or at least that's what I'm chanting to myself.

We're adults. Life comes up. Family is priority.

And anyway, I know he will understand.

Because we're adults. Life comes up. Family is . . .

On and on the broken record goes. As I dash up the creaky

front steps of Pennington Publishing in my heels, I fumble with my purse for my keys. The foyer is dark through the glass. No light on to be seen through the entire building.

But that's okay. That doesn't mean he's left.

I move to check my watch, then remember my wrist is naked after I convinced Olivia, in a momentous moment, to take off her watch. To lose track of time. And steps. And be free.

She insisted we do it together, then giggled nervously at me as though we were illegally going skinny dipping in the frozen lakes of Michigan. When it came off, she actually whooped.

I don't need to know the time anyway. All I need to do is get this door open.

After a bit more fumbling, the door opens, and I glide up the stairs by the light of my phone flashlight. With every set of steps my hope loses a bit more air. When I reach the ARC room, I push through the filing cabinet and into our secret room, and the air finally escapes entirely.

Nothing.

Not even a set of lights aglow.

All that's left is a note on top of the manuscript: Sorry I missed you.

And then I drop down onto the beanbag, feeling really crummy. Because he's not even going to put any of the blame on me here, but act as though he's the one who missed me.

I look around for a pen.

And start writing.

I'm so sorry I wasn't able to meet you for dinner. I tried my best, but there was a family crisis I had to attend to—a crisis that is eating all my ice cream in tears back at the apartment, in fact. And long story short, I have a sister who is no longer engaged and an ex-boyfriend who, in the most underhanded way imaginable, proposed to me instead. It's been a mess. But while it's a temptation to use my family situation as an excuse for my tardiness, I can't help but feel there was something else at play. And the fact is . . . I can't go on without letting you know the truth.

Tonight I realized I am interested in another man.

I'm so sorry. I have loved our friendship through the pages. I just wish the relationship we had on page was the same as we share face-to-face.

Anyway, what you've done for me here is so much more than I can ever express in words. I am so grateful to you and the time you've spent with me on this project. If you'd like, I'd love to remain friends. And if you are up for that, which I hope you are, dinner tomorrow is on me. I'm turning this manuscript in tomorrow. I'd love to celebrate with you.

Waiting with bated breath,

S.

There. I sit back and look at the note scrawled down the page. It's raw. And painful. And it hurts me just to read it.

But it must be said.

Because in the events of tonight, I've learned something. Something about myself. About what I really need to remember in this life.

It turns out, racking up accomplishments doesn't mean anything. Life is not simply some game where the person with the most plaques wins. It's not about a perfectly organized home or acquiring degrees you'll never use or the number of inches around your waistline or, most especially, counting steps. Life is about movement, and pause. Work, and rest. It's about relationship. About valuing others and truly taking the time to show them they are precious. About valuing yourself, too, and your uniquely given, whispered-into-your-DNA goals and dreams.

Life is about making drippy pancakes on a Saturday morning, and leaving the dishes in the sink to sit down with Lyla at the kitchen table and talk about her new agent. It's about making a bath and spending so much time reading in it that the water gets cold and my fingers go pruny. Yes, there should be fundraisers and shoebox drives and hard work, too, but it's also about slowing down. Truly being present.

It's about appreciating the miraculous gift that is *existence*. It's about loving on others as much as you can. And yes, it is also about appreciating what organically makes you happy and, where reasonable, finding it.

Which is why, tonight, I had to write to Sam.

Because I realized what would make me happy.

I want another dart game with Will.

I want to sit in his truck and drive through town, talking about our past.

I want to run through a tunnel of people with flying rice and fat snowflakes, holding hands.

And unlike people like Ferris, I can't go on dancing with other partners while really only wanting the real thing.

Chapter 20

*M*essage Sent.

Just two little words, and how the earth quakes beneath my feet.

Message. Sent.

I stare at the words in the bubble in my in-box and for a long moment sit in silence.

My manuscript is now in the in-box of Claire Donovan. My hopes entirely in her hands. It all comes down to this.

I suck in a deep breath and look around the room. Something feels different about the space. The same late-afternoon sunshine makes the floating dust specks glitter; the books all around still hold their musty, leathery smell. But the air is cooler, and the February chill rattles at the sparrow glass in a solitary way unlike before.

It's funny. When all this first started, I was angry at discovering someone else was using my haven. I treasured the privacy of my little cove. I treasured the solitude and the time I had it all to myself.

Now, I can't help feeling alone. Like I'm on my own in a chilled room in a musty old attic space where the strands of lights wait cold and lightless.

For three days I've kept the lights off, waiting to see a sign of his return. Holding off on sending this final email in hopes that I could do it after we've had that talk.

But so far, nothing. No coffee brewing. No lights glowing. No candlewick flickering and the scent of gardenias filling up the room.

No notes.

Nothing.

And while I wouldn't take back what I said, every run-in with Sam in the flesh only confirming our lack of chemistry, I can't help but wish he would write to me here. Again. If not for a relationship, at least as a friend.

Worst of all, it pains me to think he could've felt I took advantage of him.

That's the hardest thought of all.

That I just took all his time and energy for my own gain. That I let eager conversation fill up the margins. And the moment the manuscript was done I left him waiting up here, alone. I never intended that. Never in a million years. And everything within me wants to make sure he knows.

It hasn't been easy, though, to get the message across. Sam has avoided me like the plague these past three days. And while I'm trying to respect his wishes, I can't help but feel like it would be best for the both of us to clear this up. I won't keep it long. I won't overstep. But he needs to get a proper thank-you from me.

And as for the manuscript itself, I never did get that final kiss right.

I read through a dozen classic scenes, watched four iconic eighties rom-coms, and read a dozen articles on the topic. And still the words fell a little flat. Better. But still . . . flat.

And I wasn't about to ask him to help me.

Anyway, I think, snapping my laptop shut and standing, *what's done is done.* It may not be the best kissing scene in the world, but the story as a whole is truly the best I could give. Kisses can be edited in the end if it's acquired.

All I can do now is wait for her answer.

⌣

"You're wanting . . . to include a photograph of your son . . . riding a go-cart . . . on the cover of this book."

Even as I walk into the office I can hear the slow, long intake of breath through Lyla's nostrils. When I look, her eyes are screwed up so far toward the ceiling her false lashes are brushing against her newly waxed brows.

"Dr. Shaw. Sweetie."

My antenna rises as I hear Dr. Shaw's name. *My* author, Dr. Annabelle Shaw, revered professor of anthropology, to whom I sent the cover for her new release, *Extraterrestrial: How Theories of Life Beyond Earth Have Affected Culture.* (And yes, after editing her book, I do look up at the sky a little more warily these days. And I do sometimes get a little nervous as I brush my teeth while looking back at myself, and the shower curtain behind me, in the mirror.)

The point here is Lyla is talking. To my author. On my phone.

Lyla pinches the crown of her nose with her eyes closed. "As adorable as your son is in your family albums, this isn't the vibe we're going for with your book." There's a pause. There's silence as she listens. Then Lyla opens her eyes. "Because it's a book about extraterrestrial theories through culture and history. Now, unless you want to inform me that your son is actually an *alien*, I don't know how slapping a picture of your son across the cover applies—"

I scold Lyla with my eyes and hold my hand out for my phone.

She sees me and swivels in her chair toward her computer. "And I understand that you are a respected anthropologist in the field. But I know *my* market."

I step forward and swivel her back toward me. She digs her heels in on the floor so the chair won't budge.

"And I understand that your son is also a human being. But what I think you don't understand here is that while *you* may think your son has the most endearing smile, nobody else in the world cares. *Nobody*—and I cannot emphasize this enough—is going to buy this book because a random eight-year-old with a cheeky smile is sitting inside his *Christmas present* on the front cover. And can I be frank?"

"*Lyla!*" I hiss and yank at the chair. Grab the long, twisting cord connecting the base of my office landline to the phone clasped tightly to her ear.

Her brow wrinkles as she hears some clearly distasteful words on the other line. "No, I'm *not* saying that because I'm reacting to a male-centric society and hoarding anti-Y-chromosome thoughts. I'm saying it because *this book is about extraterrestrial theory in culture and your son has nothing to do with it!*"

Her voice has risen now, so much so that Marge and Rob in the office directly opposite have looked up from their computers.

And with no other options, I lunge for the phone.

She clings to it as tightly as a mother protecting her young. *"Stop,"* she whispers sharply, holding it to her chest. "She has to *know!"*

"That you're bat crazy?" I shoot back, trying my best to yank it from her chest.

"This woman wants to put her family members on the cover like some *family album!*" she barks.

I put my elbow into it and, centering squarely on her rib cage, leverage myself with another yank. Just as I do so, I register her glance above my head and feel her fingers releasing the phone. It's like slow motion: her long, pink nails letting go, the phone pulled into my stomach by my own strength, and then the force of my momentum throwing me back.

Back, back, back, until I become fully aware that my feet are unable to catch up with my body and the only place I'm headed is to the floor.

With a *thump.*

Followed shortly by the *thump* of the phone being yanked off the desk, the line itself ripped from the wall.

For a moment I sit there, wondering about internal injuries. When nothing but a painful throb begins on my backside, I move to stand. As I do, I register the shoes beside me.

Will's shoes. Will Pennington's black, shiny, emotionless oxfords.

And my reaction is a confusing mix of elation and fear.

Professionally: fear.

But on a personal level . . . Well, obviously this isn't the most attractive way to see him after three days, but the point is he's back. Back from another trip to NYC.

I rush to my feet, the phone still clutched to my chest. "Will.

Hi." My voice comes out a thousand times more breathless and wanting than I intended. *Pull it together*.

But, a bit to my surprise, the grin—and the glance my direction, for that matter—is such a short flicker, it hardly counts. His eyes move back to Lyla, who, with her dramatic red lips open to reveal an *Oops* smile, looks as guilty as ever. "My office," he says, pointing down the hall. "Now."

I open my mouth. "It's good to see you again," I say, butting myself into the conversation as Lyla stands. "I was, um, thinking through some more ideas for staff while you were gone. I'd love to talk them over with you and get your opinion—"

"I can't right now, Savannah."

"But I was just thinking—"

He stops me. And, for the first time, really looks me in the eye. "Please. Later."

I pause, my brow creasing. His eyes are grave, serious, as though he's doing me a favor by taking the briefest moment out of his busy day to cut my advances off then and there.

He keeps his eyes on me until he seems sure he's gotten his point across and then turns his attention back to Lyla. As they turn to go, he calls over his shoulder. "Email me your ideas. When things clear up, I'll read them."

Email him.

Later.

Don't meet him. Don't sit in his office or drive around town on his business errands or chat while playing darts in some saloon.

Just wait, like I'm nothing more to him than his employee.

Which, I suppose, is exactly what I am.

And he couldn't have made it clearer that that's all he wants.

Chapter 21

Every hour of the last two weeks has crept by like a creaky carousel on its last legs.

When I was under a month-long writing deadline, the days flew by, terrorizing me. Now every minute crawls by, also terrorizing me.

"You know, you're acting kind of crazy," Olivia says as I hit the Refresh button on my email for the 4,586,345th time of the day.

To her credit, she's sitting on the couch, having discovered something I introduced her to three days prior: popcorn covered in chocolate chips. And she's enjoying herself.

The result of the microwave popcorn and thorough dousing of chocolate chips is a sticky, melty chocolatey mess—a fact that normally would have led to a half-hour lecture about salt, sugar, and the importance of eating at the kitchen table. But here she is, in actual pajama pants at ten in the morning, eating popcorn on the couch.

Honestly, I have never been prouder.

"And that's coming from *me*," she adds, giving me a little eyebrow wiggle before popping another piece of popcorn into her mouth.

Two nights ago, after she caught me checking my email every other minute, I finally let her in on my little secret. Told her the truth about how I've secretly longed to establish myself in the book world, not just as an editor but as an author. And to my surprise, she didn't balk at it. Not even when I told her my chosen genre.

"I've always secretly wanted to go into fitness," she said when I told her, digging her way through a bowl of popcorn in her yoga pants.

"Fitness?" I exclaimed. "Like . . . as a job?"

She looked at me and shrugged. "I know it's not the most *unique* idea out there, or profitable, but I love working out. I love everything about it, really. The smell of a newly unrolled mat. The look of those large glass doors I walk through when I enter the gym. The sweat rolling down my arms as I push to new limits. I love it. I've always wondered what it would be like to own my own."

I stared at her. It was the first time in my life she had ever said anything, *anything*, about *anything* outside finance, and yet . . . it made sense. In fact, as soon as she said it, I couldn't imagine her doing anything else.

"You should do it. You should own a gym."

She gave an incredulous laugh. "Yeah, right. Why work on two degrees when you could be working on two degrees while opening your own business? You sound like me."

"No. I mean, drop out of school. You've only got so many

hours in this life. You may as well spend them doing something you're passionate about."

She raised a brow. "You're stealing from my speech now."

I grinned. "I've heard them so much, the words just pop out of my mouth sometimes. I'm like a walking motivational poster."

"Yeah? Then here's another one that you should consider," she said and glanced at the phone in my hand. "Waiting impatiently for something that will inevitably happen either way is a waste of time. Enjoy the journey, not just the destination."

And begrudgingly I put my phone away that evening and sat beside her for the movie.

It was a movie we'd seen several times before but that, as I could hear it for once without the Peloton whizzing in the background and the distraction of captions in French, felt like the first time.

But the fact is now, despite all the positive messages about enjoying and living for each moment, I can't escape the reality that it has been fourteen days with no email from Claire.

Fourteen.

And regardless of how much better off I'd be embracing the mild Saturday morning without checking the screen, the fact is I *need* to know.

I *need* to see what she thinks the second the email arrives.

I *need* to finally have this torturous waiting end.

One way or another, even, I *need* to—

I stop.

Because there, as if willed into existence by my longing, the new email blips onto the screen.

A little heart-stopping *ding* goes off.

A little number *1* pops up beside the word *In-box*.

1.

1 new email.

From Claire Donovan.

Even Olivia has heard the *ding* and noticed, probably by my petrified face, something is up. "Is it her?" she says.

I can't say anything. I just nod.

My arms feel all prickly.

And I just stare at the bold subject line: **RE: Manuscript**.

This is it.

In regard to my manuscript. From Claire.

"Well?" Olivia says.

My finger hovers over the mouse, but it has trouble clicking.

Because all of a sudden I am acutely aware that I'm standing on the precipice of knowing and not knowing.

And really, the not-knowing land was not such an imposing land to live in after all, when you think of it. In not-knowing land there was still hope. There was still a chance that things would work out for me. In knowing land, though—if I step into the Land of the Know—I'm going to know without question. And if the answer isn't what I want, I can't strap hope back onto my back for safekeeping. No, hope is for those who stay in the Land of the Not Know.

Vaguely, I realize Olivia is now hovering over my shoulder.

"It's going to be okay either way, Sav," I hear her say quietly and feel a squeeze on my shoulders. "C'mon."

I press my lips together. "You know, I do often tell authors that the longer it takes for me to reply, the better the odds are in their favor. It takes me a second to send a rejection when I know something won't work. But working through a manuscript with real potential . . . There's a lot to it. It takes a lot of time."

Olivia nods encouragingly. "And she's already said how much potential your book has," she adds. "Way before you made those revisions."

I nod, slowly garnering courage to press the button. "That's true."

"I read some myself. It hooked me from the start."

"Mmm," I murmur, although I can't help being aware of the fact that if that were entirely true, she'd have finished it two days ago when I gave it to her.

"I'm all the way to page 86!" she exclaims as though that really says something.

And to be fair, she's never been a big reader. At least, not of material that talks about anything *fun*. In her world, that probably really does mean something.

"C'mon," she urges and lifts her face into a grin. "I'll take you out to celebrate tonight. Just for opening it. Either way."

The excitement in her eyes is the penny that tips the scales, and with a final nod, I turn to face the computer. And click.

From: Claire Donovan
Received: 10:03 AM
To: Savannah Cade
Subject: RE: Manuscript

Dear Savannah,

It is with deep regret that I must tell you that Baird Books will not be moving forward with your manuscript. Although I was greatly impressed by the final product you sent, my own opinion seems to vary from the team as a whole, and I have been unsuccessful in my efforts to sway them. These are hard days, as I'm sure you know. The competition is quite fierce. Nevertheless, I have no doubt you will find a wonderful home for your story. You truly do have much to be proud of.

Best wishes,
Claire Donovan
Chief Editor, Romance
Baird Books Publishing

For a long minute, neither of us speak.

I read the email again. And again. Quite solemn. Quite still.

My book is rejected.

My dream . . . crushed.

After my fourth reread, I realize Olivia is no longer standing behind me but is in the corner of the living room, a phone pressed to her ear.

"Yes, I'd like to order for delivery, please. What are your specials?" She pauses, listening. "Yes, that'll be fine. Bring it all. Yes. All of it . . . All."

Chapter 22

The next week goes by in a blur.

I try to be positive. I try to hold tight to the words Olivia has bestowed on me through at least a dozen randomly placed Post-It notes and, if I let her, long monologues over breakfast. I try to remember that there are "other fish in the sea" and that "Baird Books isn't the only publisher out there" and "Isn't it just good to know *she* loved it? Isn't that just a great new step worth appreciating in this journey?" But at the end of it all there still lies the fact of the matter: my dream publisher turned me down. And I have no contract. And no potential contract in sight.

Because that's what was also so amazing in it all.

I don't have a literary agent. I haven't spent years drafting proposals and querying agents and building up a competitive social platform. I don't have thousands of people on my news-letter list, itching to hear from me every week and to buy my book the instant it's out. I have nothing. *Nothing.*

Except a manuscript.

And nobody is going to want me like I am now.

Baird Books was the golden-ticket moment because I met Claire in person, an opportunity that barely ever happens. Aspiring authors pay thousands of dollars for a fifteen-minute pitch session with an editor at a writers' conference, and I—fortunate of fortunates—had been given an hour.

And she liked me. And the hook of my story. And was just powerful enough to potentially take on my project without all that other stuff, because she was with Baird Books. They could make anything sell, even hermit authors with no social media accounts and no previously known name.

But me? Savannah Cade, now having to take a long, hard look at what it will really take to get my manuscript in front of reputable literary agents and editors and have anyone take me seriously? It'll take years. If not decades.

Even so, I'm trying to swallow the idea bit by bit. Like Olivia keeps telling me, "How do you eat an elephant? One spoonful at a time."

I hate the imagery. I've always hated the imagery. But the point is true. And at the end of the day, I do feel joy in the writing.

Writing is what makes me happy. Writing, even, is how I feel I contribute to the world. Reminding people of what's important. Letting them escape the harsh parts of life, even if just for a few hours. Helping them feel happiness through watching happily-ever-afters unfold. Remembering truths. Recalling their self-worth. Loving others. Living well. Learning.

I want to do that.

So, I will press on. Even if the road ahead is harsh and the journey long, I will keep on.

Seeing the clock strike noon, I push away from my desk. As

I slip my laptop into my computer bag, another Post-It note slips out and I bend to retrieve it.

It's a doodle of a stick figure, smiling while holding a spoon next to a half-eaten elephant.

It's disturbing, particularly as the stick figure seems so happy about it.

I grin.

"Wanna come grab some Thai with me?" Lyla says, moving for the door. "I'm meeting with Ryan. You could join us."

When I look up I see the genuine concern in her eyes.

"No, that's okay," I say, smiling slightly at the Post-It before giving it a spot next to the growing collection on my desk. "Best he doesn't remember me and you have to explain yourself," I say, imagining her manager seeing me stroll up with her to the table.

"Oh, he'd just turn it into some compliment about my ingenuity or other," she says, waving a hand at the thought. "And besides, he's bound to run into you with me sometime."

"How about when you're officially on tour." Because to be honest, the moment she signed with Ryan, things have started to happen pretty quickly. She's already had four bookings. Locally, but still. Four. With real money. And lunches with bubble tea on him. "Then we can reveal the big surprise."

"Fine," she says, clearly grinning at the idea of being on tour. "But I'm coming back with eggrolls."

Picking up my half-drunk, lukewarm coffee in the green mug, I move toward the hall, laptop bag over my shoulder. I no longer expect Sam to show up in the ARC room's hidden chamber. He's avoided me so far; I've come to realize nothing is going to change.

I shuffle down the hallway, giving friendly smiles to everybody heading off in separate directions for lunch as I do.

Will's office at the end of the hall is open, a rare sight. He's been gone a lot the past two weeks, more often than usual, always leaving with no warning and no information about his return. Sending emails to everyone just as much as he would in office, keeping us all on our toes. Maybe that's just how it's going to be with him. He's going to be out of the office, corresponding through clipped emails forever.

My foot hesitates at the bottom step, and I brave a glance through his door.

He's typing away at his computer, his eyes focused and intense as he stares at the computer through his rectangular glasses. And for a moment I feel that twinge of lost hope and longing.

But then his eyes flicker, and he spots me.

And for one long moment, as people pass by, our eyes lock on each other.

A ghost of a smile passes my lips.

Sure enough, he looks like he's about to stand, to come over. His phone rings. He ignores it, and for a wonderful second I feel my hopes rise. But then his eyes dart to the number. And, with an exhale and an apologetically bleak smile my way, he turns and takes the call.

I hesitate a moment longer, but as his words string on and on without any hint of ending, I move up the stairs.

And while I would normally let that thought linger through the day, I can't help noticing, as my feet pad past bookshelves among bookshelves, the little glow at the end of the room. For the first time the filing cabinet is wide open, revealing the little cove inside.

Hurrying, protectively even, I step into the room, my thoughts pressing me on.

Did someone else discover it?

Why is it unprotected?

But as I quickly assess the empty room and shut the door behind me and feel my pulse start to slow, I notice the note in the center of the floor. I move to the rug, pick up the piece of paper. All it says is: Did you get an offer on the manuscript?

I flip it over, but nothing.

Hastily, I scribble an answer. *No. They turned it down. But even so, I can't tell you how much your help has meant to me. Thank you again. Truly. And... welcome back.*

For half a minute I think about leaving more, writing more, asking how he's feeling about everything and trying to open up the conversation again. But then I still myself. Remind myself of the first rule he made: stick to the point.

And so I do.

I hope my response is emotionless enough, and as far away from the topic of our relationship enough, to beg him farther into the start of a new conversation. Though where this conversation would go, I don't know. But does it matter? Not really. I'm just glad he's back.

Even the room looks glad he's back.

There's a pot of brewed coffee in the corner, full of sweet, dark caffeine, and I refill my mug. Take a sip. Grab the lighter and light the candle.

Stand back and admire its glow.

Not everything is right right now.

In fact, a lot is wrong.

But even so, I can't help but feel a little glow as I sit on my beanbag and get to work on the long, long trek that has only begun of writing my own book proposal. All the while, the room glows around me.

And in that moment, I pause to look around, appreciating the journey.

Chapter 23

A s it turns out, everyone—me included—in the publishing industry is evil.

I open yet another automated rejection email from the twelfth literary agent this week, and with everything I have left resist banging my head on the table.

Do these people *realize* how much work goes into a proposal? Much less a manuscript? Honestly, I think of all the times I've flippantly written rejection letters to hopeful writers and their respective agents, and I cringe.

I'm horrible. A horrible, horrible person, and I never even knew it.

Forget about the manuscript. Just the amount of time it takes to figure out how to make a website, get a website host, find and buy a domain name, create a newsletter mailing list, create a newsletter mailing-list template, and figure out how to "create a brand" when you don't yet have anything to sell . . . It's enough to make your brain explode. I'm halfway into the "Become an Influencer in Thirty Days!" class led by some peppy seventeen-year-old girl who wears a lot of shiny pink lipstick and talks excessively with her hands, and I'm still lost.

And the question running through my mind in all of this is, How on *earth* am I supposed to be able to manage a website, run a bimonthly newsletter, talk daily on Instagram, Facebook, TikTok, YouTube, and Twitter, and still have time to actually write books? What are these insane expectations?

I blame it on those rejection letters.

Now, mind you, 99 percent of the rejections are just automated emails. But the rare ones, the ones where the agent has actually taken the time to leave a sentence or two as to *why* you are being rejected . . . Well, those say the same thing. *Nice story here but need to have a more stable social platform for consideration.*

So, I took the advice and tried a few things.

But for goodness' sake, it's like getting a college degree just to figure out how to get *anyone* to follow you on social media. For two weeks I've given it all I've got, and so far I have one homemade-looking website with broken links, one Twitter account with zero posts because I always get lost on the home page, and thirty-two followers on my Instagram page. And for the record, before all of this I had thirty-four. I have actually lost two family members in the process.

And worse, it's been radio silence in the ARC room. That brief spot of brightness from his presence—gone.

So, I've forged on alone. Working late into the evenings, taking breaks during lunch to try to figure out some other mind-numbing technological skill for which I'm ill equipped but that I'm apparently supposed to have to be an author in the current industry.

I don't see Will much. As is usual now, he's gone half the

time, and when he's back he always seems busy, mysterious conversations going on behind his closed door. Sometimes on the
phone. Sometimes when the accountant steps in. Sometimes—
and that's when things get loud—with his mother.

I yearn to see him, to talk to him, but whatever glimpse of
hope I had back on the staircase was a blip, and he's no more
interested in making something happen with me than Sam is in
patching things up.

Seems I was quite off with both of my interpretations of the
situation that day.

Still, I have Olivia back, in a new way I haven't felt since we
were girls. She even went out of her way to drag me to our parents' house the previous week, all but holding the antithetical
version of an intervention to declare she was very, *very* sorry for
all the ways she hurt me the past few years—particularly with
Ferris—and all but insisting Mom and Dad apologize too. It
was domineering, in her usual way. But also . . . touching. Sweet.

So I have her and a positive lifestyle shift with my family.
And Lyla.

And they all have been a balm to my soul these days.

I have much to be thankful for.

I see the time and click out of my in-box.

"Ready to go?" I say, standing from my chair.

Lyla, deep inside that genius mind of hers, is drawing a line
on a new design she's working on. She's working so intently she
doesn't seem to hear me.

I step toward her. Tap her on the shoulder.

She jolts. Lifts her head. Pulls the earbud out of her ear.

"Time for the meeting," I say.

"Can't," she chirps. "I'm still on probation."

Evidently after Lyla had it out with Dr. Shaw, Will put her on "probation" for the foreseeable future from all meetings, all phone calls, and all emails with any human being at all. She's basically in work jail, spending her nine-to-five time designing with zero communication with human beings (aside from myself and Will, who is evidently acting as her email liaison), and I've never seen her happier.

"Oh, right. Okay . . . then. I'm off," I say and move for the door.

"Have fun," she replies vaguely, her eyes back on her computer.

I move down the stairs. This isn't an ordinary meeting. Ms. Pennington's assistant, Brittney, sent out the memo just yesterday, informing everyone of an all-staff meeting the following morning. All appointments were expected to be canceled. Any traveling plans for the day to be put on hold. Whatever announcement to come must be important, and everyone (barring probation-Lyla happily sketching away upstairs) is expected to be there.

I walk into the Magnolia Room and faintly recall, as I take my place in the back, how I stood here the day Will was first introduced to the company. How I tripped on this very carpet, and Will picked up my manuscript page. Handed it back without a word.

I thought he was terribly intimidating that day, the first time I stood up and discovered myself staring into the chest of the man who was to be my boss. Daunting with his intense, icicle-blue eyes. His perfectly tailored suit.

But now . . .

Will Pennington takes the podium, looking exactly as he did that first day. Tailored suit. Intense expression. All hints of cheerfulness far, far away.

The room stills as he looks around at the staff members gathered within.

"Thank you, everyone, for meeting on such short notice. My mother"—he gives the briefest nod to Ms. Pennington, who sits upright in the front row, her legs tightly crossed at the ankles and a begrudgingly approving smile on her lips—"and I have called you here today to discuss the situation with Pennington Publishing and its future."

A ripple of murmurs passes through the room, no doubt led by fear.

"It is no secret that the publishing industry everywhere has been impacted by the recent economic struggle, and smaller houses like ours have been hit even more so. But while Pennington has tightened its budget and even its staff over the course of the last year, it still hasn't been enough." Will looks down at his paper and continues reading. "By my forecasts, along with those of both our in-house accountants and legal expertise on the out-side, Pennington Publishing, if continuing in the manner it has been this past year, will go under within three months."

This time the murmuring grows into a wave of worried con-versation, so much so that Will puts his hands out to try to calm everybody down. "Please."

He looks around the room, waiting until it's so quiet a single droplet of rain could land on the roof and still be heard.

"When I left Sterling a few months ago, I didn't come on a fool's errand. I came because I believe in this company. I believe in its goals. I believe in its people. And I came with a plan."

Will *left*?

Will wasn't let go?

"A plan, and a new venture for the company, that will not

only allow Pennington to keep its roots as the place to look to for quality literary fiction and nonfiction but allow every single employee here today to not only stay but hopefully thrive. As of April 1, Pennington Publishing will be sold to Archer."

"*Archer?*" Even I can't help muttering in shock. But Archer is . . .

"Yes," he says, nodding as the volume in the room goes up once again. "Archer is a company specializing in commercial fiction. And there will certainly be some adjustments. Some of you will be afforded the opportunity to turn your specialties to more commercial works, like westerns, cozy mysteries, and romance. Others—particularly those of you who are passionate about your chosen fields and possess the greatest experience—will stick to your current expertise. For many of you, though, this will mean a genre shift."

He lets that settle in, and a bit to my surprise, not too many people are scowling at the idea. In fact . . . quite a few faces are brightening up. There's even some elbow rubbing with neighbors. Is even *Yossi* grinning?

"So . . . we'll have to build a whole new directory of places to push our press releases?" Marge raises her voice and asks.

Will nods. "For those of you in publicity who are switching fields, yes. You'll have to build a whole new set of relationships."

"And if we move over," Tawnya chimes in, "we'll be editing completely new fiction. Works from people like Debbie Macomber. Francine Rivers."

"Yes. If you are called to move over, yes."

And to my surprise, Tawnya breaks out into a huge grin, almost as if she's won the lottery.

Will observes her. "Does this make you . . . happy, Tawnya?"

"Does it?" she says and pulls three small, thick paperbacks

from her bag, lovestruck couples on each cover of peppy blues and pinks and greens.

And for the first time—in a long time, really—I see Will crack a smile. For the first time, his shoulders start to ease. "I'm glad to hear that. And I'd like to thank you for that nice segue into my next point. In addition to these changes, the ArcherPennington division here will be starting a second brand-new line of commercial fiction. A line devoted to publishing sweet, uplifting romances. It's going to be called Archer Heart."

My heart almost stops.

A new line. A . . . romance line.

"I've been working with your CEO and my mother for some time regarding its development. And while my mother, as many of you know, may have some quibbles with entertainment fiction as a whole, she has come to see the value in stories that are enjoyable for the masses to read but also offer some of the fundamental messages our literary greats have shared in their own time. Messages of unity. Of overcoming evil with good. Of love conquering all. And I can think of no one better to represent this line as an example of what the world at large can expect from Archer Heart . . . than an author I've been privileged to know for some time. Holly Ray."

Now my heart really does stop.

I grab the chair in front of me for support.

"Holly Ray? Have you heard of her?" I hear from someone across the room.

"Oh yes, I read her for a book club. Quite good," says another.

"Ohhhh. *Holly Rayyyy*," whispers another, as though she just mentioned someone who's been a favorite of hers for decades.

Will catches my eye then. There's an unmistakable upturn

of his lips peeking from his professional posture as he continues, holding the paper, shifting his gaze back to the audience.

"I have read and vetted this manuscript personally, and after multiple discussions with friends and colleagues in the mass markets, I sent the novel to Maggie Samson"—he pauses to give a nod her way—"who will be heading up the Archer Heart imprint. In short, she loved it." He pauses again, and his grin grows. "And I am pleased to announce on her behalf that she and her team intend to pull together a competitive contract offer for a three-book deal. Now all we need to hope is that Holly takes it."

An appreciative chuckle moves around the room.

Meanwhile I can't breathe. Can't move.

Will at last sets down the paper in his hand. Puts his speech aside as he addresses the room. "So, expect things to start shuffling around pretty soon. It'll be a bear working out our new positions. And I have no doubt there will be tensions at times. But overall, my mother and I are very pleased with this decision and hope you are as well." And then, with an unsolicited smile my way, he raises his green coffee mug in the air. "To ArcherPennington and a promising future."

And while the meeting moves on to other, more logistical matters, I can't hear any of it. Because the world around me has quaked so heavily whole columns that were holding up my previous beliefs have crumbled, leaving me unable to do anything but stare at the crushed pieces at my feet. My mystery editor wasn't Sam. It was never Sam.

It was Will. All those notes, all those messages, were for him. From him.

It's been him all along.

The energy in the air crackles as the meeting comes to an

end. People all around are talking excitedly to one another, a buzz of questions including, "Who is going to take over each division, then?" And "Does that mean we get to pick which genre we'd like to specialize in?" And even "He's not going to make me read thrillers, is he? Because I won't, Gertrude. I won't."

As for me, I may as well have my shoes nailed to the carpet, because I don't think I can walk.

Nearly everyone has trickled out by the time Will reaches me.

My head is whirring, my brain still trying to compute everything that has just happened and been confirmed, and failing.

As he walks up to me, his steps are wary. He's grinning, but despite that, there's some uncertainty in his eyes.

"Let me get this straight," I say as he stops in front of me. "You're offering me a contract."

He shakes his head. "I am not offering you a contract. Maggie is offering you a contract."

"Yes, right. Maggie." I nod, then give about six extra nods to myself while glancing Maggie's way. "Does she know it's me?"

Again he shakes his head. "I'll leave that up to your discretion."

"Sure." I nod again, letting this settle in. So Maggie chose my manuscript. Not because we shared a yogurt in the breakroom one time. Not because I purposefully went with pumpkin syrup in my coffee once because I knew she wanted the last of the vanilla. Not out of workplace-sister solidarity. But because she liked my book. *She liked my book.*

And then, because I am apparently incapable of letting a good thing lie, a little rain-cloud thought forms, and I narrow my eyes. "So basically you handed her the manuscript, and she liked it because she had to. You're her boss."

At this he chuckles, almost as though he expected as much

from me. "Actually, Savannah, I purposefully sent her a dozen proposals. Particularly for that reason. She chose yours."

I can't help it. The idea that she actually chose mine over others is elating, and I can't help grinning. "And where, exactly, did you get a dozen proposals?"

"Why, from Claire Donovan," he replies. "An old friend. Of course."

When I stare at him, he continues. "I wasn't making it up when I said in that meeting that Claire is a friend, and one whom I intended to meet with before her retirement. I did get that meeting to discuss a potential project—which, as you know, was this one—and she happily offered up several rejected proposals she thought had promise but that she'd been unable, for one reason or another, to take on."

"And of the stack of proposals . . ."

"Maggie decided to pursue three, yours being the most promising."

And here his temples crinkle with his smile as he watches my bewildered face, and his voice softens. "Which isn't surprising. Because I meant it when I said your story is a good one. And that it deserves to be heard."

"Even though . . ." I can't help pressing the point. I can't help wanting to be absolutely sure he realizes what he's saying. "It was turned down by Baird Books."

"Their loss," he parries, undeterred in the slightest. "Savannah, I have had a decade at Sterling in the book business. Beyond that, I was quite literally born into this book business. I know the industry. And I know that if you let us give your book a chance, we can sell it to the world."

If I let him. *If.* He has to know there's no question. Doesn't he?

"I must tell you, I'm really awful at TikTok," I say after a lengthy pause. "I've been at it two weeks and have five followers. And I'm not sure any of them are real people."

He's pressing his lips together, trying to smother his smile. "I think we will be able to succeed despite that setback."

"And I created a newsletter. But right now the only subscribers are my sister and parents."

"I'm sure you have terrific open-and-click rates, then," he responds. "And for that matter, I'll let you go ahead and subscribe me to that list."

He's serious.

He truly believes in my book, despite all those other things. There is truly a contract on the table.

And for a long second I can't think of anything else to say. All I can do is try my best to gather up the threads of this conversation in a big heap in my arms and hold tight to them as the tangle they are until I can slip away and take the time to unravel it all. And take a snapshot in my mind of this moment. So I can remember everything about the way he's looking at me now.

His crinkly smile lessens, and his expression shifts as the banter falls away. "I want you to know that none of this is because of my feelings for you. You truly have written a wonderful book, and despite how things have shaped up for us personally, on a professional level I have nothing but respect and admiration for your teachable spirit and creative ideas. I really do believe that under Maggie's expertise you can succeed here, and—"

I lift a hand. "I'm sorry. I think we need to back up to a critical piece of this puzzle."

And just then I see Brittney come up behind Will and tap

his shoulder. Sam is standing by her side, looking anxious and uncomfortable.

Will turns.

"May I have that back, please?" she says, looking pointedly at the mug in Will's hand. "It has sentimental value."

"It's fine, Brittney," Sam says, chuckling uncertainly. "They just want to borrow them."

"Sam. For the fifteenth time, it isn't borrowing if someone takes it without asking and keeps it for weeks on end." She turns her gaze back on us with a sweet smile.

I'll admit, I don't think I've ever heard Brittney talk out loud since she joined the company as Ms. Pennington's personal assistant. All I've seen her do is run after Ms. Pennington, scribbling furiously with her pen and pad. It's funny. Her voice doesn't sound anything like I would've imagined. Much less . . . delicate.

Will and I drop our eyes to the mug in his hands.

"So . . . this isn't yours?" he says, looking at me. "You didn't add this to the room?"

"I didn't," I say immediately, putting my hand on my chest. "I thought it was *you*." I laugh. "I mean, I did think it was pretty cheesy of you to add them, now that I think of it, but—"

"Hey, now," Brittney says, frowning as she holds out her hand.

Will promptly hands her the mug.

Slowly, new questions form. If the mugs are theirs . . .

"So . . . what about the lights?" I say.

"Me," Brittney says.

My eyes widen. "Candle?"

"Also me," Brittney says, starting to sound proud. "I thought the place needed a little glow."

"I liked it," I say quickly. "It was a very nice touch."

Brittney gives a little-girlish smile and raises her eyebrows at Sam as if to say, "See? I told you it was better."

My eyes flicker over to Sam. "So . . . the two of you are a couple, then. Who found the ARC room too."

Brittney grins and says as loudly as ever, "Yes, we did. I found it last June when running an errand for Ms. P. The door was open—"

I can't help but wince, vaguely remembering second-guessing myself one day last summer with the question of if I had actually shut it or not.

"—and I was just about bowled over when I discovered what was inside. But I never really had a reason to use it—"

A reason? What does she mean, "never really had a reason"? It's a hidden room!

"—until Sam and I started dating," she continues. "And yes, we are dating. Didn't want to announce it until Giselle was gone. But now that she's moved on to . . ."

"Hostessing at the Painted Pony Saloon," I say, filling in the blanks for her.

"Right." She nods. "Now that she's at the Painted Pony, we are happy to make the news official." She reaches for Sam's hand and holds tight for good measure. "Going to that little room every once in a while was just our way to have some nice little meet-and-greets in secret until we could share."

"Not that our work has suffered," Sam adds suddenly, looking directly at Will. "We made very sure of that. Just like you all did, too, I'm sure."

At that point Will and I glance at each other.

"Of course," we both say at once.

"Right," Will adds.

"And for that matter, you were obviously *doing* work in there, as I now understand," Sam says, loosening up a bit now that he's been openly cleared. He looks at me. "Isn't that right . . . Holly?"

His eyes twinkle oh so slightly with the name.

"Don't worry," he continues, no doubt seeing my cheeks flush. "I'm a lawyer by trade. I'm used to confidentiality. The secret's safe with us."

"We could be like ARC buddies," Brittney adds, her cheeks glowing with the sudden inspiration. "It could be like our own secret fraternity."

I nod on and on as the conversation turns enthusiastically toward homemade T-shirts with our secret club logo stamped on the front, group handshakes, and double dates. It stops on the question of double dates, and my eyes shift to Will.

His, too, look uncertainly back at me.

"Brittney, how about we go get that coffee mug from Savannah's room and have a go at them?" Sam says, clearly seeing the situation at hand.

And as they move out of the room, it's just Will and me.

"I thought it was Sam," I confess immediately and rub both hands up my temples. "Oh, this is all so confusing. I thought my editor was Sam."

"*Sam?*" Will says incredulously. He looks like he's been slapped in the face. "How could you think *I* was *Sam?*"

"Well, I kept running into him up there, just as he was coming and looking so guilty every time I saw him, and—oh," I say, closing my eyes. "It all makes sense now. So . . . let me just run this through out loud. You're him."

"I'm him."

"And he's you." I open my eyes.

Will tilts his head, as though clearly finding me amusing. "He's me."

"So . . . what," I say, venturing toward a new thought. "You knew about the secret room because you're the son. You probably know every square inch of this house. Of course you knew."

"I know about the room because I made it my first summer in middle school," he says. "It was originally just an offshoot of the ARC room. Dad spent a lot of time with me over the years, teaching carpentry skills, how to use my hands. One day when I was cleaning out the room for some odd jobs, I realized that if I covered up the old door with that cabinet and did some basic maneuvering, I could just about erase the room from existence. Turn it into my own getaway."

"Did many people know about it?"

"A few. Most of them gone now. But my mother is one."

I raise a brow. "Your mother? Your mother knows about the room?"

"Who do you think supplied the rug and furniture?" Will grins and lowers his voice as he leans down. "Mother's a bit of a Narnia fan."

Well, I'll be. Ms. Pennington likes happy fiction. Playful, whimsical fiction without any despairing ending or anything.

As he steps back, he frowns. "So you really didn't think it was me. All this time. I admit, I'm having a hard time processing that right now."

"I *wanted* it to be you. But no. And then I found myself fighting with myself, because I found myself so . . ." I hesitate.

His forehead creases. "So?"

I exhale. Confess. "So attracted to the person on the page,

and yet whenever I was with you face-to-face I felt the same way, and it was all so confusing, believing I had feelings for two totally different people and having to choose. And yet . . ." I break off.

"Yet?"

"Yet here you are. And it turns out . . . I don't have to choose at all."

"Hold on." He seems to recall something and puts up a finger. "Does that mean . . . when you told me on paper you cared for someone else—"

"That I was rejecting you because I liked you? Yes," I supply.

He is quiet for a moment and then laughs. A hearty, rich laugh that makes the carpet shake. "You know, you should write a book about that. That's a pretty good plot twist."

I grin and tilt my head. "*Meet Me in the Margins.* It has a nice ring to it."

And as we stand there, smiling at one another, his eyes transition from holding mirth to something more. As though he remembers something. Something . . . inviting. He considers me. "So. Did you ever get that kiss scene sorted out?"

Biting my bottom lip to keep a feeling of hopeful trepidation from rising, I shake my head. "I guess that means Maggie can't publish the story after all, doesn't it?"

"I'm afraid so. Can't publish a romance without a proper kiss scene."

And then I realize he's touching my elbow.

He's taking a step toward me.

I can smell the old scent of cedar and grease around me now. Can almost feel the warmth of his old truck and the morning routine of choosing from one of his four coffeepots as he watches the flakes fall past his window. I want to be a part of that life. I want to be in it.

"But . . . ," he continues softly, gazing down into my eyes now, mere inches between us, "if you're open to it, I'd be happy to give you some suggestions."

I have an intake of breath as his finger grazes my chin and gently lifts it. My eyes rise and, with them, my hope.

"Well, for the sake of the manuscript . . . ," I manage to all but whisper and lift oh so slightly on my toes.

And then, as though he's been waiting all his life for those final, acquiescent words, his hands cup my jawline, and he draws me in.

I feel his breath mingling with my own as his lips meet mine.

If there was any doubt before, any room for wondering, I feel with certainty now the answer in his kiss. He wants me. Has wanted me all along, perhaps. Savannah Cade. The girl with the fungal-feet stories from the gym. The girl who throws small temper tantrums when her characters' names are put into question. The girl who shows up at bars impersonating booking agents on behalf of her best friend and can't fit into size 2 warrior-blue dresses and likes to rewatch painfully corny movies even though they always make her cry.

The way his hands move to cradle my neck, holding on to me, now says he knows all of these things about me, has known these things for a long time, and they only make him want me more.

Which is convenient, as I feel the same.

At last his lips turn playful as his mouth turns into an almost bashful smile. As we part, his hands slip down to hold both of mine. And while his smile is timid, his eyes are on fire, as though apologizing for demonstrating such surprising and uncaged desire, but at the same time gazing at me now like he would do it again in a second.

"Well," he says. And leaves it there.

My cheeks tingle. The nape of my neck, freshly released from his strong hand, is hot.

For a long moment we just look at each other. Until . . .

"Yeah . . . that was okay," I say nonchalantly, although highly aware of the fact I'm grinning ear to ear.

And that does it. That breaks the spell.

"Just *okay*?" he says incredulously. "Just . . ." There's a question in his tone. This time he's really asking. " . . . okay?"

"Well, I mean . . ." I take on an instructional tone. "Where were your hands? I'm pretty sure they just stayed there, clipped to your sides"—my eyes twinkle—"like you were made of cardboard."

"*They were holding you!*" he retorts. "What do you mean, where were my hands? They were holding you!"

"Were they?" I say innocently, as though I can't remember— *quite* clearly, in fact—*exactly* where his hands skimmed the back of my arms, tugged me close, cupped my cheeks and then my neck the past three minutes. I shrug. "You know, the important thing here, I think, is practice. I can tell we're going to have to practice a lot. Indoors. Outdoors. We'll just have to keep practicing as much as we can until we get it right."

There's a long pause as Will surveys my words.

A long pause followed, at last, by a short nod. "Seems fair."

And as he drops me off at my office door a few minutes later, surrounded by the incoming and outgoing traffic of people walking around us in the hall, I can't help but smile as he leans against the doorway and asks, "So. Meet you in the ARC room at two?"

Epilogue

TWO YEARS LATER

*Y*es, we do carry book-club kits for librarians on our website, or you can find it on . . . at . . . at . . ."

"HollyRay.com," I finish, smiling serenely at Gabriel.

Gabriel is our newest acquisitions editor. She's twenty-two. She's lovely. And she's completely terrified she's going to screw up.

"I'm fine here, Gabriel. How about you take a break and get some coffee?" I say, watching the girl give an entirely overwhelmed look at the exhausting line of librarians at our booth.

They are all here for my signing. Correction: Holly Ray's signing.

Of her second book in a series.

Funny how of all people in Nashville, I'm the one who ended up with a stage name.

I write half days these days, and spend the other half as acquisitions editor for the mainstream ArcherPennington line. I've considered dropping my editing job a few times, but the perks are too great to ever let that be a real possibility. For one, I still share an office with Lyla (whose probation, barring LOA events, has just become the general rule for her). I still edit books, although my client list has shrunk now to a manageable six, and I am just as passionate about their cozy mysteries, YA, and speculative works as my own.

And I still have my little getaway in the hidden room, although now Will joins me. And sometimes Brittney. And sometimes Sam—who has turned out to be a truly lovely man after all.

And we all really do have a secret group handshake.

I'm listening to a woman talk about her two grown daughters as I finish off my signature on my new book when I hear Lyla's voice rise above the general hum.

"Protect the castle! Protect the castle at *all costs!*"

I swivel my head around and see Lyla in a tug-of-war with the same librarian from two years ago who was so bent on stealing Oswald's foam-board headshot. Lyla still has the same old Dolly Parton hair, which swings violently all around her. She also has a protruding belly showing she's about five weeks from her due date. Three weeks into her first tour she realized she might not be cut out for the country-star life after all. Now she sings on the weekends here and there, and Will and I, along with Garrett, and even Sam and Brittney, go out to show our support.

"Excuse me," I say politely to the woman before me and hand her the copy.

I spot Yossi and Marge in the corner, covered up in conversation. Gabriel just left for coffee. Will is off at an appointment. It's up to me.

I jump up and rush as quickly and professionally as I can over to Lyla. I grab her shoulders and say calmly, "What did we just talk about in the car, sweetie?"

Lyla stiffens without letting go. Her lips purse and her nose wrinkles.

"What was it?" I prompt again. I stare at her, smiling, until she gives.

Lyla, after glowering at the librarian, finally looks at me.

"Remind ourselves," Lyla chants dully, "that people have feelings. And they are more important than things."

"What things?"

Lyla raises her eyes to the ceiling. "Books. Pens. And foam boards."

"And what is Will going to do if he catches you chasing another nice librarian down the aisle?"

Lyla exhales. Lets go of the foam board and folds her arms across her chest. "Make me stand in front of everyone at the next meeting and compliment each person one by one."

"That's right," I say, rubbing her shoulders soothingly for several seconds. I then turn to the librarian and give her a broad, we're-all-sane-here smile. "I'm so sorry, but that board isn't part of the merchandise we are giving away today."

The elderly miscreant, for her part, only wrinkles her brow distastefully at me, with zero regard that it's my own face she's currently stealing.

"I'd be happy to give you my book instead. Signed personally," I add.

She, holding the foam board, takes a step backward.

Beside me, I hear Lyla hiss.

"You know what?" I'm stepping on Lyla's toes. "How about I just sign that for you and you can take it? I'm happy to."

But as I turn to grab my Sharpie, the small woman swivels faster than I imagined was possible and makes a squirrely rush for the crowd.

Well. Sometimes that's how it goes.

I return to my seat, and to meeting with librarians, many of whom I've specifically come to know over the past twenty-four months as the sweetest, most encouraging, and most powerful cheerleaders for my books. And by the end of the signing, my aching, smiling cheeks reflect it.

"Thanks, Miss Michelle," I say, passing her the book. "I'll be looking forward to it."

Miss Michelle, a kind librarian out in East Tennessee, takes the book and slips it into her bulging tote, along with all the other ARC reads for the day. "Thanks, Savannah. We're all really excited for our chat with you."

"Me too," I say and smile at her, meaning it. Some authors, like Oswald (whom I ended up retaining despite the company shakeup, simply because he was so overwhelmed at the thought of a new editor), find social gatherings around their books terrifying. Not me. Chatting with book clubs is quite possibly my favorite part of the job.

The librarian drifts into the stream of traffic, and I sit there on my little barstool, snagging a moment to take it all in. The hum of energy. The eager faces.

A few moments later there's a break in the stream of passing people, and I see Will standing on the other side.

He's just looking at me, as though he's been standing there for some time, taking it all in as well. An easy smile plays on his lips.

As he saunters forward, I see two hardcovers in one hand.

Recognizing the bold orange cover, I suck in a breath. "Is that . . . ?"

"Green's latest? Yes. Got one for you. One for your mom. I had to barter, though. Green was pretty particular about what he wanted."

He gives a wry smile, and I feel impossible thoughts forming in my head. "He didn't . . . want . . . mine?" I say incredulously and with growing awe.

"No," Will says, clearly having no problem dashing my hopes. "Guess again."

My eyes dance around the tables beside me, covered in our titles. "Jackson's?"

Will shakes his head.

My eyes dance around again. "Hugh's?"

Will shakes his head again. "Oswald's," he says at last, grinning so much his eyes crinkle. "Evidently, Trace is having some sort of vole problem and thinks Oswald's the guy for the job."

I'm momentarily stunned, imagining Green—who is truly on another level—perusing Oswald's book under lamplight from some massive leather chair in some massive home library. But then another idea lights. "Get a blurb from him. Get a blurb, and we'll put it on Oswald's next cover."

"Already asked," he says, stepping around the podium to stand beside me. "And while we're on it, I finished your manuscript last night."

I raise a hopeful brow. "And?"

"The timeline has some issues. The secondary characters are weak. But, I'll grant, the hook is strong."

"Is that so?" I say and give him a playful punch on the arm.

"Gently, Mrs. Pennington." He rubs his arm with a grin. "You're wearing diamonds."

And it's true. As I pull my hand back, I can't help admiring the single solitary diamond twinkling beneath the high fluorescent lights of the conference building. A gift from Ms. Pennington—Martha, I amend mentally, although it seems I'll never get used to calling her that. And the band from my own mother, passed down from her own.

Will leans down, and there, as I've come to experience regardless of ambience, regardless of fluorescent lighting or park trees or glowing string lights all around, I experience the perfect kiss.

The perfect kiss, because it's with the man I love—and will love forevermore, over scrambled eggs and wedding china.

Acknowledgments

The idea came for this book while I was first touring the offices of my own publishing house, Thomas Nelson, with my then editor, Jocelyn Bailey. The ambience of the office was delightful. The hum of activity and floors of people all dedicating their energy toward one goal—the publication of life-giving books—was inspirational in itself. Then I visited a little unassuming room, not much bigger than a closet really, where shelves of ARC copies were stored. The room was glorious. Hundreds of books that had not yet been released to the public, there for the taking. And then my editor waved at the shelves and said two magic words, "Take some." That moment, combined with witnessing the budding romance between a certain charming lawyer and a certain endearing editor, and I knew I had my next story. What better place to write about than here? What better place to start than in a tucked away ARC room in all the excitement of the publishing business?

So there is nowhere I can begin with my gratitude than with everyone at Thomas Nelson. For not just helping to get my stories out in the world through talented cover design, editing, sales and marketing efforts, and publicity, but by being the inspiration for this story itself, thank you. Thank you. Thank you. For Lynn Buckley's stunning cover design of this book, thank you. Particularly to those with whom I have the joy of communicating with often—Laura Wheeler, Leslie Peterson, Kerri Potts, Kimberly Carlton, Amanda Bostic, Becky Monds, Savannah Summers, and Margaret Kercher—thank you.

And for my forever-first editor who took me on, walked with me through this story and so much more, and has since moved on to other life adventures, Jocelyn Bailey, thank you.

To my agent, Kim Whalen, thank you for always being so available and encouraging.

To Ashley Hayes, for being such a wonderful comrade.

To Nicole Coley, for walking alongside me with creative support of my books.

To Christine Berg, for always being my first and favorite reader.

To my husband and family for constant support, thank you.

To those bookstagrammers and bloggers who have shared my books in the most gorgeous of ways, you truly move the needle, and I am indebted to you.

To Christ, for giving me a reason to write.

And to every single reader who encourages me on social media, replies to my newsletter emails, shares my books, writes reviews, tells your book clubs, and just makes me feel like I'm part of a cozy community, thank you. I appreciate everything you do more than I can say.

Discussion Questions

1. Savannah is in a family of chronic multitaskers. How do you handle multitasking? Do you have a healthy or unhealthy mental way of handling all the tasks in your life?

2. Have you ever seen accomplishments as a bad thing? How, in the book, was hitting an accomplishment sometimes demonstrative of a bad thing? When, in the book, was hitting an accomplishment a good thing? What's the difference?

3. When Savannah loses her longtime boyfriend to her sister, what do you think of her family's reaction?

4. Point-of-view is a powerful thing. From Savannah's perspective, losing her longtime boyfriend overnight to Olivia and "Cupid's arrow" was devastating, but if the story had been told from Olivia's point-of-view, it could have been viewed as dramatically romantic. How have you seen this work in your life, or perhaps when

you listen to two very different stories from those in conflict?

5. Given how subjective each person's point-of-view is to an experience, how should you react when other people relay different experiences from yours?

6. Savannah and William end up in one of those challenging, but understandable, work relationships where the boss and employee are attracted to one another. What is your opinion of such relationships and situations? Have you ever seen it be a bad or good thing?

7. Just before the final staff meeting, Savannah accepts the fact that she's going to have to do a lot of work over several more years in order to continue pursuing her writing passion. She decides that she won't let rejection get in her way. Have you ever had that moment? What were the consequences of such perseverance?

8. What would you do if you stumbled into a hidden ARC room? How would you decorate it? Would you tell people?

9. Which character's weakness do you identify with most? Why?

10. Which character's strength do you identify with most? Why?

11. What does Savannah learn about herself in the end that changes her? How?

12. Who was your favorite character, and why?

About the Author

Photo by Taylor Meo Photography

*M*elissa Ferguson is the best-selling author of titles including *The Dating Charade, This Time Around,* and *The Cul-de-Sac War.* She lives in Tennessee with her husband and children in their growing farmhouse lifestyle, and writes heartwarming romantic comedies that have been featured in such places as *The Hollywood Reporter, Travel + Leisure, BuzzFeed,* and *Woman's World.*

She'd love for you to join her at www.melissaferguson.com.
Instagram: @our_friendly_farmhouse
TikTok: @ourfriendlyfarmhouse
Facebook: @AuthorMelissaFerguson